The Hiking Trip

Jenny Blackhurst lives in Shropshire where she grew up dreaming that one day she would get paid for making up stories. She is an avid reader and can mostly be found with her head in a book or hunting Pokemon with her son, otherwise you can get her on Twitter @JennyBlackhurst or Facebook. Her favourite film is Fried Green Tomatoes at the Whistle Stop Cafe, but if her children ask it's definitely Moana.

D1150315

Also by Jenny Blackhurst

The Girl Who Left
The Hiking Trip

The
hiking
trip

JENNY BLACKHURST

CANELO

First published in the United Kingdom in 2023 by

Canelo
Unit 9, 5th Floor
Cargo Works, 1-2 Hatfields
London SE1 9PG
United Kingdom

A CIP catalogue record for this book is available from the British Library.

Print ISBN 978 1 80032 928 7
Ebook ISBN 978 1 80032 927 0

This book is a work of fiction. Names, characters, businesses, organizations, places and events are either the product of the author's imagination or are used fictitiously. Any resemblance to actual persons, living or dead, events or locales is entirely coincidental.

Cover design by Lisa Brewster

Cover images © Shutterstock

Look for more great books at www.canelo.co

Printed and bound in Great Britain by Clays Ltd, Elcograf S.p.A.

1

Chapter One

It took just three little words to ruin my life the second time around.

Human remains found.

It's a Saturday, which is a particularly inconvenient day for my life to be ruined, because I have both of the children with me. Faye, seven, and George, four, are sitting in the back of the car arguing over whether Mr Tumble is a poo-head as I line it up ready to reverse into the last parent and child space at Asda – score – when a guy in a black Mercedes drives from behind the spot, straight in.

I slam on the brakes and wind down my window as Mr Mercedes jumps, child-free and blatantly conscience-clear, out of his car and presses the key to lock it.

I lean out of the window and wave. 'Sorry, I was just about to park there,' I say, in case for some reason he can't see my shiny silver people carrier stuck out in the road.

Another car stops, the driver looking impatient for me to get out of the way, but she's going to have to wait.

'No worries, love,' Mr Mercedes says. He's wearing a suit that doesn't quite hide his middle-age paunch and is tall, hair shaved because he thinks it will hide the fact that his hair has receded, with any luck into his nose and ears. He has that kind of all-year-round tan that he hopes will

I

say 'summer in the Med' but instead screams 'tanning bed three times a week'.

'I didn't actually mean that I was sorry,' I say, opening my door to get out and ignoring the woman in the waiting car who has started to make frantic hand gestures. 'I meant that was my space. And you don't even have children. It's a parent and child space.'

He looks at me as though I am a persistent mosquito and I swear I can feel my blood actually start to boil. 'I *am* a parent,' he says. 'I just don't have my kids with me. And I parked in the space first. You can see that, because my car's in there, isn't it?'

'But I was just about to—' I start.

'But you didn't,' Mr Mercedes cuts in, his voice infuriatingly low and calm. 'So get back in your car and find another space. You're causing a traffic jam and being very selfish.' He carries on walking towards the supermarket.

I stand watching him go, stunned.

'*I'm* selfish?' I shout to his retreating back. '*I'm selfish?* You utter PRICK!'

One of the drivers in the queue waiting leans on their horn heavily.

I let out a huge huff and get back into the car, my face burning red. I spin the wheel around and drive past the line of cars, my hand up in a conciliatory gesture.

'Swear jar, Mummy,' Faye says sweetly.

The space I find is about a mile from the front entrance, but it has a curb next to it so at least I'm able to open the door wide enough to heft George out without hitting anyone else's car.

As I lock the door, I slide the keyring into the palm of my hand, the key sticking out from between my fingers, the way women learn to hold them when they walk around after dark. *Don't play on your phone, don't wear headphones, don't drink too much and if anyone tries to grab you, jam your key into their eye.*

'Come on, babes,' I say, taking George's hand with my free one. Faye grabs his other one and we hurry across the car park.

'Mummy, you're going the long way,' Faye complains. 'The door is over there.'

'Yes, I've got something to do over here,' I say, heading for the black Mercedes. As I pass it, I let my cardigan fall over my hand and jam the key in-between my fingers into the shiny black paintwork. I drag it a few inches, pressing as hard as I can. It makes a satisfying screech, but I make a point not to look down at the damage I've just caused. I've chosen the side of the car opposite the security camera, but I'm not about to make it obvious by bending down to inspect my handiwork. He'll know it was me, that's enough.

I rub my thumb over the paint left on the key and slip it into my pocket, my hand still hidden from view.

'What did you have to do, Mummy?' Faye asks, oblivious to the petty act of revenge her mother has just committed.

'Mummy had to show someone that they can't treat her like dirt and get away with it,' I reply. 'I learned that a long time ago, from an old friend.'

–

Buoyed by my act of defiance, my quick shop goes well, Faye and George on their best behaviour. I'm back in my car before Mercedes Man, and although I feel slightly disappointed that I'm not going to get to see his face when he notices the damage, it's for the best – I don't need another angry showdown in front of the children.

'Can we have *Frozen* soundtrack on again?' Faye asks. I groan inwardly.

'The CD player is jammed, sorry, sweetheart,' I lie. 'Daddy will fix it later. Radio is all we have for now.'

'On your phone?'

I hold up my phone as if to demonstrate. 'Battery is dead.' Another small white lie.

I switch over to the radio before the Bluetooth can connect and give me away. The voice of my favourite local host makes me smile; listening to him is like having a chat with a friend.

'That was "Suspicious Minds" by the king himself, Elvis Presley. What a classic. Now it's time for the eleven o'clock news with Piper Brent. Morning Piper.'

'Morning Jim. Here are our top stories today. The Prime Minister has said that he won't apologise for comments he made during yesterday's Prime Minister's Questions, stating only that "any offence has been taken, not given". There are calls from the opposition for his resignation.'

'No chance,' I snort.

'And authorities in Vancouver say they are close to identifying the human remains found on the famous West Coast Trail back in October this year. There is no word yet on whether it could be the body of missing British backpacker, Seraphine Cunningham, and the Canadian Mounted Police are under growing pressure to—'

In the back, Faye and George scream as our car slams into the Waitrose lorry in front.

Chapter Two

She should have known, really, when she'd arrived at the airport and her friend hadn't been waiting outside the automatic doors of Departures, sucking frantically on the last cigarette she'd have for twelve hours. Or when she'd gone inside to wait out of the biting cold and seen that their desk was open for check-in and there was no boisterous brunette regaling the queue with stories of the 'worst train journey ever' to get there, or the 'hideous taxi driver'. Ruth always had a 'from hell' story, whether it was the housemate from hell, or the boyfriend from hell or the job from hell.

And when Maisie dialled Ruth's number from the payphone by the airport doors and heard her friend's voice answer, she knew that the feeling of dread which had been building inside her chest all morning had been justified. She'd been right. Ruth wasn't coming.

'I'm *sooooo* sorry, Maisie. I'm having the week from *hell*. Harry said if I go to Vancouver we're finished and I just can't risk that, sweetie. You understand, right?'

Maisie had placed the receiver back in the cradle, not even bothering to reply. There was no point in calling back to try to change her friend's mind. It wasn't like Ruth was going to be sitting by her phone waiting for Maisie's forgiveness. She was probably shagging wonderful, too-good-to-lose Harry right at that moment. Maisie wouldn't mind, but she knew full well that Ruth had been head over heels for a guy called Kent less than a month ago, so Harry was a completely new venture.

What was she going to do now? As predictable as it was for Ruth to let her down, Maisie had truly believed that they were going to be going on this 'trip of a lifetime' together. It wasn't like it was an entire summer: including travel there and back, it was a ten-day trip. Just ten days for childhood best friends who had been separated by Ruth going off to university, leaving Maisie behind. But no, this month's shag was more important. And what made it worse, far worse, was that her mum had warned her this was going to happen.

'She'll let you down, that girl. She always does.'

Of course, the fact that she was right was little consolation to Maisie. Her mum had only been saying it because she couldn't bear the thought of having to look after the rest of the kids in the house by herself for ten days, or get the tea ready, or make the beds. It suited Mum just fine that all of Maisie's friends had gone away to university. It meant that Maisie was stuck at home alone, only a couple of mates from her job at the café to go on the occasional night out with.

Maisie looked up at the departures board. There was still time to check in, or still chance to turn around and go home. Home to a shared bedroom at the age of nineteen, waking up at 5 a.m. with her four-year-old sister because her mum had been up all night with the baby, home to more nappy changes than it was reasonable to expect of a nineteen-year-old who had never even had sex. This was supposed to be her escape from the responsibilities she'd been saddled with.

But she had never done anything like this alone. She would never have booked the trip in the first place if Ruth hadn't begged her to go.

'I feel like we haven't seen each other in forever Mase,' she'd said, her voice a cajoling whine. 'This will be the trip of a lifetime, you and me together again, besties reunited.'

And Maisie had fallen for it because she'd been flattered that Ruth could have asked any of her classy new university friends but instead she'd opted to invite her. Now she realised too late that Ruth's university friends had probably got the measure of her far faster than Maisie ever had.

Although that wasn't true, was it? Maisie had always known what her best friend was like, ever since they were thirteen and Ruth had left her in town on her own after spending all their money for the bus back, to get in the car with a group of boys.

'Only one seat,' she'd said, squeezing in. 'You'll be all right, won't you?'

Not that her mum was any better. Maisie thought back to just a couple of hours ago, when her fourteen-year-old sister had chased her out of the house, banging on the window of the taxi.

'Did you leave any money? Mum overloaded the washing machine again and it's fucked.'

No, Maisie wasn't going back there with her tail between her legs. Without another thought, she picked up her bag and walked over to the check-in desk.

Chapter Three

'No we're fine, honestly,' I repeat for what seems to be the millionth time. 'Thank you.'

The Waitrose delivery driver, a young lad, perhaps early twenties, looks petrified, despite the fact that it had been me who had driven into the back of him. 'Are you sure? The kids seem quite upset, and you went into the van quite fast. Maybe there's someone I should call or something? An ambulance?'

'No,' I shake my head, 'thank you, but we're fine. An ambulance would be overkill. I'll call my husband to come and get us, we'll be fine. Honestly.'

He looks relieved at the thought of a man coming to save the day, and nods. 'Well, if you're sure. I'll just give my boss a ring, find out if there's anything else I need to do. Oh wait.' He disappears round to the side of the van, and I roll my eyes impatiently. I could really do with him going away now. I've pulled my car to the side of the road, calmed the children, reported the collision to the police so they can check the road for debris, called my local garage to arrange for the car to be towed and ordered a taxi through their app. The manchild reappears carrying two ice lollies. 'These were on the substitutions list and the last woman didn't want them. For the kids. They've had a shock.'

I immediately feel bad for mentally telling the driver to get lost. 'Thank you,' I say, taking the ice lollies. I open the back door of the car and lean in. Faye has stopped screaming and the pair of them look at me, wide-eyed and in shock.

'Are we going to jail?' Faye whispers.

Human remains.

I don't know how I'd missed it. Human remains found on the West Coast Trail in October. Close to being identified.

I force a smile. 'No, sweetheart, it was an accident. The nice man gave you these while we wait for the taxi.' I tear open the lollies and thrust them at the children.

'You said you would call Daddy,' Faye says. 'I want Daddy to come.'

'Want Daddy,' George parrots. He spends half of his life just repeating what his older sister says.

I hesitate. I could call Rob, and he'd be across Reading like a shot to get us, of course he would. But the fact is, everything is taken care of. I don't need him here.

'No point in disturbing him at work,' I say. 'Not if you want him to make enough money for that giant trampoline for your birthday.'

Faye grins, her face yellow and sticky from the lolly, all thoughts of the crash, and calling Daddy, gone from her mind.

'We don't need Daddy, Georgy,' she says. 'Mummy's got it all under control. We want the trampoline, don't we?'

All under control. *That's what I thought too, kid*, I think. Only now I'm not so sure.

As we wait for the taxi, I google: *West Coast Trail body found*.

It seems that it was all over the news in October, I must have been blind to miss it. Human remains had been found three miles inland from Cribs Creek and speculation was that it could finally be the remains of British backpacker Seraphine Cunningham. Seraphine had been hiking the famous West Coast Trail in July 1999 when her friend and fellow British traveller, Maisie Goodwin, reported that Seraphine was missing following an attack by another hiker, Mitchell Dyke.

There had been a couple of small follow-up articles but nothing major until today, when police declared that tests are almost complete and an identification was imminent.

And there it is. The past I have worked so hard to put behind me, tugged to the fore once again.

No one knows who you are now, the voice in my head urges. *Only you. It doesn't have to drag anything up. It's been twenty years. There won't be any evidence left. You are not going to prison.*

As soon as the words enter my head, my hand shoots to my mouth to hold in the bile that rises. I can't go to prison. Not now that I'm Laura Johnson, I have Faye and George, and Rob. I have a life now, a family. Back then, I had nothing to lose. Maybe I should have come clean then, taken my punishment, done my time. But then I never would have met Rob, my children would never have been born. Everything I have now I have because of the lies I told. And looking at my children, I know I'd do it again if I had to. I would do anything to protect the life I've made for myself. Even kill.

After all, I've done it before.

Chapter Four

Maisie had expected to start panicking the minute she stepped onto the plane and there was no turning back, but all she felt was a complete feeling of peace. It was only then that she realised how most of her stress had come from the knowledge – however much she hadn't wanted to admit it – that Ruth was going to let her down at some point. Granted, she hadn't thought it would be the minute she'd arrived at the airport, but she thought now about all the years she'd spent making excuses to herself for her best friend's behaviour, and how many of her memories were tainted by Ruth's selfishness.

The thought of not having to traipse round after some boy her best friend had decided she was in love with, or walk an extra fourteen miles out of their way to find a phone box so she could speak to Harry, was so freeing that Maisie found herself falling asleep as soon as the plane took off. She'd spent so many nights lying awake worrying about how her sisters would cope with their mother's increasingly erratic behaviour, or all the ways Ruth might get them arrested or lost, but now she was on her way and nothing from the world below made any difference. For the nine hours of the flight, at least, she was free from all of her chains.

She woke after a couple of hours, her neck sore from the way she'd been lying.

The middle-aged guy sitting next to her gave her a smile and offered her a sweet.

'I'm okay, thanks,' she said. 'Hope I wasn't snoring.'

'Not that the people in the front row would hear,' he said, winking.

Maisie shuddered. Perhaps this was what Ruth was useful for after all; she'd have told him he had something in his eye, or just visibly shuddered and said 'gross'. Instead, Maisie gave an embarrassed smile, reached into the carrier bag of things she'd bought at the airport and, in what she hoped was a pointed gesture, pulled out a magazine.

She was glad now that she had always been the organised one. All of the maps and trail plans, the transportation details, everything was booked in her name, and she had printed out copies of it all, which were in her bag. If Ruth had been a little more reliable, or trustworthy enough to take care of the details herself, Maisie might have had nothing now. Then again, if Ruth had been a little more reliable, Maisie wouldn't be taking their 'girls' trip of a lifetime' on her own.

As the plane began to descend towards Vancouver International, Maisie began to feel those familiar jitters start up again. Was she crazy to be doing this on her own? Was she going to end up on *Crimewatch*, or on the *News at Ten*? *Don't be ridiculous*, she told herself, bracing for the landing. *Thousands of people do this hike every year. It's statistically unlikely you will end up eaten by bears.*

Or killed by Hill People like in one of those horror movies her sister loved so much.

Or…

'Stop it,' she muttered to herself, and the man next to her looked up. 'Oh, not you, sorry.'

'Travelling alone?' he asked.

'I've got friends picking me up at the airport,' she lied.

He raised his eyebrows at her defensive tone and went back to his phone. Poor guy was probably just making small talk and she'd practically made him feel like a serial killer. Her mum was right, she really needed to loosen up. Maybe this was the trip where that would finally happen.

—

The view from Vancouver International was simply breathtaking. Maisie felt like she could stare out of the huge glass windows for hours, then go home happy that she'd seen the most beautiful views she was ever going to see. She'd never been abroad before, barely seen more than the Yorkshire town she'd grown up in, except a trip to Scotland once to visit her dying nan, which had hardly been the holiday of a lifetime. Looking out now at the glistening turquoise sea on one side, and snow-capped Rocky Mountains on the other, she knew she'd made the right choice to come alone.

The security officers had told her where she had to collect her baggage from and where she needed to go to get her transport from.

Maisie felt like baggage claim was the most exciting and stress-inducing thing she'd ever done, and waiting to see if her gigantic rucksack was going to slide through the flaps, she felt sick with anticipation. In reality, this was the last bit of her trip where she would be 'looked after', where there was someone she could call on if her luggage didn't arrive, or if she couldn't find the taxi rank. Once she stepped out of those airport doors, she was on her own. She hadn't anticipated, either, how fast the bag would fly past her, or how many people would surge forwards at once to check if it was their name on the label. Surely they knew what their own bags looked like?

'It's mine!' she tried shouting, but no one moved to let her through. 'Excuse me, that's my bag!'

But it carried on trundling past unclaimed, back into the darkness from whence it had came, and Maisie had to wait another ten minutes for it to come back past. This time, though, she was ready. She shoved her elbow into the path of the man next to her, who had started to reach over to check the label, hooked her arm through the handle and heaved it off, stumbling backwards but clearing a path for herself and her bag. She felt like whooping in excitement. She'd done it, the bag was hers and she felt invincible.

Chapter Five

November 2019

I can't put off calling Rob any longer. After all, when he gets home and sees that my car isn't on the drive, he's going to ask questions and I want to tell him myself before my motormouth daughter has a chance to rat me out.

'He just slammed on the brakes, I don't know what he was playing at,' I say, the cracks in my voice genuine as tears threaten to spill out over my cheeks. I held it together all the way home, long enough to get the kids settled with some snacks, before sitting down at the kitchen breakfast bar and resting my head against the cold marble, trying to stop the thoughts crashing and colliding around. Still, I hadn't wanted to cry until I heard Rob's voice, and I'm not sure if I'm crying over the crash, or the news, or the death of someone I knew twenty years ago. Maybe all three.

'Hey, don't worry, the insurance will sort it,' Rob's voice soothes, as it always does. If I am the fire in the relationship, Rob is the ice, always there to cool me down when my temper flares, always ready to stop me diving off the deep end. He would never have let me key someone's car for stealing a parking space, that's for sure.

'Except it's my fault, isn't it? Even if he stopped suddenly, it's my fault for going into the back of him. I'm such an idiot.'

'Lollypop, stop it.' His nickname for me makes me feel like a child, and yet I've always liked it. Now more than ever. It makes me feel safe, loved, more than I ever actually felt as a child. 'That's why we have insurance. Because accidents happen. Even to you, the Indestructible Laura Johnson. Now, are the kids okay?'

That's the other thing I love about Rob, although I could never tell him, because it would make him sound like a terrible father if I were ever to say it out loud. He puts me first. He loves the children, anyone can see that, and he is a perfect dad – exactly the type I would have wanted for my own if I could have chosen. He plays with them, teaches them things and takes them places. He's far more patient than I am. But at the end of everything, he always makes me feel like I come first. I am his everything.

I know I don't award him the same satisfaction, I put my children first above everything else. It is clear that I would give my life – or Rob's – for theirs in a heartbeat. And while I know Rob would die for his children, I have never been quite sure that my husband would trade *my* life for theirs. No one has ever elevated me quite so high. And all of that will come tumbling down if he finds out the truth about what I did.

I take a deep breath and nod, even though I know he can't see me, my eyes still watery. 'The kids are fine. Faye is in her room bossing her Barbie dolls around – I think she's pretending to be a personal trainer – and George is watching *PAW Patrol* in the front room.'

'See? Everyone is fine. Do you have any pain in your neck? Whiplash, maybe? You didn't hit your head?'

'No, I wasn't going fast enough for any of us to be hurt.'

'There you go then. Everything is okay. Love you.'

'Love you too, baby, see you later.'

What I really need for everything to be okay is information. If I have information, I can feel in control again, formulate a plan. Is it too soon to be making plans? To be thinking about fleeing at this early stage?

Human remains found.

No. I was stupid to google it the first time, let alone use my laptop to leave a search history. I'm going to need a SIM-only phone if I'm going to keep on top of updates. The Canadian authorities will be in charge of the situation, I'll have to set up alerts for all of the Vancouver press. I can almost feel my panic ebbing away as the list of things I can do to stay in control grows.

I grab my purse and my keys from the countertop.

'Kids!' I shout, knowing that my calls will be ignored. 'Faye! George!' I poke my head around the staircase. 'Faye Johnson! Bring your brother, we need to go out!'

Faye's head appears at the top of the stairs. 'We just got in! I'm playing. And you broke the car.'

'We can go on the bus. It'll be an adventure!'

My head hurts at the thought of dragging my children onto the bus on a Saturday afternoon, but the need to claw back some control and avoid spending the rest of the day trying not to google incriminating information on my phone is too much. There's no way I'm going to sit around and let my life be ruined a second time.

—

We brisk-walk to the bus stop at the end of the road, George's pudgy little hand in mine and Faye lagging a little way behind. I hope no one will see us waiting for the bus and ask where the car is. It isn't that lying is a problem for me, but, unfortunately, Rob and I have raised children who feel very differently about the importance of telling the truth. Faye would grass on me in an instant, and although it doesn't matter in the slightest, I suppose, the news report has already started working on me, closing me off from those around me, making me want to retreat into my safe cocoon with my little family. It is starting, and I need to get control of the situation before the police turn up, or worse – the media.

No one knows where you are, I tell myself as I walk. *No one knows* who *you are. You were thorough. You did a good job. You've been left alone for twenty years. You are going to be okay.*

The bus arrives within minutes and as I bustle the children on, enthusing about how great it is to be on a bus, how much fun, I can't help but relax a little. The kids are being agreeable, Faye is enjoying sitting up straight on the grown-up seats, George just like his dad, laid-back, content to go wherever he is taken. But so incredibly loving. He often puts his face to mine, looks deep into my eyes and announces in his adorable way, 'I love you more the world.' He will stroke my hand while we watch TV, or twist my hair around his fingers. Now he is sitting on the same seat as his big sister, wedged in and waving to people outside of the bus.

What will happen to them if I am arrested? How will Rob cope? Who will George love more than the world? The thought has always been there, of course, but until today it has been one of those fleeting considerations, easily batted away, the kind every mother has about what her children would do without them. Now, though, it is closer than ever to being a reality.

Human remains found.

All of a sudden, my future is unclear, my plans irrel-
evant if the truth is uncovered. How long until they
uncover the identity of those remains? How long until
they come for me?

Chapter Six

July 1999 – Maisie

Maisie found the transport to the trail head without any
trouble and dropped her bag next to a trio who looked to
be her own age, perhaps a little older, and terrifying. Two
men and a woman, all three dressed completely in black,
all with jet-black dyed hair. The woman's dreadlocks were
adorned with all kinds of silver jewellery, pentagrams, and
wiggly symbols. She wore ripped black jeans and a black
T-shirt bearing a picture of a sexy woman with tattoos
and goat horns eating a bright red apple. Blood dripped
from the girl in the picture's lips. The woman wore a long
black hooded cardigan over the top. One of the men wore
a black Metallica T-shirt and faded black jeans, with huge
Dr. Martens; the other the same, except his T-shirt had a
triangle symbol with some swirls on the ends. Maisie had
no idea how they were going to walk anywhere in boots
that looked so heavy.

'Hey,' the woman caught Maisie looking and lifted a
hand.

Maisie's face flushed deep red. 'God, sorry. I didn't
mean to stare,' she said, horrified to have been busted.

The girl smiled. 'Don't worry about it. You dress like
this and you get used to people staring.' She held out a

hand. 'I'm Kaz. This is Mitch and Keddie. Are you hiking from Gordon River too?'

Maisie shook her head. 'I'm going the other way, Pachena Bay.'

Kaz smiled. 'So the next time we see you we'll be halfway through! Probably wet and exhausted.' She shrugged. 'Between you and me, I'm not sure all three of us will make it. My money's on Keddie to break an ankle.'

'Oh cheers,' the guy in the triangle tee remarked. 'Thanks for the vote of confidence, Kaz mate.'

The other guy, Mitch, gave Maisie a knowing smile. 'She's right. He's the clumsiest hiker ever. Keddie is the only person I know who is steadier on his feet when he's drunk than sober.'

They all laughed. Maisie thought it was a shame they were starting from different places; it would have been nice to have a group like this to tag along with. Sure, they looked different, but she didn't care about that. She was different too, and she'd only just started to realise how lonely hours and hours of hiking on her own was going to be. With any luck, she would get to spend the evening with them at one of the halfway campsites, and who knew, maybe she'd fall into step with another solitary hiker along the way.

She gazed around at the rest of the travellers waiting. A lot of older people. Maisie had expected it to be full of students, but apart from Kaz and her companions, there was only one other couple who looked to be the same age as her. A female and a male, who, now she looked closer, seemed to be arguing. The girl's sun-streaked blonde hair hung messily around her shoulders. Blue eyes, tanned skin. The straightest nose Maisie had ever seen. Everything about her face was perfectly proportioned, as though she had been hand-crafted for maximum visual satisfaction. The man she was with seemed oblivious to her heart-stopping beauty, however, and was remonstrating with her as though she was just a regular person. He gestured wildly with his hands, and as Maisie moved closer, she heard him saying, '…are we going to do now?'

'I'm sorry,' the girl said, her face crumpling as though she was about to cry. 'I had it in the front of my bag. Someone stole it! You can't blame me if I was robbed.'

'What, you can't be trusted to look after something for five minutes? Now all our money is gone. Jesus…' He said something that Maisie couldn't hear and then '…sister!'

That makes sense, Maisie thought. No wonder he wasn't drooling at this girl's feet – they were siblings. And it sounded as though she'd lost their money.

'Final call for Pachena,' the bus driver called out.

Maisie looked over, shocked. Had he been shouting this whole time? She'd been so enamoured with this couple that she'd almost missed her ride. And if they didn't get on, they'd miss it too. She realised with a strange jolt that she didn't want them to miss the bus. She didn't want to leave them behind.

'Excuse me, the bus is going now,' she said, without knowing why it was suddenly so important to her that they got on. 'You're going to miss it.'

The man turned his face to her, and she saw in an instant that the genes for beauty must run in the family. His hair was darker, but his eyes were just as blue.

They both looked at her in surprise, as though they had forgotten the rest of the world existed.

'Well, we're not going anywhere, thanks to this idiot,' he said, gesturing to the girl who scowled. 'She lost all our money.'

The girl looked miserable.

'I'll loan you the bus fare,' Maisie found herself saying. The minute the words were out of her mouth, she regretted them. She'd saved for so long for this trip, using money she'd been stashing away since she started work at fifteen. Now she was just going to give away a good chunk to people she'd never even met? But despite regretting the offer, when the girl looked at her in surprise, she found she desperately wanted her to say yes. And then she smiled, and her beauty was elevated above anyone Maisie had ever seen in real life.

'Do you mean it?' she said, her voice breathy and eager. The girl looked at her brother. 'Did you hear that? She can lend us the money. We can still go!'

'We're not borrowing the money from a stranger,' he said irritably. He looked at Maisie and shrugged. 'No offence, thanks for the offer. We need to get out of here, Scra.'

'Are you kids getting on or not?' the bus driver shouted, a scowl on his face. 'I'm leaving right now.'

The girl let out a low moan and looked at her brother beseechingly. 'Let's go with her, Ric. It's probably in my bag somewhere anyway. I'll get everything out when we get there and have a look. We can pay her back.'

'Your sister's right,' Maisie said, half hoping he'd say no. It was madness to pay for these people she'd never met. But the other half wanted them around a little longer. She shrugged. 'Pay me back at the end of the trail. It's no problem.'

Ric looked at Maisie, then at the bus driver, who was glaring at them. 'You sure about this?' he asked quietly. 'Don't let my sister emotionally blackmail you. She does it to everyone.'

'It's fine,' Maisie lied. 'Come on, before the driver has a heart attack.'

He smiled and Maisie didn't even care if their bus fares took up her entire budget. Food was already planned into the cost, so she didn't really need money anyway. And hopefully the girl – Sera, had he called her? – would find their money when they got the chance anyway.

'Oooh yay!' Sera squealed, jumping up and down on the spot. 'Thank you, thank you!'

They boarded the bus, Maisie well aware of how many people were looking at them with hostility for keeping them from their trip of a lifetime for an extra few minutes. Only Mitch gave her a friendly wave.

Maisie found an empty couple of seats in the middle, and much to her surprise, the girl plonked herself in next to her.

'Thank you so much,' she said again, giving Maisie's shoulders a hug. Maisie didn't know what to do. She hadn't grown up in a particularly tactile family; hugs had never been a spontaneous act. 'I'm Seraphine, but everyone just calls me Sera. You literally saved me. My brother can be such an asshole.'

'I'm sure he's not that bad,' Maisie murmured, looking at where Ric was sitting a few seats in front on his own, long hair falling into his face as he read his book.

'Oh God, don't be fooled by his brooding intensity,' Sera rolled her eyes and threw her head down dramatically on her arm. 'You have to be on my side. All my girlfriends back home take his side.'

'Where is "back home"?' Maisie asked. She couldn't place Seraphine's accent, but Maisie couldn't imagine her anywhere other than LA or California, she looked so effortlessly glamourous.

'We've been in Australia for the last five years,' she said, 'but we were born in Nottingham.'

'Are your parents still in Australia?'

Seraphine shook her head. 'We were living with our aunt out there. But that's more than enough about me. What about you? I want to know *everything* about my guardian angel.'

Chapter Seven

August 1999

FEARS GROW FOR MISSING BACKPACKER

Sunday Echo

The hiking companion of missing British backpacker Seraphine Cunningham has told others that she 'fears the worst' for the nineteen-year-old, sources say, despite still refusing to speak to the national media about the case.

Student Maisie Goodwin met Cunningham on the famous West Coast Trail in Vancouver and says the pair became friends. Just three days later, the now infamous 911 call was made to Canadian Mounted Police to say that a woman had been killed on the trail. That woman was Seraphine Cunningham.

Police arrived at the scene, where they found signs of a struggle, but Cunningham was nowhere to be seen and hasn't been sighted since. Searches of the area yielded few clues to the backpacker's whereabouts and her belongings were recovered from the campsite where she was last seen.

Canadian police say a thorough investigation is underway and they are exploring all avenues. They refuse to say if they have any suspects at this time, or even if they believe Seraphine is still alive. Police are also refusing to confirm rumours of a 'sex cult' and acts of satanic worship playing any part in Seraphine's disappearance.

A police spokesperson for Goodwin says she is refusing to talk to any media about the incident because she 'doesn't trust them not to twist her words and make her look like a liar'. The spokesperson went on to say that at the current time they have no reason to doubt the story that Ms Goodwin has told, but they are 'exploring all avenues of enquiry'.

Chapter Eight

November 2019

The town centre is busier than I've seen it in a long time. I usually avoid it on a Saturday, especially with the kids in tow, and I'm not used to having to navigate through groups of teenagers blocking the high street.

'Can we go to Smiggle?' Faye asks.

'If you're good while Mummy does her shopping.'

'What are you getting?'

My shoulders tense. How am I going to explain getting a new phone to Faye? If she sees what I'm buying, there's always the chance she'll mention it to Rob, and there's no way I'll be able to explain that away. He'll think I'm having an affair – which is preferable, of course, to him finding out the truth, but would still be a nightmare. I can't let this impact on my family in any way – that's the promise I'd made to myself and I'm going to keep it.

I glance at the phone shop, almost directly across the street from Smiggle. I'll definitely be able to see Faye from inside the shop, as long as I don't turn my back.

'Okay,' I say, bending down to address my daughter so she knows I'm serious. I open my purse and pull out my debit card. I have fifty pounds in cash that I retrieved from the thick envelope I keep inside a hollowed-out hardback copy of *Rebecca*, but I need that for the phone. 'You can spend twenty pounds in Smiggle. Twenty – two, zero – do you understand?'

Faye nods. She might only be seven, but I've been teaching her to deal with her own money since she was George's age. *Never rely on anyone else.*

'Now, this is very important, Faye: I'm trusting you to be grown up. You do not leave that shop until I come and get you. Even if you've spent your money, you just wait by the counter. I can see you from the shop I'm in. Mummy just needs to get a new cover for her phone.'

Faye nods, thrilled to be given such responsibility, as well as my debit card. 'Promise.'

'Right, go on then.' I gesture with my head to Smiggle and watch Faye take off into the shop, her glossy curls bouncing as she runs.

Moving as quickly as I can, ignoring George's protests of 'Wanna go Faye,' I dart into the mobile phone shop across the road. I can still see Faye, poring over rows and rows of pink unicorn-adorned pencil cases and strawberry-scented pencils.

The two advisors in the phone shop are busy and I mutter a silent curse for this happening on a Saturday afternoon. George is tugging at my hand and I let him go to play on the row of phones lined up on display as I look for what I need. SIM only, internet access, it's as simple as that. There, that Samsung one will do.

I glance across at where Faye has moved on to the backpacks. Those are definitely more than twenty quid, so she'd better not even think about picking one of those up. I'm trying to catch my daughter's eye to tell her as much when the salesperson behind me asks, 'Can I help?'

'Oh yes,' I snap around. 'Can I just get one of these please?' I gesture to the cheapest Samsung phone on the rack with internet capability. 'I don't want a contract or anything. It's for my mum,' I add, by way of explanation. 'She just wants something basic that she can top up and use Google.' I laugh in an 'oh bless her' kind of way.

The sales advisor smiles. 'With our contracts, they actually work out cheaper than our pay-as-you-go models. I can show you some tariffs that would be perfect for your mum?'

'No,' I practically snap. I glance across the street, where I can see Faye's yellow coat behind a stand that declares 'Four for Five Pound!' 'No, sorry, I'm in a bit of a rush. Can you just get me this one please?'

The assistant gives a faint smile as she watches her commission float away. 'Sure. I'll be right back.' She disappears through a door in the back.

George is making shooting games noises whilst tapping furiously on a tablet and Faye is in the corner of Smiggle, likely racking up charges that I have no way of explaining to Rob. I'll get away with letting Faye in the shop on her own by passing it off as 'treating her like a grown-up', making out that I was outside the shop the whole time. That excuse isn't going to wash if Faye charges the entire range of unicorn poo to our debit account.

'Mummy, look!' George shouts, thrilled with himself despite missing every one of the targets he's aiming for. God, life is so simple at that age.

'You're doing great!' I enthuse, glancing again at the door the sales assistant had disappeared into. What's taking so long? Is she actually making the damn phone herself? I picture the sales assistant hunched over a desk with a pair of goggles assembling my device.

After what seems like an eternity, the assistant returns with a box and takes it to the counter.

'Do you need any help setting it up?' she asks as I hand over the cash.

'No, no thank you,' I smile, shoving the phone into my oversized handbag. Okay, first bit done. Now I can at least get information without leaving any kind of search history. 'Come on, George,' I bend down to take his hand, but he pulls it away.

'I'm playing.'

I sigh. George is usually so well behaved, but when he digs his heels in, he can be as stubborn as his sister. Please don't let this be one of those times, I am not in the mood for a tantrum.

'Look, Georgie, let's go and see what Faye's got and you can get something from Smiggle too.'

Yes, I have resorted to bribing both of my children. This could get costly.

Thankfully, George relents and puts the tablet down without causing a scene. I take his hand and lead him out of the shop towards where Faye is playing with something that flashes annoyingly. Fingers crossed she isn't going to ask for one of those.

Except That isn't Faye's light-yellow coat. It is a yellow coat, but now I get closer, I can see that it isn't the same shade as Faye's, and closer still, I see that the girl's hair is lighter than Faye's and I realise with sickening, heart-lurching clarity that the little girl I've been watching from across the street hasn't been my daughter at all.

Chapter Nine

July 1999 – Maisie

By the time the bus arrived in Pachena Bay, Maisie felt as though she really had told Seraphine absolutely everything about herself. She didn't think she'd ever talked so much and had someone just listen. Usually, people she spoke to were customers who just wanted their breakfast or morning coffee, or colleagues who were just waiting for their turn to talk, or her mother who was too busy to listen to anything she said. Talking to Seraphine was like a breath of fresh air, almost like a therapy session, Maisie thought. Well worth the nearly hundred dollars she'd paid for her and her brother to make the trip. She'd also discovered, to her delight, that Ric and Sera were on the same planned hike as she was.

When the bus pulled up, Maisie expected Sera to rejoin her brother and for them to disappear off on their own. She was ready for it; she knew she couldn't be lucky enough to have found people who wanted to spend the rest of the hike with her so easily. So she truly couldn't believe it when Sera linked arms with her and dragged her to the booking-in desk.

'Maisie Goodwin,' she said to the woman at the desk.

The woman gave her a wide toothy smile and handed her a pack. 'Orientation at noon,' she confirmed. Maisie

32

gave her own nervous smile and moved back with the rest of the group. She watched as Seraphine stepped up to the desk and began conversing with the receptionist. She pulled something out of her pocket and held it up for inspection.

The woman nodded and gestured to the waiting area while she disappeared. After about ten minutes, she returned.

'Mary Whittaker? And Albert Hennessey?' she called, and to Maisie's surprise, Sera bounded over to her.

'What was that all about?' Maisie asked her when Seraphine rejoined her. 'Mary? And Albert?'

Seraphine grinned. 'My aunty paid for my hike,' she explained. 'But she booked it in her name, for some reason known only to her and God. I knew I should have done it myself. Ric's mate booked his. Don't you think Mary suits me?'

Maisie laughed. 'I don't know about a Mary, but your brother definitely looks like an Albert.'

'He does at the moment, don't you think?' Seraphine gave her a nudge and nodded her head towards her brother, who had a scowl on his face. 'Like a right grumpy Albert.' They both fell about laughing. Ric looked at them sharply and Sera gave a little finger-wiggle wave. Maisie broke down in further giggles as he gave them the middle finger and approached the desk.

'You'll have to change your bracelet,' Maisie said, grabbing Sera's wrist and holding it up. She'd noticed Sera's childish friendship bracelet on the bus and thought how sweet it was. Braided colourful threads held white beads with the letters SERAPHINE printed on them.

Sera rolled her eyes. 'Not exactly New York chic, eh? Ric got it for me at some market stall. I used to moan that nowhere ever sold anything with my name on it and there was this woman selling these "make your own" ones. Now I have to wear it.'

'I like it,' Maisie replied. 'I think it's adorable.'

'I'll send you one,' Sera promised. 'When we get out of this hike alive.'

–

Orientation would have been frankly terrifying, had Maisie not had Sera next to her, making silly comments throughout. The hike leader made it sound as though they were trekking through the Amazon rather than 'some beach in Canada' that Ruth had assured her it was. She'd read the brochure front to back, but even that hadn't been quite as doom-mongering as she was hearing now – warnings of slippery ladders, twisted ankles, broken legs.

'On the trail, help can take up to twenty-four hours to get to us,' the guide warned. 'So please watch your step and take your time. Take the time to look up and around every now and then – enjoy the scenery, just do so safely.'

'It's like having my year seven teacher taking us on a school trip,' Sera complained.

Maisie snorted. The guide looked at her sharply.

'Your waterproof tide timetables are in the pack you were given at book-in,' she continued, raising her voice as though they really were naughty schoolgirls. 'You don't want to get stuck in rising tides, so make sure you check it regularly. When you set up camp, be sure to make use of the campsite food boxes unless you want to share your food with a hungry bear.'

Someone close to the front put up their hand.

'Yes?' The guide pointed at them.

'Are there wolves on the trail?'

'There are a number of animals that call the forest around the trail home,' the guide said, as if she'd rehearsed for that very question. 'Which includes bears, wolves and cougars. You might see a bear, but they want to avoid us as much as we want to avoid them. There hasn't been a bear attack on the trail since I started working here six years ago. I've never seen a wolf or a cougar – although I have heard them, and I have known people's incorrectly stored food to be ransacked by the local wildlife. Store your food properly and you won't have any problems.'

'Brilliant,' Seraphine said as their guide asked them to line up to collect their park passes. 'Just bears, wolves, tides, tsunamis, broken bones and grumpy Albert to contend with.' She looked at Maisie and grinned. 'What could possibly go wrong?'

Chapter Ten

November 2019

I stand staring stupidly at the little girl in the coat that is so similar to my daughter's and let out a strangled sound that is half cry, half sob. There is barely anyone else in the shop, nowhere Faye can be hiding. While I had been in the phone shop panicking about losing everything, I had actually lost everything. My daughter is gone.

'Excuse me,' I shout to the woman behind the counter, trying not to let panic take over my entire body. 'My daughter was in here – she was wearing a yellow coat like that little girl, I got confused… She's gone. Where is she?'

The woman steps out from behind the counter immediately, obviously realising the gravity of the situation. 'She was talking to your husband when I saw her,' she says, looking around the stands. 'Then when I looked again, they were gone.'

Your husband. Your husband. Your husband.

'I'm not shopping with my husband,' I say, the words tasting bitter in my dry mouth. 'That wasn't my husband.'

'Oh Jesus,' the woman mutters. 'I had no idea. She didn't look distressed. Don't worry, we've got a very strict protocol to follow, we'll find your little girl. What's your name?'

'Laura,' I say, trying to comprehend what is happening. *Faye is missing.* The words pound in my head, unable to fully take root. This has happened before, as it does to all mums. You turn around at the park and your child isn't where you thought they were. A few heart-pounding seconds before you spot them, safe, on another swing or a climbing frame. In that instant, your world falls out from under you, but you still don't fully believe – not in those few seconds – that they are truly gone. Just like in this moment I don't believe… I expect to turn round and see her, her grinning face in a 'gotcha!' She isn't gone, she can't be gone.

Your husband.

'What did he look like?' I demand, but the woman is already on the phone to someone – the police? If she is calling the police, then this is real… this is serious. Part of me wants to grab the phone from her hands – she's overreacting, being stupid, Faye isn't missing. I have to find her.

I grab George's hand and run out onto the street, looking up and down for her yellow coat, my heart feeling frantic. Would he already have taken her coat off her?

'I've alerted the centre management.' The woman appears by my side. Despite opening onto the street, the shop is still technically part of a shopping centre. 'They've sent security to every entrance. Someone is on their way here to get a picture of her and the centre manager is going to phone the police. How old is she, six? Seven?'

'Seven,' I confirm, barely able to comprehend anything she's said. I don't just need the centre closing off, I needed a cordon around the whole town centre, before it's too late.

'Oh!' The woman grips my arm and I spin around to see what has startled her.

Faye.

'Mummy!'

Faye is standing in the street, waving frantically at me. She looks as relieved as I feel. There is a woman standing next to her smiling.

'Wow, you got us a bit worried there!' the woman says, as though we are old friends. I have no idea who she might be. She's taller than me, with bobbed light brown hair and blue eyes. She's wearing a long beige coat and tailored black trousers with a black polo-neck jumper and an expensive, oversized handbag.

'Faye!' I shout, throwing myself at her. At my side, George begins to cry and I feel tears fill my eyes as well. The adrenaline pounding around my body is making me feel sick. She's here. She's alive. I haven't lost her. Already it feels like a second chance, a chance to make the right decisions next time. I hold her little body to mine and begin to sob.

When I pull away, the woman from the shop pats Faye's head and grins. 'Are we glad to see you, young lady.' She looks at me. 'I'll call off the tracker dogs.'

'Thank you,' I say, truly grateful at how quickly she'd acted. I hold Faye at arm's-length. 'Why did you leave the shop? I told you to stay in there until I came.'

Faye's smile drops. 'Sorry,' she says, her voice reverting back to the little baby voice she does when she thinks she might be in trouble. 'The man said you said it was okay.'

'The man?' I look at the woman who had been with Faye for an explanation.

'I saw Faye talking to a man,' she says quietly, as Faye hugs George. 'I heard him say that her mum had said it was

38

okay for them to grab some sweets while she waited for you. She didn't seem to know him, so I kind of followed them... I wasn't sure what to do and I didn't want to make a fool of myself, but it didn't feel right.'

'Oh God,' I mutter. 'Thank you so much. I don't... I didn't...' I feel bile rise in my throat and think I might be sick. Who is this man?

'I thought as much when I approached them. I pretended to be a friend of yours and he got really agitated, said he was taking her for some sweets. When I asked her if she knew him, she said no and he just took off running. When we got back to the phone shop, you were gone, but we spotted you over here and I realised you must have noticed that she was missing. I'm so sorry to have got you worried.'

The woman looks so concerned that I almost laugh, but the noise won't come out.

'You saved her life,' I half whisper. Faye and George are looking in the window of Smiggle now and can't hear me, but I still can't bring myself to say it out loud. 'That man... he was trying to abduct her, wasn't he? She could be gone... so far away now if you hadn't been smart enough to realise something was wrong. I don't know how to thank you.'

'God, that's terrifying.' She looks as though only now is she grasping the gravity of what she's done. What she's prevented.

I picture the town swarming with police, my daughter's face on the news, on the fronts of the tabloids. I picture her being shoved into a van and driven away, so far away that I can never reach her. My legs threaten to give way underneath me.

The woman grabs my arm to steady me. 'Are you okay?'

'Yes, sorry.' I steady myself against the shop window. 'We should still report this though, to the police. He might try it with another child.'

'Shit, yeah, I hadn't thought of that,' she says. Up close, she really is very pretty. Her skin is clear and creamy – no hint of a tan and the merest touch of make-up, just a little blush on each cheek. I have a crazy urge to hug her, needing comfort from the sheer hell of what could have happened. 'Shall I call them?'

'We'll get her to do it,' I say, gesturing back at the woman behind the counter. 'She's pretty amazing in a crisis, I've got to say.'

I put my arm around Faye's shoulders and take George's hand in my other. I never want to stop touching either one of them again.

The woman in the shop agrees to call the police as soon as we explain what's happened. She instructs us to wait in the coffee shop a few doors down so I can recover – the blood hasn't fully returned to my face, it seems, and I'm not sure it will for a while.

'I'm really sorry about this,' I say to the woman as we head out of the shop. 'You've done a good deed and now you're going to have to wait for the police.'

The woman looks uncomfortable. 'I'm really sorry, but I can't stay.' She makes an apologetic face. 'I've got a hospital appointment in an hour and if I don't get back to the car and get up there, I'll never find parking on time.'

'But you're the one who saw the man,' I say. 'They'll want to speak to you.'

'I'll write down a description,' she promises. 'And I'll leave my name and number with you – that way, they can call me. This appointment…' She looks for a second as though she might start to cry. 'It's pretty important.'

'Of course,' I say quickly. This woman has done such a wonderful thing for me, she shouldn't be forced to miss what is clearly an important appointment to help me further. 'And there will be CCTV they can get. Hopefully you scared him out of trying it again.'

I loose hold of George's hand for one second to take hers. 'I can't express how grateful I am to you. Honestly, I thought I'd lost her forever. You must think I'm a terrible mother.'

'I just did what anyone would do,' the woman smiles. 'And you aren't a terrible mother. There are truly awful people in this world, and I'm pretty sure you're not one of them.'

As we say goodbye and I thank her for the millionth time, I can't help thinking about how right her instincts had been about the man who had tried to lead Faye away, and how wrong they are about me.

Chapter Eleven

July 1999 – Maisie

To Maisie, the trek into the forest felt like walking into another world. Growing up in a city centre, she hadn't had a lot of experience of the great outdoors. There had been no Park Dean holidays in her childhood – money had been too tight to mention, and her mum's various illnesses meant that even the few opportunities there were for Sunday afternoons in the woods were missed.

Here, everything was green. Despite the warmth of the day – their guide had informed them that the next couple of days at least were forecast to be sunny – the air still felt moist, the ground beneath her feet slightly damp and muddy in places. Tree roots snaked over the narrow dirt path and Maisie had to concentrate on not landing on her face more than on the beauty of her surroundings. The air was cool, what little sunlight that could break through the canopy of leaves overhead dappled the pathway in front of them.

This was the freedom she had been craving so badly. Okay, so her backpack was already cutting into her shoulders, and the duct tape she'd put on her heels to prevent blisters was less than comfortable, but it was a small price to pay for the ability to do exactly what she wanted at any given time. How fast she walked, how often she stopped, where she set up camp – it was all her choice. And to make things even better, Sera and Ric seemed to be happy to take the hike at her pace, not complaining if she stopped to take a photo, or readjust her pack.

She'd told them a few times that they didn't have to stay with her – they had swapped details so that the money could be repaid – they didn't have to take her along with them out of a sense of loyalty.

Sera had laughed, dimples showing in her cheeks. 'Are you trying to get rid of us, Maisie?' she'd asked, giving her a nudge. 'If you want us to leave you alone...'

'I'm not saying that,' Maisie had replied quickly, before Sera could get the wrong idea. 'I just don't want you feeling like you owe me anything.'

'Oh I wouldn't worry about that,' Ric had remarked, raising his eyebrows. 'My sister doesn't ever feel any sense of obligation to anyone. She was born without the gene for moral duty.'

'Don't be an asshole.' Sera had squeezed Maisie's arm. 'But he's right. I generally do what I want to do, so if I'm here with you it's because I want to be. When I don't, I won't be.' She gave a little shrug and smiled.

Maisie's mouth had dropped open. She had never even realised a person could live that way, doing exactly what they wanted with no thought to whether it was the right or good thing to do.

–

It took three hours, over slippery boardwalks and up wooden ladders through the forest, before the trees seemed to part miraculously to reveal their first glimpse of the beach.

'Oh yes!!!'

Seraphine, who had been quiet for the last hour or so, dropped her bag and ran, whooping, onto the sand. Maisie laughed and Ric rolled his eyes. Sera pulled off her jumper, then her shorts and dashed, in her pants and vest, into the surf.

Maisie dropped her own bag and sat down on a rock, watching Sera dance in the clear blue water. Ric dropped down next to her.

'God, I wish I could be like that,' Maisie admitted, nodding towards Sera.

'Like what?'

'Like her. Just do what I feel like doing, whenever I feel like doing it, without worrying that people are judging me, or that I look stupid. Or worse, that I'm letting someone down.'

'Why can't you?' He was staring at her now, and her face reddened.

She knew that the only reason he was paying her attention and not drooling over Sera was because they were related, but still, it was nice to be in the company of a male who actually wanted to talk to her, instead of just her mate. Maisie had been the 'bring a friend' her whole life. Like whenever Ruth was dating a lad and he wanted to bring a friend along, Maisie would be trotted out like a prized cow and have to endure an evening of torturous small talk while Ruth and her date snogged one another's faces off.

She shrugged. 'I've always worried what people think. And I've always been the responsible one, it's who I am. I've got younger sisters who rely on me. Our mum, she gets ill, depression, so if I don't look after them, no one else will. And my friends... they're just used to me being the reliable one.'

'Is that why you're here on your own?' he asked. His voice was gentle and it made Maisie feel like crying, although she wasn't sure why. She thought she'd been fine about Ruth letting her down, she'd thought she was used to it. But now, here, having to explain to someone else that her best friend didn't care enough not to let her fly nearly five thousand miles away on her own... it just felt too sad for words.

'My friend, the one I was supposed to come with, she had an emergency.'

Ric nodded as though he knew that there had been no emergency. 'I've got mates like that. Why do you think I'm here with my sister? She looks crazy, and, true, she does exactly what she wants to do, but she's the only constant I have.'

'How come you moved away from your parents?' Maisie asked before she could stop herself.

Ric frowned. 'Did Sera tell you that?'

'Yeah, sorry, I didn't mean to be nosy.'

He shook his head. 'It's fine, she just talks too much. Come on.' He stood up and offered his hand. Maisie held hers out and he pulled her to her feet, her skin feeling warm at his touch. 'You're going to do exactly what you want to do, right here, right now, without worrying anyone will judge.'

Maisie shook her head. 'I'm fine here, really...'

Ric raised his eyebrows. 'If you want to stay here, stay. I'm not allowed to tell you what to do. But if you're going to take the first step to freedom, there is no better place to do it.' He held out his arms. 'We're all alone.'

He took off his jacket, revealing a black T-shirt underneath, and dropped it to the floor. Maisie froze as he unbuttoned his walking trousers and dropped those to the floor too, then stood in front of her in just a pair of black boxers and a T-shirt. His legs were tanned with just a hint of muscle – not like the weedy boys she'd gone to college with. She could tell that under his T-shirt his body was athletic, toned, she couldn't drag her eyes away.

'Are you just going to stand there and watch me undress?'

Maisie felt her cheeks burn again and Ric laughed.

'You know what Sera would do?' He jerked his head at his sister, who was out to her waist now. 'She'd tell me to go fuck myself, take off her shorts and get in the sea.'

Maisie contemplated for a second taking off her shorts and running straight into the sea, just like he'd suggested. But she wasn't Seraphine, and what she actually wanted to do was take her shoes off and lie on the sand.

'Go fuck yourself,' she said, sitting back down. 'I want to stay here.'

Ric hesitated a second, then grinned, as if she'd passed some kind of test. He hadn't wanted her to do exactly what his sister would do, he'd wanted her to do what *she* wanted to do. To be her real self, instead of what she thought other people wanted of her. 'That's more like it,' he said. 'Say hello to freedom.' He darted off towards the sea.

Chapter Twelve

October 1999

WHO IS MYSTERIOUS STRANGER?

Vancouver Post

Missing British backpacker, Seraphine Cunningham, who disappeared from the West Coast Trail last July, was seen arguing with a mystery man at a bus stop before joining the hike, witnesses say. The man, who has been described as 'early twenties, with longish brown hair', is yet to be located by police.

Maisie Goodwin, who claims she joined Seraphine at the beginning of the hike, denies any knowledge of this man and didn't see Seraphine arguing with anyone. Goodwin told police: 'We were both lone hikers, that's why we hooked up. If Seraphine had argued with someone, she never mentioned it to me.' Seraphine is believed to have booked in alone, using a cloned credit card under the name of Mary Whittaker.

Fellow hiker Mitchell Dyke is due to stand trial next year, accused of Seraphine's murder.

Chapter Thirteen

November 2019

'I still don't understand why you were in town after you'd already been to the supermarket. And on the bus? What was so urgent that *you* used public transport?'

I can't even get irritated about the emphasis on *you*, Rob is right. I haven't ever used public transport in all the time I've known him.

'I'd forgotten to get a present for Faye's teacher,' I sigh, the lie coming out easily after all the truths I've been forced to tell this afternoon. 'She's leaving to have a baby and Monday is her last day.'

'And you left Faye in Smiggle because…?'

'Jesus, Rob!' I snap. 'Don't you think I feel bad enough without you giving me the third degree? I've already had to explain my extreme lapse in judgement to the police and almost had my daughter snatched. I won't ever forgive myself for what happened today, so you can't possibly make me feel any worse.'

'Hey,' Rob says. He walks behind my seat at the dining-room table and starts to rub my shoulders. It feels amazing. 'I wasn't trying to make you feel bad. It's fine. Faye is fine. She doesn't even really have any idea about the danger she was in. In a few days, this will all be a bad memory.'

I think back to the afternoon I've just spent being interviewed by the police, having Faye recount her description of the man who she'd spoken to... all of it making the possibility of what could have happened so much more real coming from my baby's lips. I can't imagine it fading from memory any time soon.

And yet, still there is the threat of what might be to come. More police, news crews... Oh God. I rub a hand across my eyes and sigh.

Taking it as stress from what has happened today, Rob squeezes my arm. 'Why don't you go and have a bath?' he suggests. 'I'll bring you up a glass of wine and you can try to relax.'

'That's a great idea, thank you.'

I don't particularly want a bath and I definitely don't want alcohol – taking the edge off is the last thing I want to do – but what Rob has just offered me is half an hour to myself, where I can regroup and not have to make up any more lies for a few minutes. I'd forgotten how quickly one lie could spiral into another, and another, until you need a spreadsheet to keep up with them all.

The main lie I've told this afternoon has been to the police. *Is there anyone you can think of who would want to harm your daughter, Mrs Johnson?* At first, my horror had been genuine. I've played the part of the innocent housewife for so long that the thought of anyone wanting to harm me or my family seemed shocking even to me. But, of course, there is someone who would want to harm us, someone who, when I thought about it, fits the description Faye and Cally gave perfectly. But that man is in prison, and I can never tell the police why he might want to hurt me.

Upstairs, I lock the bathroom door and run the water scalding hot and full of bubbles. As it flows, I slide the phone I bought that afternoon – the one I almost sacrificed my daughter's life for – out of my dressing-gown pocket and set about putting the SIM card into it. Just as I'm fumbling the back off, there is a bang on the bathroom door.

'Your butler with your wine, madam,' Rob calls.

I panic, shoving the phone and the box under the folded towel on the toilet seat. The box immediately drops to the floor with a thunk.

'Just a minute!' I shout through the door, opening the cabinet and practically launching the box into it. Several bottles of things we never use fall over.

'Everything okay?' Rob sounds concerned. I usually love his concern, but at the moment it is just making my life difficult. 'I'm allowed to see you naked, you know.'

I pull open the bathroom door, still fully clothed.

He frowns and tries to peer around the door. 'What took you so long?'

'I was having a poo, if you must know,' I snap.

He grins and hands me the glass of wine. 'Sorry I asked. Enjoy your poo-scented bath. I'll put the kids to bed and maybe we can watch a film?'

'Yes, thank you.' I take the wine and back into the bathroom, not wanting to risk him inviting himself in. As soon as the door closes, I lock it again.

The phone takes longer than it should to take apart and insert the SIM. Realising that if I don't actually have a bath Rob is going to notice, I strip off my clothes and, still clutching the mobile, sink down into the scalding water, holding the phone in the air. The water burns my skin, but it feels amazing.

The minute the phone has loaded and I've selected my language and all the other preferences EE needed to know,

I load up the search engine and type in his name. I thought I knew what I would find: a ton of old articles on the trial, my face in all the newspapers, his arrest and subsequent full life sentence. What I'm not expecting is what loads onto the screen in front of me.

SERAPHINE CUNNINGHAM KILLER
APPEAL CONFIRMED

MITCHELL DYKE FULL LIFE
SENTENCE OVERTURNED

MITCHELL DYKE RELEASED

And there it is. The man who I sent to prison for a murder he didn't commit is free.

Chapter Fourteen

It was 6 p.m. by the time they reached Michigan Creek campsite. Five other tents were already pitched, eleven people in all, hanging clothes from the trees, boiling up water on stoves and starting fires. It already felt like a mini community had sprung up.

Seraphine unceremoniously dumped her pack on the floor. 'Where shall we camp?' she asked, looking around for a spot.

'Oh, I'm not stopping here,' Maisie said. She felt a pang of disappointment that this might be the last she saw of the siblings, but Ric's advice from just an hour ago still rang in her ears. This was the trip where she became her own person – where she did what she wanted to do without relenting to others.

Seraphine looked surprised. 'Where will you camp?'

Maisie lowered her voice. 'There's a campsite a couple of kilometres further on, Darling River Falls – I'm going to camp there.' She'd found out about the Darling River Falls campsite through a customer at the café where she worked and had felt particularly pleased with herself – it was barely mentioned in any of the guidebooks she'd bought from Waterstones. A 'hidden gem', the customer had called it, and although she didn't mind sharing her

53

plans with Seraphine and Ric, she didn't want to shout about it.

'Oh.' Sera scrunched up her nose and Maisie was secretly thrilled to see that she looked disappointed. 'Well, can we come with you?'

'Of course.' Maisie tried not to sound too eager, but it was practically impossible. Had she really just made a decision for the group?

She saw Sera look at Ric for confirmation and he gave her a slow, lazy look.

Maisie would wonder later if that was the look that made her do it, the look that made her lie to protect him. That feeling of someone who wanted to spend time with her just for her, not because her mate was hooking up with his mate. She wasn't going to be the hanger-on anymore – they were hanging on to her. She'd never experienced that before.

'Is that okay with you?' he asked, raising one eyebrow. 'Do you mind us tagging along?'

'It makes no odds to me,' she said with a shrug. That was the first lie she told that trip, but it wouldn't be the last.

–

Maisie had felt the pressure as they'd got closer to where Darling River Falls was marked on the map. What if it turned out to be no more than a muddy spring? She'd been promised a beautiful waterfall and an 'out of the way' campsite, but she'd been promised a lot of things by a lot of people in her life that were rarely delivered. If she'd been on her own, it wouldn't have been so bad, she was used to disappointment, but now she'd dragged Sera and

Ric along with her, she was desperately hoping it panned out.

She needn't have worried. It was Sera who saw it first, and Maisie could tell by her reaction that the waterfall had lived up to expectations. She'd been walking behind with Ric when Sera gasped and called out. They'd spent most of the walk together, talking and laughing as Sera trekked ahead, throwing them apprehensive looks every now and then. Maisie got the impression that Sera had wanted to claim her as her friend and was annoyed that her brother was giving Maisie so much attention. It felt good to be squabbled over for once.

'Hurry up!' Sera urged them. 'It's beautiful!'

They picked up the pace through the trees and into the clearing.

'Wow,' Ric breathed. 'You weren't wrong about this place.'

The waterfall was nestled in a cove of jagged rocks, flowing into an emerald pool of water at its base. Maisie – who had thought what she'd seen of Canada so far was beautiful – was awestruck.

'What are you waiting for?' she asked, suddenly feeling daring. She wedged her pack against a rock and began stripping off her clothes.

Sera whooped and followed Maisie's lead, and before long, all three of them were in the pool, washing off the grime of the day.

'How does it feel?' Ric asked her as she floated on her back, gazing up at the sky through the canopy of trees.

Maisie turned her head to look at where he was sitting in the water, watching her. 'How does what feel?'

'Being free.'

Maisie considered the question. 'Wet,' she said.

They made camp on the beach that night, exhilarated but exhausted, and the only ones at the campsite. The tents took an age to put up. Maisie had practised a few times with hers before coming away, but Ric and Sera looked at theirs as though they had never seen them before. When they were finally done, Maisie got out her stove and boiled up water for food. Unsurprisingly, neither Ric nor Sera had brought any food with them, expecting instead that there would be cafés on the trail.

'The Canadians are missing a trick here,' Sera said. 'How about we come back and set up a café of our own, hey, Mais? We could make a fortune.'

'Sure,' Maisie grinned, handing Sera a portion of chicken tikka. She'd packed extra because she'd known Ruth would be cadging food off her. 'And we're going to hike out here with the food every day, are we? Or are we going to live in our tents?'

Seraphine frowned. 'We can work out the details later.'

Maisie laughed.

The temperature had dropped and she shivered and went over to her tent to grab a hoodie from her bag. When she went back, Sera and Ric looked like they'd been arguing.

'Everything okay?'

'Fine,' Sera said, her voice tight. 'I'm just really tired. You don't mind if I turn in, do you?'

Maisie looked between the two of them. Ric gave his head a small shake.

'Of course not. I'm exhausted too, I'll probably turn in now as well.'

'Let me help you pack this away first.' Ric picked up the empty bowls and cutlery.

Sera glared at him and walked towards her tent.

'Goodnight then,' she called. Then she climbed in and zipped up.

'Have I missed something?' Maisie whispered as they carried the plates to the freshwater creek to wash up.

Ric shrugged. 'She doesn't like not being centre of attention,' he said. 'I think she feels like maybe we're getting on too well. She thought you were going to fall all over her like everyone else does.'

'She's very beautiful,' Maisie said. 'And she's certainly charismatic. I can see why people love her.'

'You wouldn't believe,' Ric replied. He crouched down at the spring and filled the collapsible water bowl. Maisie began handing him plates. 'It's ridiculous to watch sometimes, how she gets her way with people. Of course, she doesn't realise that she's just trying to make up for how little attention our parents gave us.'

This took Maisie by surprise. He'd chastised Seraphine earlier in the day for even mentioning their parents, now here he was blaming them for his sister's attention-seeking.

'Were you neglected then?' she asked after a pause. 'Is that why you went to live with your aunt and uncle?'

'We ran away,' Ric said flatly. Maisie sucked in a sharp breath. 'We ran away to live with our aunt and uncle. And I don't think our parents ever bothered to look for us. I don't think they even called my aunt to find out if we were with them.'

'God, how shit,' Maisie said. She cringed at how utterly terrible she was at deep and meaningful conversations. That was the problem you had when the most meaningful conversation you had was to ask if someone wanted Earl Grey or English Breakfast tea.

'Utterly shit,' Ric replied with the greatest sincerity. He met her eyes and they both burst out laughing. 'Look, I might not have any food with me, but I've got a few joints,' Ric said as they carried the clean plates back. 'Let me pay you back for the meal?'

'Oh, I don't know, I've never… I don't really…'

'It's just an offer,' Ric said, putting a hand up. 'No pressure. You're doing exactly what you want on this trip, remember? Not what you think other people want.'

–

Seraphine's tent was silent when they got back from rinsing the plates, and Ric put a finger to his lips and gestured to his tent, which was further away from his sleeping sister. He dragged his sleeping bag out and motioned for Maisie to follow him away from the beach and into the trees.

'I found this clearing when I went for a piss,' he said, taking Maisie by the hand. He led her to where the trees were slightly less dense and moonlight shone through the sparse leaves overhead, dappling the ground with a silver glow. Generations of hikers before them had arranged the rocks so that they formed a smooth seating area, cold but not uncomfortable.

Ric laid the sleeping bag on the rocks and gestured for her to join him. When Maisie sat down, he pulled the sleeping bag around her shoulders and she felt as though he could probably hear her heart thumping against the inside of her chest.

Ric reached inside his shirt pocket and pulled out a joint. Lighting it, he offered it to her.

'Ladies first,' he said.

'I've, um… I don't smoke,' Maisie said, feeling her face flush.

'Do you want me to show you?'

He put the joint to his lips and breathed in, demonstrating how to hold the smoke in and draw it slowly into her lungs.

Maisie tried it and fell about coughing and spluttering. Ric laughed, and when she recovered, she joined in. With him, it didn't feel like he was laughing *at* her, they were laughing together.

Eventually, though, she got the hang of it and found she liked it much more than alcohol. Sure, her head felt super spinny, and she didn't fancy her chances of standing up, but she didn't feel like she was going to puke… just a little sleepy and majorly hungry.

'You okay?' Ric asked, slipping his free arm around her shoulder. His body was warm and hard, and without thinking, she reached out a hand to touch his chest. She'd been wanting to do that all day.

Ric snorted back a laugh. Maisie realised what she was doing and snatched her hand back.

'God, sorry,' she said, mortification creeping over her. 'That was so uncool.'

'It's okay,' he said, taking her hand and placing it back on his chest. 'I like that you're not cool. I like you the way you are.'

He leaned in closer and Maisie knew that this was it – he was going to kiss her.

His lips were warm and moist on hers, and his mouth tasted of weed and curry, but it was the most wonderful kiss she could have ever imagined. Nothing at all like the sloppy, fumbling kisses she'd had with boys at school, who were only snogging her because there was no one else around. Ric was soft and slow, gentle and tender but passionate at the same time.

When they broke apart, he didn't try to shove his hand up her top, or grasp desperately at her belt to fumble her jeans down. He took her hand and they wandered back to the camp, where he led her into his tent, pulled her close, wrapped the sleeping bag around them both and rested her head on his shoulder.

Maisie fell gently asleep to the sounds of the ocean in her ears, the smell of his aftershave in her nostrils and the taste of him on her lips.

Chapter Fifteen

November 2019

I don't know how I've let this slip past me and I'm furious when I realise how complacent I've become. The beautiful home, the doting husband, two gorgeous children. I even have the perfect job. I work from home creating bespoke gifts. And as the years passed, knowing that Mitchell Dyke was behind bars I allowed myself to forget what had happened in Canada and put what happened firmly behind me. She is in my past and she can't hurt me now… that was what I believed. But I've been stupid, naive. What happened in Canada is never going to be behind me, that is clear now. Not until I face Mitchell head on. I discovered a long time ago that I wasn't going to become a sad little victim. When I'm pushed into a corner, I fight back and that is exactly what I'm going to have to do. Again.

'Faye, sweetheart, come on, get your shoes on!' I shout up the stairs. 'George! School!'

Monday, everyone's least favourite day of the week except mine. On Mondays, I get to drop the children off at school and do what I love best: paint. I'm working on a particularly tricky commission that I'm dying to get back to, anything to just forget what has gone on at the weekend. I spent all of Sunday obsessing about tracking down Mitchell, and what I was going to do when I did. I don't really believe the man Faye spoke to was him – there's no way he can have found me so quickly. I thought I'd made sure that I'm untraceable. He's only been out for six months and if he's really come to find me here, that would be a huge mistake. He should know that after what I've been through I'm not just some middle-aged yummy-mummy pushover. I won't run off to be sick at the drop of a hat like the heroine in a book and my hands won't shake if I have to do whatever it takes to protect my family.

'I didn't do my reading,' Faye says as she shoves her feet into her shoes. Are they getting a bit tight? I mentally add shoe shopping to the list of things I have to do this week.

'You didn't tell me you had to read,' I counter. That doesn't wash with Faye as I'd known it wouldn't.

'I have to read every night. Or I don't get my stamp. You know that.'

'Read in the car and I'll write it in as last night's,' I say, picking up her school bag.

Faye looks horrified. 'That's lying,' she accuses.

I try not to sigh. Good mothers teach their children not to lie.

'Not if you read tonight as well – you've still done the same amount of reading.'

'I don't think Mrs Ramsey will see it that way,' Faye insists.

This time, I do sigh.

'Tell her you were in a car accident,' I say, hustling her and George out of the door. 'Look, we're even having to get a taxi to school. She'll definitely understand that.'

Faye's eyes narrow, but even she can't argue with that. No lying involved and a get-out-of-reading-free card. She's sold. Maybe she is her mother's daughter after all.

Miss Murray – or Tamra to the parents – the new school secretary, comes out to meet us at the gate. She's only been here about six months, but she's so beautifully unconventional that it's impossible not to like her on first sight. She's in her early twenties, I think, her shoulder-length hair is bleached blonde down to her ears with a striking blue/black at the bottom, and when it moves, you can see bright red hidden underneath. All perfectly acceptable hair colours by the school board's rules, and they are unable to find anywhere where it says she can't have all three at once – and I have it on good authority that they've tried. Not everyone in the school approves of her, I know that, but I think she's a delight, and brilliant with the kids. Today, she is wearing a plain black shift dress with a frilly white collar, and black-rimmed glasses in a parody of a stern secretary look, only she's paired it with bright red tights and lipstick to match.

'Laura, sweetheart, I heard about your crash,' she says, taking Faye's bags from me in one hand and George's hand in the other. 'Are you all okay?'

'We're fine. Who told you?' I try not to sound annoyed. This school is a nightmare for keeping secrets – not ideal when your whole life is based on one. At least she doesn't seem to know about what had happened in town afterwards – if she knew that Faye had almost been taken by a strange man, she wouldn't be asking me about a little bump to my car. I wonder if Faye will tell a version of the story in class. I hope not.

'Veronica saw Steve at the shop who said Rob had told him,' Tamra says, not a hint of embarrassment at the shameless gossiping that had been going on. 'Is the car totalled?'

'It wasn't even a real crash,' I assure her, shunting Faye forwards to get them moving. 'The car will survive. My insurance – not so much. Rob's going to do pick-up tonight though, save taxi fares.'

'Oooh, that will be a treat for the mums.' Miss Murray winks theatrically, making me grin.

'Not you though. I heard about your new fella?'

Now it's my turn to unashamedly gossip. One of the other mums had seen Tamra in a bar with a guy, but she's always talked about being single.

Her face reddens, I've embarrassed her. 'He's just... well, yes, I suppose you could call him my boyfriend. It's early days. Eek! I've said too much. I'm not supposed to jinx it.' Then she turns to the children. 'Come on you two, let's get you into class. George, is that a new teddy? What's his name?'

I wave them off, George looking slightly teary-eyed as usual, dragging his new bunny alongside him. It's almost worse than if he had full-blown tantrums every morning, that quiet, watery-eyed acceptance that I am leaving him again. Sometimes I really wonder if I've ruined him just by loving him too much. I've made myself the centre of his universe and I panic often that it is unhealthy. What if something happened to me? Even at such a young age, I have this notion that Faye would cope; she would be sad, of course, but she is a survivor. George, on the other hand, I just have this image of him ceasing to function without me, physically not having anything to tether him to this world. Or perhaps it's projection, because he is my tether. He is the one who needs me most, or the me that I've become – Laura Johnson, mummy – and that anchors me to this new world I've created. They – the children and Rob that is – stop me slipping back into the person I was.

Deceitful, distrustful, dishonest. The problem I face now, after what happened with Faye at the weekend, is that if I'm going to protect my family from Mitchell Dyke, the old me is exactly who I need to be.

–

The taxi drops me back at home, where I let Archie out of his crate and boil the kettle while he bounces around my legs.

'All right, baby, I've only been out for half an hour!' Still, he nudges at my legs until I bend down and scratch him behind his ears where he loves to be fussed the most. He's just over eighteen months old now and while he's still a little devil most of the time, he knows his routine and he likes to stick with it. In the week, I drop the kids off at school, come home, make coffee, and decamp to my studio at the bottom of the garden, where Archie curls up on the sofa and waits until lunchtime when he gets a walk. Today is no exception – despite what's gone on this weekend, I've still had orders placed and I can't afford to let my customers down.

My business – personalised gifts that I sell through Etsy and eBay – has been growing slowly for the last three years. Very slowly at first, as I could only accept commissions that could be fit in around a baby's naptime, but once George was old enough to join preschool, I began to take on more and more, until our dining room started to resemble a warehouse and packing centre. That was when Rob had declared 'enough was enough' only in a half-mocking tone and found me a summer house to go at the bottom of the (already not huge) garden of our three-bedroom semi-detached house. He spent a whole weekend insulating it and putting electrics in. He painted it himself and sanded and stained the floors, then presented it to me in a mock-grand opening, with a bunch of flowers and Faye cutting the ribbon. It had been quite emotional.

Although Rob had spent what felt like a week in IKEA to make the perfect craft studio, with whitewashed walls full of shelves lined with baskets and the multicoloured rug he knew I'd love, over the next year the summer house became something of a haven for each one of us. If I needed to get something done at a weekend, George would come and sit at the end of my long wooden desk and colour in pictures of *PAW Patrol* or Marvel heroes (although one time Rob caught him colouring in from my sweary adult colouring book and put a stop to that. I didn't see the big deal – it's not like George can read anyway), or if Faye had a project for school that involved making anything, she would come and pore over all of the ribbons and sequins, washi tapes and pom-poms I'd collected. Most of it was unnecessary for my work – people wanted Cricut stickers and hand-painted family trees, but I scavenged and saved everything I could because every minute my daughter and I spent crafting was so precious. I'd never had any time like that with my own mother and so I always made sure those sessions with Faye were protected.

Then, on the odd occasion that I would need to work in the evenings, after reading the children to sleep, Rob would bring me a glass of wine out to the studio, sit on the tatty old reconditioned armchair I'd insisted on dragging in there and complain about how out of place it was in the perfect space he'd created. Then we'd talk about our day, or the children. Our favourite thing was to invent stories for the people I was personalising gifts for. How Andrea's personalised map of Australia was her boyfriend's way of telling her he was leaving her to go travelling, or Roger's personalised stationery set was his wife's way of saying she knew he'd been sleeping with his secretary. I think those times, when it was just me and Rob – and sometimes Archie if he hadn't fallen asleep in George's room – were my favourite parts of mine and Rob's relationship. Of course, it was exciting when we first met in our late-twenties, all whirlwind romance and holidays and sex in the daytime, but those times are easy, aren't they? It's the bits later on I wanted to hold onto and cherish, the bits after children and age had made our bodies squishier and our under-eyes darker. When we still managed to carve out time and space to really be us again, even if it was only for half an hour. The parts you have to work for.

It's all these thoughts that go through my head every time I approach the wooden cabin that we painted forest green, so it blended into the hedges behind and it automatically makes me calm. I see Rob in the chair and Faye with her head in the sequin box, and little George perched at my desk. Today Archie runs beside me, giving a little skip and a jump like he knows the routine.

I pull the key out of my pocket, but when I get to the door, I don't need to use it. The bolt is on the floor and there is a gaping crack in the wooden door. Someone has broken into my studio.

Chapter Sixteen

Maisie woke the next morning feeling as though she'd slept for days. It took her a minute to remember where she was, and what the cause of the elation running through her entire body was. She was waking up on the beach, in Canada… in Ric's tent.

Ric was no longer lying next to her, but unlike the old Maisie, of only two days ago, this didn't seem to bother her in the slightest. There was no instant paranoia or shame – they had only kissed and she was plenty old enough to do that with whoever she liked. She wasn't panicked that he was full of regret and had run away, never to be seen again – after all, this was his tent. But it wasn't just that, even if Ric told her that the whole thing last night had been a terrible mistake, she didn't think it could ruin the way she felt now. For the first time in her life, she had had an experience she felt like she had been in total control of, and it had been perfect. She was free.

She lay there a moment longer, not wanting to lose the feeling. Inside the tent was warm and she could see the bright sunlight outside. Checking her watch, she realised it was 9 a.m. Jesus, she had slept well. Pushing herself up and out from under the sleeping bag, she unzipped the tent and peered out. Her own tent was still closed up, and she realised with a bit of a jolt that she'd left her bag and belongings in it unguarded all night. It was funny though; she couldn't even bring herself to be overly bothered about that. Que sera and all that.

Speaking of Sera, her new friend was standing in the surf, just twenty metres or so away, talking to her brother. Maisie cringed, wondering if Sera had noticed that her tent was empty and wondered where she had spent the night. She didn't know why, but for some reason she didn't want Sera to know what she and Ric had shared the previous evening. It felt imperative, almost, that she kept it a secret.

Sera's back was to her, and Maisie padded silently over to her own tent, cringing at the noise the zip made as she eased it open. Then, from inside, as though she had just poked her head out, she called, 'Morning!' to the pair.

Sera looked round at Maisie, almost seeming surprised to see her. Then she smiled and waved, turned to say something to Ric and then bounded over with all the energy Maisie had come to expect from her.

'Morning!' she said, throwing herself down at the front of the tent. Damp sand clung to her legs and her skin smelt of salt and sun cream. 'How did you sleep?'

There was no hint of innuendo in her voice, no little wink wink, nudge nudge. Perhaps she really was none the wiser that Maisie had spent the night in Ric's tent. Or perhaps she just wasn't bothered in the slightest. Maisie only had sisters, but she couldn't imagine wanting to know about their sex life. Not that her and Ric had a sex life. Not yet anyway.

'Really good actually, considering I'm not much of a camper back home. How about you?'

'Like the dead,' Sera said, a huge smile on her face. 'We camp loads, so I'm used to sleeping on the floor. It's a different experience on sand though. Anyway, you have to come with me. I found these rock pools full of starfish and weird barnacle things, and some people walking past a bit ago said that sometimes you can see whales from this part of the beach.'

'That's amazing,' Maisie replied. 'Although I'm starving.'

Sera waved her hand towards her brother. 'Ric can do the food. Just leave your bag outside your tent and he'll take care of it.'

Maisie noted once again that Sera expected her to provide the food for breakfast. She wondered what they would have done if they hadn't bumped into her. Starved, it seemed. Still, she didn't feel much like cooking and if Ric was happy to do it, then she didn't mind sharing some food. She just hoped she'd packed enough to last the three of them the entire trip.

'Come on,' Sera urged, and Maisie climbed out of her tent, looking like she'd spent the night in yesterday's clothes. Again, if Sera noticed, she didn't say so. 'You are going to love this.'

Chapter Seventeen

November 2019

My first instinct is to push open the door and check my things – my computer, my Cricut machine, my laminator… My whole business is in there and my heart sinks when I think about the loss. The studio is technically classed as a shed, and only things that should usually be stored in a shed will be covered by our home insurance. That does not include my iMac. *Shit.*

It's only when Archie gives out a little whine that I whip my hand back as though the door handle is on fire. What am I playing at just walking in there? What if there's someone still inside? After all, I've only been gone forty minutes or so and I'm certain it wasn't like this before I left.

I back away as quietly as possible, gesturing for Archie to come with me and I'm relieved when, for once, he complies straight away. Back at the house, it takes me longer than it should to decide what to do. There are just too many factors at play; this might not be any normal break-in. If I call the police – which I should – and it's Mitchell Dyke in my studio, the truth is bound to come out. And if I call Rob, he's going to tell me to call the police, like any normal, law-abiding person would do. Of course he won't understand if I say I can't. So I leave my phone where it is and I move around the kitchen island to where we keep the knives and lift one from the block. I bounce it lightly in my hand a few times, feeling the weight of it, wrapping my fingers around the smooth black plastic handle. Can I use this?

'You don't have much choice,' I tell myself. 'He's here to hurt you. You have to defend your family.'

I take a deep breath in through my nose, hold it for a few seconds and let it out slowly. Locking Archie back in his crate – he's not exactly a guard dog and I don't want him getting hurt – I close the back door.

'The police are on their way,' I say loudly, hoping the neighbours aren't in their garden. 'I'm going to stand back and give you a chance to run now. If you stay in there you will be arrested.'

It sounds like the world's worst lie. If I'd called the police, then obviously I would have locked myself inside the house and waited for them, or left and gone to a neighbour's. I wouldn't be standing in the back garden giving the burglar a chance to escape. And if it really is Mitchell in there, well, he'd know for certain that I'm not going to call the police on him.

Silence.

I wait another few seconds, then slowly make my way to the door. I'm not bothered about fingerprints or forensics; this isn't a police matter anymore. This is between me and Mitchell. There's only one reason for him being here – he blames me for spending half of his life behind bars. And why wouldn't he? But he crossed the line when he tried to take my daughter. And it's too bad for him that he failed, because now I know what he's capable of, I'm not going to give him another chance to get his hands on her. He'll have to get his revenge by picking on someone his own size. Me.

Without hesitating, I lift my leg, kick the door to the studio and stand back as it flies inwards. No one rushes towards me; no gunshot rings out. My back to the wall, I edge in, like I've seen them do on TV, and swing around the door frame.

The studio is empty.

The only place to hide would be under the desk, and if he's done that, he's dead already. He can't jump out at me from there. Still, I tread carefully until I'm close enough to see underneath. Nothing. My machines and computer are still in their places. Nothing seems to have been…

And then I see it. The piece I was working on, a laser-cut photo frame for a couple called Susan and Nick for an eight-year anniversary. It should have their pictures on, and their names underneath, but instead their photographs have been replaced with newspaper photographs of two girls. Two girls I know very well. And underneath, where the names of my clients should be wrapped in a heart, are two names that I couldn't forget if I wanted to.

Seraphine and Maisie.

And underneath, someone has scrawled the words LYING BITCH.

Chapter Eighteen

July 1999 – Maisie

Sera had been right. The small rock pools that had formed on the beach had held crabs and starfish; there was even a baby jellyfish in one. Maisie had been delighted. She looked over to the rocks where Sera was now scanning for pieces of the shipwrecks that made the West Coast Trail so famous.

'You look like you've never seen a starfish before,' Ric grinned, swatting her on the arm.

'Well, maybe that's because I haven't,' Maisie admitted. When Ric raised his eyebrows, she laughed. 'What? We can't all be intrepid adventurers like the Cunninghams. My mum couldn't afford holidays, and even if she could, she's rarely well enough to take us.'

Ric's face took on a serious look. 'You sound like you've spent your whole life trapped by your mum's illness,' he said, placing his tanned, smooth hand on her pale knee. Maisie turned away, not wanting to start crying in front of him.

'She can't help it,' she said, attempting a nonchalant shrug. 'She didn't ask to get depression.'

'No,' Ric nodded, as though he understood completely. 'But you didn't ask for her to get it either. It's not your responsibility to make sure everyone is looked after, you know.'

'That's easy for someone like you to say,' she snapped, feeling anger begin to rise inside her. 'You don't have to think about anyone but yourself. What am I supposed to do, abandon my family? It's not that easy.'

'Actually, it is,' Ric said, without looking offended at her words. 'You just walk away and don't look back. Are any of them looking out for you?'

Maisie reached forwards and brushed her fingertips against the starfish, which rippled underneath her skin. Ric made it sound as though the world was her oyster, as if there weren't invisible ties binding her to her depressed mother and her dependent sisters. What if it were true? What if she never went back? Perhaps her sisters would be removed from their mother's custody. It would hurt her — her mum wanted to be a good mother; it wasn't her fault that she couldn't cope sometimes — but what if Ric was right? Maisie wasn't the one who had made the decision to have more children than she could look after, and she wasn't the one who went on and off her medication whenever she felt like it. If she walked away from her life, someone would have to take her place in looking out for her sisters. Social services, or her aunty Fiona, who she hardly ever saw but knew was a good person who loved her sister and nieces.

'So tell me,' she said, her voice quieter now. 'How does one just walk away from their life and start anew? And, for argument's sake, let's pretend you are a nineteen-year-old girl with about a hundred pounds left in the bank.'

'How did you discover my secret?' he teased.

Maisie smiled but wasn't letting him off that easily. 'Go on,' she urged. 'Where would I go? How would I get there?'.

'There are plenty of ways to get along without having thousands of pounds in the bank,' Ric said. He picked up a stick and began to draw lines in the wet sand next to him. 'Let's say you decided to stay here, in Canada, for a while. You could stay in a hostel, get a job in a bar washing pots. Then, when you've made enough for some bus fare, you go and find another hostel, another bar. Pretty girl like you, you'll always find some work. You could sell jewellery on the beaches in Bali. Paint sunsets in Milan. Pick pockets in Rome.'

Maisie's eyes narrowed. 'Is that what you and Sera do? Get by picking pockets?'

He shrugged. 'On the odd occasion, we've had to.' He must have seen the frown on her face because he laughed. 'People do what they have to to get by in this world, Maisie. If someone is born with rich parents who can afford to fund their start-up business and their fancy meals in nice restaurants, then great, they need never do anything that you find so distasteful. But what about the rest of us? Those of us with parents who wouldn't piss on us if we were on fire? Who have never provided us with even basic food and drink, let alone caviar and champagne? Should we starve on the streets because of circumstance? It's a roll of the dice what kind of life you're born into, and it's not always fair. So those of us who got a bum deal have to do stuff that is frowned upon by those who have never had to go hungry a day in their lives. And who are they to look down on us? To judge us? Walk a mile in my shoes, Maisie, and then frown when I tell you how I stay alive.'

She felt a wave of shame wash over her. He was right – her life hadn't been easy, but she had always had a roof over her head, there had always been food in the fridge – even if she'd had to use Mum's benefits to go and buy it for them. And if she'd had to steal to feed her sisters, then she knew she would have done without a moment's hesitation.

'You're right, I'm sorry,' she said, gazing off across the sea. It still didn't feel real that she was actually here, in another country, a world away from home. Here, anything felt possible, even this life of freedom Ric was describing. After all, if this was possible now, then why shouldn't it be possible tomorrow, and the day after that, and the day after that? 'What if…' She hesitated. She wanted to ask him what would happen if she wanted to stay with them, him and Sera, instead of going home to her old life. How would it work? Would she just not get on her flight back home? But she was scared. If he told her no, that would be the end of the dream. She would never go it alone.

'What if what?' he pushed. He looked like he knew exactly what she wanted to ask him and he was playing with her. 'You're supposed to be a new woman. Take risks, get what you want. So go ahead. Ask.'

She felt her face redden. 'What if I came with you after the trail is done? Just for a while,' she added quickly. 'Just until I find my feet somewhere. Get a job…'

Ric grinned. 'One kiss and you're willing to follow me anywhere. I must be a better kisser than I thought.'

'What? I… You…'

He held up a hand, laughing. 'I was kidding, jeesh. I'll talk to Sera, but I don't think it will be a problem. I think she likes you.' He looked across to where Seraphine was now sitting on the rocks, gazing out to sea, and he leaned forwards, quickly placing a kiss on Maisie's lips.

–

However reluctant she had been to break the spell and move on, Maisie knew they had to cross one section of the Klanawa hike below 2.7 metres or they would be stuck another night until low tide. Sera made little complaint about pressing on – she grew bored quickly, it seemed – and they hiked on until they reached the cable cars at Klanawa River, then on to Tsusiat Falls. It was nearly dusk by the time they reached the falls.

'Oh wow,' Maisie breathed as the trees parted and the fast-flowing water was revealed in all its splendid glory. 'If I live to a hundred, I know I'll never see a more beautiful sight.'

Ric looked at her in wonder, as though she was the tourist attraction. 'It's just a waterfall,' he said, his voice betraying his surprise. 'Haven't you ever seen a waterfall before?'

Maisie shrugged, her cheeks colouring. 'I've seen a couple of little ones back home. None that are higher than my head.'

Ric put his arm around her shoulders and squeezed. 'I promise you right now, if you stick with me, that waterfall will be the least memorable thing you see on this trip.'

Maisie grinned and shrugged down her pack. 'Well, until you decide to show me something memorable, Mr Cunningham, this is all I have. So I'm going to make the most of it.'

For once, Ric and Sera were the sensible ones, convincing her to at least stop to put the tents up before jumping into the pool and underneath the waterfall. She was glad they had when the sky began to turn a petulant grey, and fat raindrops landed on their heads.

'Oh bloody hell,' Sera complained, scowling at the sky. 'I thought we were going to avoid the rain.'

'Well, we're wet already,' Maisie said, ducking her shoulders under the cool water. 'So it doesn't matter much, does it?'

'Yeah, lighten up, Sera,' Ric said, his voice teasing. He pushed a strand of wet hair from Maisie's eyes. 'I thought you were supposed to be the free spirit.'

'A free spirit doesn't have to enjoyed getting rained on,' she said. She swam over to the side. 'I'm getting out. You two can mess around like children in the sodding rain for all I care.'

'I don't think she's loving this hike,' Maisie whispered.

Ric sniggered. He drew himself closer to her and under the water reached out a hand, brushing his fingertips against her hip. Maisie shivered, and it wasn't from the cold of the rain.

'The thing you should know about Sera,' he said, wrapping his finger around the fabric of her bikini bottoms and tugging her closer to him. 'Is that she's not really the person she wants to be. Never has been. I don't think she has any idea who she really is, to be honest. She's never been allowed to be anything other than what her parents wanted her to be. It's like her personality is made up of bits of things she's seen on the TV and in films, depending on who she's with, and what she thinks they want of her. One day she can be Eliza Doolittle the flower seller, the next she's My Fair Lady.'

'Don't tell me you've seen *My Fair Lady*,' Maisie scoffed. She didn't want to talk about his sister anymore, she wanted to feel those fingertips over the rest of her body, his lips on her skin. She slipped her leg in-between his thighs and nudged them open.

'It was my favourite ever film,' he said, his eyes wide in mock offence. He opened his legs to let her in-between them, sliding his finger lower and nudging her bikini bottoms to one side. Maisie gasped as his fingertip circled her clitoris and ground herself into his hand. 'There's no need to rush,' he murmured into her ear. She saw him looking over to where Sera had disappeared into her tent and then he bowed his head and covered her lips with his. As she trembled under his kiss, he pushed his finger inside her, making her gasp out. Her entire body quivered as he arched her backwards to reach the perfect spot, then began to move his finger, slowly at first, then faster and more urgently. A pressure began to rise within her, a pressure she'd never felt before. It felt like exquisite torture, a longing she'd never known.

A loud cough and the sound of a woman's giggle ripped Maisie back to the present moment. She pulled away from Ric to see a couple of hikers looking awkwardly at the falls.

'Sorry to interrupt!' the woman called, waving.

Maisie realised that all they had seen was the pair kissing, they had no idea that they had just interrupted the first orgasm she'd never had.

'They don't look sorry,' Ric muttered, and Maisie burst out laughing.

'Come on,' she said, taking his hand. 'Let's get dry.'

'Ah man,' he complained. 'I quite like you wet.'

Chapter Nineteen

November 2019

I take a hammer to the photo frame, gather up the tiny fragments and take them to the bin by the bus stop. I won't pretend I'm not shaken by what's happened – my worst fears have been confirmed, after all. Someone – Mitchell – knows who I am, and where I am. He knows where I live, what else does he know about me? He must have followed me into town the other day and been watching the house to know when I take the kids to school and what time I get back. So what is he playing at? I get why he'd want payback, but if I was out for revenge, to be honest I'd just go straight to the big stuff. Either burn my house down or out me to the media, don't mess around with old photographs and mean words. It's a clear warning – he can get to me, my family, my home, any time he likes. And that puts me on the back foot straight away because I don't know where he's staying or what he's planning and yet he seems to know so much about me.

You can't let him get to you, I think as I check the locks on the front and back doors. *You need to get ahead of him. That's how you've had to live your whole life, one step ahead.*

My call to Rob's mobile rings and rings, and when it goes to answerphone, I just dial again. After a couple of rings on the second try, he answers, his voice sounding concerned.

'Everything okay?'

'Not really, no,' I tell him truthfully. 'When I got back from pick-up, someone ran out of our back garden. They'd been breaking into the studio.'

'Shit, are you okay? Did they hurt you? Have you called the police? I'll come home… I'll be back in half an hour.'

'No, Rob, there's no need,' I interrupt his barrage of questions. 'They ran off. They didn't come near me and nothing was taken – I must have disturbed them. They're long gone. It was just a shock, that's all.'

'I bet it was. What did the police say?'

'I didn't call them. Before you start,' I say, 'they won't do anything anyway, especially as nothing was stolen. They'll take a week to get here and all that will happen is that our home insurance will rocket.'

There is a pause on the other end of the line and I know I've got him with the home insurance comment. I considered just getting the door fixed and not telling Rob until I realised that if I play this right, I can get what I need from the situation.

'I'm just glad your car wasn't there,' I say, and hold my breath.

'What, do you think he'd have tried the car?' The fear in his voice is palpable. Rob's car is his pride and joy – he wouldn't have been quite so forgiving if it had been his Mercedes I'd crashed rather than my Nissan.

'Didn't I tell you? I spoke to Gina a couple of doors down and she said there had been someone trying car door handles a couple of nights back. They're getting security cameras put up, I think she said. And a Ring doorbell,' I added for good measure.

'Bloody hell. Do you think we should get some cameras ourselves?'

Bingo. My wonderful husband is nothing if not predictable.

'I don't know, do you? It might be a good idea. More for a deterrent than anything. If he sees we've put cameras up, it might stop him coming back.'

And if it doesn't, I think, then at least I'll see him coming.

'I don't know, Lolly, I don't really have time to sort all that and he's probably long gone. I bet you scared him off.'

'You're right,' I agree. 'Gina's just paranoid. I mean, you know how much Adam loves his car. And I don't think their security would be the reason he chose our house instead of theirs...'

Rob sighs and I feel a bit guilty for stressing him out like this.

'Look, why don't I take a look at some cheap cameras and one of those doorbells?' I suggest, as though I'm taking a massive weight off his shoulders. 'Everyone's got one these days, I can't imagine they are too expensive.'

'Would you?' Rob sounds relieved. 'Don't go over the top though, Lol. Like I said, he's probably long gone.' We're not short on money, but that's mainly because Rob doesn't like to waste it.

'Mmmm,' I said, already scrolling through pages of monitoring devices on my laptop. 'Long gone.'

Chapter Twenty

Transcript of True Crime Addict Podcast. 21 September 2017

Episode 78 – SERAPHINE CUNNINGHAM –
Disappearance on The West Coast Trail

Stacie: Hey, true crime fans. I'm Stacie Plant.

Kellie: And I'm Kellie.

Stacie: And we're going to tell you the story of the mysterious disappearance of Seraphine Cunningham from the West Coast Trail on 30 July 1999 – one of the most infamous 'no body' cases successfully prosecuted – along with the disappearance of Peter Falconio in 2001, and poor, sweet, six-year-old Logan Tucker in 2002.

The West Coast Trail spans from Pachena Bay to Gordon River, in British Columbia, Vancouver. It's a beautiful hike, treacherous in places, slippery boardwalks and infamous ladders. Thousands of people make the hike every summer, and in the summer of 1999, nineteen-year-old Maisie Goodwin decided it was her chance to escape her regular life and find herself on the beaches of Vancouver. Having planned to take the hike with her old friend, Maisie found herself travelling alone when her friend cancelled at the last minute.

Reports vary on how Maisie met up with nineteen-year-old Seraphine Cunningham. Goodwin herself testified that they met at orientation, but there were reports of witnesses seeing the pair getting onto the bus together from the airport. Records suggest the two were on separate flights and they come from vastly different backgrounds, so it's unlikely that they knew one another before the trip.

Seraphine Cunningham has always been something of an enigma, which is one of the reasons the case has gained so much infamy. Few photographs of the nineteen-year-old exist – Sera had been travelling for the previous two years and her whereabouts during this time are largely unknown. Her parents, a wealthy couple from the UK, had reported her missing at seventeen years old, before police had informed them that Seraphine was alive and living in France, and had no desire to see them ever again. From there, it is unknown where Seraphine spent the next two years, and it's possible that her disappearance from the West Coast Trail would have gone completely unnoticed if she hadn't befriended Maisie on that first day.

The first couple of days on the trail, according to Maisie's testimony, went without incident. So it is somewhat unusual that she can't explain why, when they camped at Cribs Creek on the third night of the trail, the pair were camping separately. Witnesses, including Mitchell Dyke who we'll hear more about later, report that Sera and Maisie barely spoke to one another on the third evening, to the extent that they were unaware that the two had been travelling together for the previous days.

The group, comprising of Kaz Rigby, Keddie Everett and Mitchell Dyke, spent the evening drinking with Maisie, until Sera joined them. It was alleged that it was Seraphine who produced the drugs that were taken that night, believed to be cocaine.

It was at some point in the evening – none of the witnesses have ever been sure of the time – that Keddie and Kaz, who had been chatting with other hikers camped at the site, noticed their two new friends were missing, along with Mitchell Dyke. Thinking nothing of their disappearance – it was more than common for people to wander off to make new acquaintances on these kinds of trips – Keddie and Kaz retreated to their tents to sleep off their intoxication.

It was somewhere around 2 a.m., as reported by the *Irish Herald*, when Kaz was woken by a low moaning sound, like someone in a large amount of pain, she testified. She and Keddie both emerged from their tents to find Maisie stumbling around in distress.

Kellie: Did she say why?

Stacie: According to Kaz's testimony at the trial, Maisie looked 'completely out of it'.

Kellie: From the drink and drugs still?

Stacie: It's possible. Maisie was unused to drugs, so it would track that they would affect her more than the others. In fact, Kaz testified that when she started talking about Seraphine being attacked, they thought she had been dreaming. It wasn't until she became hysterical, shouting that they had to find her and help her that Kaz and Keddie realised that something really was wrong.

86

Kellie: Where was Mitchell at this point?

Stacie: Well, that's the million-dollar question. Because Maisie would later claim that it was Mitchell Dyke who she saw attacking Seraphine. Yet Kaz insists that Mitchell came out of his tent minutes after Maisie came stumbling into camp.

Kellie: What about Keddie?

Stacie: Well, here's the thing. Keddie has always claimed that he has no memory of seeing Mitchell at that time, despite the proximity of their tents. This is something that has always gone against Dyke – if he was at the campsite, why didn't Keddie see him?

Kellie: Playing devil's advocate, it was dark, late, and there was a woman screaming bloody murder. Did Maisie name Mitchell on the night?

Stacie: No, she said 'he' but couldn't say who 'he' was.

Kellie: What happened next?

Stacie: Next came the search for Seraphine. But we'll cover that after a short word from our sponsors.

Chapter Twenty-One

July 1999 – Maisie

Waking up alone was beginning to become a pattern, was Maisie's first thought the next morning. The tent was warm and still smelt of sex, but Ric was nowhere to be seen. Maisie unzipped the tent, expecting to see him outside cooking breakfast, but despite the campsite being fairly quiet, she couldn't see him anywhere. Perhaps he had decided to go for an early wash in the falls, or a morning run. It occurred to her that she didn't even know if he was the type to go for a run. Maybe he was one of those fitness buffs who was up at 5 a.m. to run and meditate before the sun came up. She didn't think so, but she had no way of knowing who he really was. Just like she had no way of knowing who she really was, when she was free of responsibility and obligation. Was she the type to go for a run in the mornings? Perhaps she could be, if she didn't have her sisters' breakfasts to prepare and uniforms to get ready, work to get to. Perhaps she was a night owl, who didn't go to bed until past one and lay in until eleven. She'd just never had the space or the freedom to find out. Maybe now was her time.

Sera's tent was still closed, so Maisie pulled on her clothes and headed out with her washbag in the hope of getting some more alone time with Ric.

Last night had been simply perfect. After their inter-ruption at the waterfall, Maisie and Ric had stumbled back to his tent and stripped off their wet swimsuits, throwing them outside and collapsing onto his sleeping bag completely naked. She hadn't even had a chance to feel self-conscious; he had moved into her straight away, his mouth finding hers, then moving to her neck, and her collar, then lower to her breasts and nipples. She could practically feel it now, his tongue moving lower still until it found the place where his finger had started in the pool.

They were at the same pool now, the two of them, Sera and Ric. Maisie started, not expecting to see them. They hadn't seen her, and she moved back slightly so they wouldn't. She couldn't hear what they were saying, but neither looked happy. Sera was pointing her finger in Ric's face and her own was contorted in rage. Ric had his hands in the air in a 'what?' gesture.

She knows we slept together, and she's furious, Maisie thought. She had no idea how she knew that was what they were arguing about, but she did. She just didn't know why.

Sera threw something at Ric and spun around to where Maisie was hidden. Before Sera could walk right into her, Maisie scuttled back to her own tent. When she heard Sera clattering around outside, she pulled the zip down and stuck her head out as if she'd been in there all night.

'Morning,' she said as brightly as she could manage.

Sera looked at her as though she was about to tell her where to go as well. Instead, she plastered on a clearly fake smile. 'Morning. Sleep well?'

'Sure,' Maisie said. 'You?'

'Oh peachy, thanks.'

Maisie climbed out and pretended to look around. 'Where's Ric?'

'He's having a wash,' Sera said. 'He said something about washing off his mistakes.'

Maisie felt the words like a slap in the face. Surely he hadn't actually said that? No, this was just Sera's way of lashing out, she felt hurt, jealous that Maisie and Ric had made a connection and she had no one. Yes, jealous was what she was, and Maisie didn't have to put up with it. Once upon a time – three days ago to be exact – she'd have been devastated at Sera's meanness. But she could feel herself growing, feel herself hardening up.

'No bother though,' Sera continued, her voice casual but with a sting that Maisie didn't see coming. 'He's not travelling with us any further. There's something he wants to see off the trail.'

'We could just go with him,' Maisie said, her hardness ebbing away at the thought of Ric leaving. 'What does he want to see?'

Sera shrugged. 'He doesn't want us with him. Said we'll slow him down. He might catch us up, you never know.'

But Maisie did know. Whatever Sera had done, whatever she had said, Maisie had the horrible feeling that once he left them, she would never see Ric again.

–

Ric was different when he returned from his wash. Harder, somehow, determined. Whatever had been said lay between the three of them like a toxin in the air. They packed up their tents in silence, and when he said goodbye to her, it was as though they were strangers, which Maisie supposed they were. She wanted to grab hold of his arm, to beg him to come with them, not to leave her, but that was stupid, pathetic, and even the old Maisie wouldn't have stooped so low. Instead she watched him walk away and hoped it wasn't for the last time.

Chapter Twenty-Two

November 2019

I drag the small round table that has been folded up and stored behind the sofa into the bay window in our bedroom and set myself up with the laptop where I have a view of the entire street. Despite the paranoia that surrounds my past, and how careful I have always been, I've never viewed my house from the point of view of a potential threat before. Now I'm thinking about how accessible the back garden is, with only a flimsy side gate stopping someone gaining entry. There is a dense hedge that runs across the back and behind the studio, and although it is perfect for keeping people out, it could also be the perfect hiding place for an intruder. I have a vision of Mitchell Dyke dressed all in black and crouching in the dark space between the hedge and my studio, watching my family framed against the bright backdrop of our dining room and I want to scream at how stupid I've been. Why hadn't I convinced Rob to install security earlier? Now I'm one step behind, a bad place to be.

The first security guy I call asks for pictures of the outside of the house and then quotes me over a thousand pounds for four cameras that can be remotely monitored and controlled. The doorbell camera is only three hundred pounds extra, he tells me with a tone that says I should be eternally grateful. I've got to admit, the cost almost floors me as much as the break-in itself. The cameras I'd been looking at on Amazon are less than five hundred for a pretty decent-looking set, the issue being that I have no idea how to fit or install them. I don't want to give Rob any reason to backtrack or change his mind, and having to get up a ladder and fix things to the outside of our house would most definitely be a reason for him to change his mind. Then again, so would a thousand-pound bill.

I glance out of the window at the street below. We live on a 'nice' street, Victorian houses either side, small front gardens filled with blooms in the summer and maintained tidily in the winter. The neighbours get together on the odd occasion, without being overbearing, and everyone knows one another's names. I would definitely have noticed if one of the houses had gone up for rent, or if someone new had moved in, and even if it had slipped past me, Gina would have been straight on the WhatsApp.

So I'm fairly sure, as I gaze down the street, that Mitchell isn't watching me from one of the windows opposite. Then where the hell has he been watching me from? A man standing on the street would have caught the eye of one of the many stay-at-home mums, and there are a fair few work-from-homers as well. It's not the type of place that welcomes skulkers.

The second man I phone, Terry, turns out to be a woman, and her quote is much more reasonable. She must sense the urgency in my voice because when I ask how quickly she can do the install, she tells me that she's fully booked for nearly five weeks, but she'd taken a day off at the end of this week to help a friend move house and the sale has fallen through at the last minute, so would I like her to come then? I know I shouldn't make decisions like this without consulting with Rob first, but by now I feel pretty desperate to pull back some level of control, so I tell her I'd love her to. We agree a time of 10 a.m. on Thursday, on the proviso that I send her over a plan of the house and a rough idea of where I'd like the cameras – she'll advise me on the best angles when she comes. Do you want 360-degree coverage? she asks me. Yes, I reply, yes I do.

So the rest of my day is spent at the table in the bedroom with my perfect vantage point, drawing out plans of my house and looking for its weak spots, Archie curled around my feet like a draught excluder. Rob is picking the kids up today, so when Archie starts to grumble at around two forty-five, I reach down and give his head a rub.

'Come on then,' I tell him, taking another quick glance down the street. 'I can't hide in here forever. Let's go for a walk.'

At the sound of the magic word, Archie leaps to his feet and starts to run circles around me.

'Get out!' I laugh. 'You're going to knock me over, you bloody stupid thing.'

Even though I know he can't understand me, he gives a yip and runs off in the direction of where we keep his lead and harness.

Archie still hasn't managed to understand the idea that if he keeps still while I'm putting his harness on, then the walk comes much quicker, so with all his wiggling and mini jumping, it's another ten minutes before we're out and on our walk.

After this morning, I'm hyper alert and perhaps Archie can sense it because he's more of a pain than usual, pulling me along and zigzagging in front of me like a dog possessed. We'd been doing quite well with his training, but today I don't have the energy to correct him.

We get to the field where I can let him off for a bit and he darts away, returning every few minutes for a reward, then bouncing back into the long grass. There's a small brook that runs behind the field and I know that eventually he will disappear into that and come back filthy.

For the first time since I left the house, I can relax; the field is fairly open, I could see anyone coming towards me. I let out a sigh. Is this my life now? Watching my back at every turn? It's no less than I deserve, and yet I never meant for any of this. I never meant for Mitchell to take the blame for something I was responsible for. But he was arrested and charged and by then it was too late to tell the truth. Not that he'd see it that way, obviously. It's easy to paint myself as a victim of circumstance now, but the truth is, in anyone else's book, I'm the villain, the bad guy. In anyone else's book, I deserve what's coming to me.

It isn't until I pull out my phone at 3.30 that I realise Rob has called twice and I'm unsure how I missed it. Heart speeding up, I call him back, hoping he's not saying he's been delayed at work. Miss Murray will keep the kids at school, but I hate taking advantage of her good nature because Rob can't keep his promise to leave work early for once in his life.

'Laura, are you at home?' Rob sounds frantic and my chest fills with a lead weight. He sounds like he's driving.

'I'm at the field walking Archie, why? Are you late for the kids?'

'No, I've got George. Faye wasn't there, she's on the bus.'

95

'What do you mean she's on the bus? I told Miss Murray you were doing pick-up today.' It doesn't hit me straight away how serious this is. Rob must be mistaken; Miss Murray wouldn't have put Faye on the bus knowing that Rob was coming. She'd even made a joke about the mums being pleased to see him, she definitely knew.

'She said I'd phoned in the day to say I was going to take George to the doctors and could she put Faye on the school bus. Apparently I said you'd meet her off it.'

And that's when it dawns on me. My daughter has been on the bus on her own for nearly twenty minutes and when she gets off, no one will be there waiting for her.

It's worse than that, the voice inside my head tells me. *Because what if she gets off and there is someone waiting for her? Just not me.*

Chapter Twenty-Three

'Where did you say Ric had to go again?'

Sera sighed and Maisie knew she was being a pain in the arse, but she couldn't understand his sudden disappearance. It wasn't like he could just pop to the shops while they were out here. There was one route in and one route out — nowhere else to go unless you wanted to get lost in the forest.

'Like I said, there was something his mate had told him about that he wanted to go and see. He's faster than us anyway, he'll catch up.'

Maisie wanted to ask why he hadn't mentioned it to her, or why they couldn't all go and check out this amazing thing together, but she couldn't tell Sera why her feelings were hurt that Ric had gone off without her. For all Sera knew, he was just some random hiker Maisie had met three days ago. *And that's what he actually is*, Maisie reminded herself. *He doesn't owe you anything*. Yet still, the crushing disappointment bore down on her as they packed up their tents and left the waterfall. She felt as though she was leaving a part of her with the rushing water, hidden inside the cave perhaps. It felt like an ending of sorts, like something between the group had changed, or broken and wouldn't be repaired again. She had no idea then how right she was.

It was only when they came to the ferry a few kilo-metres on — the only way across to Nitinat Narrows — and Maisie hesitated that Sera snapped.

'He said he'd catch us up and he will,' she said, her tone nastier than Maisie had known it before. 'You don't have to sulk over him. It's embarrassing.'

'I wasn't sulking,' Maisie replied, stung by Sera's tone. 'I don't know what you're talking about.'

Seraphine muttered something out of Maisie's earshot and picked up her backpack. 'Well, if we miss this ferry we might not make it through the next bit before high tide. Are you coming? Or do you want to wait for him?'

Maisie wanted to wait for Ric, it felt odd going on without him, but given the snarky tone in Sera's voice, there was no way she felt like she could suggest they got the next ferry. Sera was right anyway; he was faster than them and could easily catch up later in the afternoon.

'I could quite easily catch the ferry back to civilisation about now,' Sera grumbled, dropping her pack onto the deck.

Maisie considered this. She hadn't seen Ric use a phone, he likely had no way to contact Sera, or she him. Which meant that if Sera got the ferry back to the trail head, Ric wouldn't necessarily know about it. He'd carry on the trail looking for his sister, and find Maisie alone.

She felt a spike of guilt for even considering it. Sera had befriended her before Ric — if she encouraged her to leave the trail now just so she could get Ric on his own, what kind of friend would that make her? No better than Ruth, the so-called best friend who had ditched her at the airport. No, she wasn't about to be that person.

'You'll regret it if you don't finish it,' Maisie said. 'Otherwise why come in the first place? What do you have to go home for that's better than here?'

'Knickers without mosquitos in them,' Sera grumbled, but she stayed put.

–

They made the short ferry journey in silence and when they were off the opposite side, Sera started the trail without looking to see if Maisie was following. She briefly considered leaving her to it, just hanging back for a bit and going the rest of the way on her own. Sera was no fun like this, and it wasn't exactly like Maisie owed her anything.

She would look back later at this moment and dream that she had taken a different path. That she had waited and let Sera go on without her, found a different place to camp and let the Cunninghams go their own way. Or even further back, at the bus stop she would beg her former self to keep moving, leave her money in her purse. But she had no idea, as she hesitated between following her new friend and going the rest of the way alone, just how important that decision would become.

Chapter Twenty-Four

'You need to drive straight to the bus stop,' I tell Rob, trying to keep the panic out of my voice. 'You might beat it anyway; it has to stop quite a few times before ours. I'll meet you there.'

The bus stop is only a two-minute walk from our house, but it's two minutes in the other direction to the field. It's a fifteen-minute walk to get to the field, but if I run, I can make the bus stop in ten minutes. I pray that Rob and Faye will be there by then.

My instinct is to start running, but I realise that Archie is nowhere to be seen. Shit!

'Archie!' I shout. 'Archie, come!'

Nothing. No sign of him anywhere. His recall is pretty excellent and usually I wouldn't panic, he probably can't hear me, but today I don't have time to go looking for him. Should I leave him? Of course my daughter is more important, but if I get to the bus stop and Rob already has her and I've lost Archie… it doesn't bear thinking about.

'Archie!' I practically scream, jogging towards the direction I think he went in. 'Archie, COME!'

But there's no sight of him and I can't wait any longer, I'm going to have to leave him. One of us has to make it to that bus stop or we may never see our daughter again.

It might be okay; the bus driver might not let her off if one of her parents isn't waiting for her, but I can't risk it, knowing that someone phoned the school pretending to be Rob. Someone has done this intentionally.

I turn and begin to run towards the entrance to the field, heart pounding at the thought of Archie returning scared and confused as to why I'm not there. Will he wait for me to get back? Or try to run home, across the roads and into traffic? The decision to leave him is agonising, but I have no choice.

I get to the entrance of the field and a mass of brown fur hurls itself past me. I almost cry when I see him, bounding ahead as if it's all a game. Bloody dog!

'Come here,' I say, stopping long enough to clip his lead on. Once again, he seems to sense my mood because he stops and drops his butt to the floor instantly. When he's safely back on the lead, I start running again, which delights Archie, of course, but just makes my heart pound even more with every step.

Please let her be okay, I think with each pound of the pavement. *Please let my baby be okay.*

At the top of the road, I see the bus, but I can't see Rob's car. There are no police – should I have called the police? If Faye gets off that bus and someone grabs her...

Archie is out in front of me again like he senses my urgency. My lungs are burning from more running than I've done in years and when I get Faye back safe, I'm booking myself straight back into fitness classes.

The bus starts to pull away and I try not to scream. Faye is there. She's right there, I can see her, I just can't touch her. And she's not alone.

Chapter Twenty-Five

December 1999

DID SATANIC RITUALS PLAY A PART IN SERAPHINE CUNNINGHAM'S DISAPPEARANCE?

Sunday Echo

Mitchell Dyke, the man charged with the suspected murder of missing backpacker Seraphine Cunningham, was a Wiccan and a Satan worshipper, former friends say.

'He dressed all in black and dyed his hair black too,' says a former school friend. 'He used to listen to all this heavy metal and if you played it backwards, there were messages from the Devil and that.'

Accusations of satanism, remain rife in the US following high-profile cases such as the Manson family murders, the case of Michelle Smith, the author of *Michelle Remembers*, the McMartin preschool trials (although the McMartins were later acquitted of all charges, many still believe in their guilt) and, more recently, the Robin Hood Hills murders. The killing of three boys in the Robin Hood Hills sent shockwaves through West Memphis that reverberated around the US. Just six years ago in 1994, three teenage boys who reportedly worshipped the Devil and conducted satanic rituals were convicted for the savage murder of Steven Branch, Christopher Mark Byers and James Michael Moore that occurred in 1993.

Officials now fear that the ritualistic practices that involve sex magic, sacrifice and drinking the blood of virgins may have found their way to the UK, following the disappearance of Seraphine. British-born Cunningham is suspected to have met fellow Brits, Mitchell Dyke, Kaz Rigby and Keddie Everett whilst travelling the West Coast Trail in British Columbia, Vancouver. The three friends are self-confessed Wiccans, and Mitchell Dyke even owned a 'Book of Shadows' – a book personal to the creator which charts their practices and journey into witchcraft and magic. Dyke's book is said to contain quotes from infamous occultist Aleister Crowley, and spells to summon vengeance daemons. Prosecutors are expected to claim that Cunningham's death was planned by Dyke as a part of one of these rituals.

Chapter Twenty-Six

July 1999 – Maisie

They made camp at Cribs Creek, the whole time Maisie thinking about how she had gone from feeling free and in control to wondering why the hell Ric had left them, and why Sera was suddenly acting like a petulant child. What had happened between the siblings before she woke this morning?

The beach was narrow at Cribs Creek and full of people setting up camp. Damp mist hung in the air, threatening rain, and Maisie longed to tell Sera where to go, and carry on the four-kilometre hike to Carmanah alone, but by the time she arrived the rain surely would have started and she would probably be biting her nose off to spite her face. Despite knowing that the campsite at Carmanah was much larger and therefore less cramped, Maisie dumped her things less than ten foot from a tent already set up and started unpacking. Sera gave her a glance, then purposely walked as far away as the small site allowed and dumped her own things down. Fine, Maisie thought, screw her. With any luck, she'd be gone before Maisie woke in the morning and she could finish her hike and get the plane home, with no more stupid notions of abandoning her old life and going travelling with the Manson family. She didn't need to get involved in their stupid arguments any more than she needed her own family. She'd already decided on this trip that things were going to change once she got home. She would move out, find a place of her own to rent, maybe even flat-share with people her own age. She would take a college course, learn a skill. Just because she wasn't going on the run with the Artful Dodger and Nancy didn't mean she had to go back home with her tail between her legs. She would go back a new person and start a new life from this moment.

Maisie's tent was up and she was about to get some food on – that ought to bring Sera running back at any rate – when she heard a group of voices arrive at the tents next to hers. Poking her head out, she saw the girl and the two men she'd met at orientation, still dressed completely in black.

'Hey!' The girl – Kaz, Maisie remembered – gave a sunny smile and a wave. 'You survived!'

'Just about,' Maisie grinned back. With how Sera had been acting today, the arrival of three familiar faces was perfect timing. 'How is it the other side?'

'We should have camped at Carmanah,' Keddie said, his voice grumpy but good-natured. 'It's much bigger than here. But these two wanted to make some more headway.'

'The trail is pretty tough in that direction,' Kaz warned her. 'But not as bad as some of the guidebooks make out. Although we did see one person get airlifted with what looked like a broken ankle.'

'But no bear attacks,' Mitchell said.

'Well, that's always a good thing,' Maisie smiled. She glanced over to where Sera was still putting up her tent, seemingly lost without her brother's help. She felt a slight pang of guilt to be all set up and laughing and joking with others while Sera struggled, but she wasn't the one who had decided to pitch up the other side of the site.

'You're on your own?' Kaz asked.

Maisie considered the question for a second. Technically she'd only known Sera a couple of days, and she'd flown to Vancouver on her own, she'd come alone. 'Yeah,' she said with a shrug. 'I was booked on the trip with a friend, but she cancelled last minute.'

'Eurgh,' Kaz said. 'I've got friends like that.'

'I seem to attract them,' Maisie said, looking again at Sera, who had managed to enlist the help of the man in the tent next to hers.

'That's why I hang around with these goons,' Kaz joked, indicating the two men with her. 'They don't have anyone better to run off with.'

'Maybe Keddie doesn't,' the first guy retorted. 'But I just took pity on you both. Neither of you can make a decent brew. You'd die out here without me.'

'How do you all know each other?' Maisie asked.

Keddie gestured to the other man. 'Mitch and Kaz went to school together,' he said. His accent sounded vaguely Australian, whereas Kaz was definitely English. 'I moved to the UK from Oz and met these two loons at college. We were meant to start uni two years ago.'

'We just took a kind of extended gap year,' Kaz grinned. 'I'm going to go back next year and study business. I know, I know, I don't look like a business student. I'll have to wash the black lipstick off and let my dreads grow out, I guess, but until then I'm free to dress like I want.'

'How do you afford to live?' Maisie asked, her voice eager. She couldn't see these three being pickpockets.

'Mitch is quite handy,' Kaz said. 'He does odd jobs. Keddie works the bars, he's a mean mixologist. I con old men out of their life savings by seducing them and getting them to change their wills.'

Maisie's mouth must have dropped open because Kaz laughed.

'I'm joking,' she said. 'I just pick up some cash every now and then for braiding and dreading some tourist's hair. What about you?'

'I...' She was about to tell them she was just a tourist, that her life back home was just regular, that she worked in a coffee shop and looked after her sisters at the weekend. But that wasn't true anymore. She'd already decided that wasn't who she was going to be. So she told her new truth. 'I'm at college in the UK,' she said. 'I was late starting too. I'm studying English Literature.'

'That's cool,' Kaz said. Maisie had never been referred to as cool in her life. 'We were just about to get some food on and we've each got a bottle of spirits we're fed up of carrying. Fancy joining us?'

Maisie looked once more over at where Sera's tent was now up, but she was nowhere to be seen.

'Sure,' she said. 'Why not?'

Chapter Twenty-Seven

November 2019

I stop running and double over, my hands on my knees holding me up. Faye's with Rob. She's with Rob.

'Oh my God,' I gasp as I reach them. 'You got here. You're okay!' I shove Archie's lead at Rob and grab Faye's face in my hands. I cannot believe that I've almost lost my beautiful baby girl twice in three days. I *promised* myself, *promised* that she would be safe from now on, but the truth is, I can't keep her safe every minute of the day.

'What the hell happened?' Rob says, and I can see that he is more upset than I think I've ever seen him. I see George playing happily in the car that I'd somehow missed in my panic. I feel like I'm going insane. I need my babies home safe, now.

'I have no idea,' I reply, and it's almost the truth. 'Let's get these two home, I need a drink and then we can sort it out. I'll walk with Faye and Archie, you take the car back.' I keep my eyes straight ahead, and I can't help wondering, is he watching us now? Was he lurking somewhere ready to snatch Faye? Or is this another warning, that he can strike anywhere, even the place we think is safest?

'Why are you mad when you're the one who said I had to go on the bus?' Faye demands of her father. 'I've been on the school bus loads of times and you're not usually this scary.'

'Just a mix-up, baby,' I tell her, clutching at her hand. 'Mummy didn't get the message to meet you, but luckily Daddy got here quick enough with Georgie and it's all okay. Poor Archie is exhausted though!'

Mollified, Faye drops my hand and walks alongside Archie.

When we walk through the door, Rob meets me with a glass of wine. It's early, but I don't care. He puts his arm around my shoulder, his blue eyes dark with concern. Usually just his touch would calm me down, but that isn't going to work today.

'You okay?' he asks.

I nod, not looking at him in case I burst into tears.

'I am now I know she's safe.'

'What were they doing sending her on the bus? Miss Murray was adamant that someone had rung the school to say that she needed to go on the bus today, but I don't understand how that can be true.'

'There's another Faye at the school.' Now I have a chance to think, the lie comes easily, but I have to say it quietly in case Faye hears and exposes me. The school isn't a big one and she would definitely know if there was another Faye. Ours is one of a kind. 'So it was probably her dad. I bet there's another set of parents waiting at the bus stop further on wondering where their Faye is.'

'What a cock-up,' he mutters. 'You want to have a word with them about that.'

'It's just a miscommunication,' I say. 'And it's all fine.' I can't tell him that there were no mixed messages, Miss Murray had done exactly what the man on the phone who identified himself as Rob had told her to do. And now I have a bigger problem, because Mitchell doesn't just know where I live, he knows where my children go to school. And the name of my husband, and probably where he works too. Mitchell knows a lot about me, and I only know one thing about him. He didn't take Seraphine Cunningham away from her family. But I think he's going to try to take mine from me.

Chapter Twenty-Eight

August 1999

FRESH AS A MAISIE

Morning Herald

British hiker Maisie Goodwin was seen for the first time this morning since she was airlifted from the West Coast Trail following an alleged vicious attack on her fellow hiker, and sources say she looked 'fresh and relaxed'. Goodwin allegedly laughed with a police officer as they took a stroll through VanDusen Botanical Garden, where they collected pastries and coffee before returning to the police station, presumably for more questioning.

Since the alleged attack that has seen the West Coast Trail closed to hikers and a professional search mounted, Goodwin has repeatedly denied requests from the media for interviews, or to give any information to the press that might help find missing traveller, Seraphine Cunningham. There have been questions about the innocence of

Goodwin herself, who is the only witness to the attack, and therefore the last known person to see Miss Cunningham alive. There are reports of a quarrel between the pair earlier in the day, and both were thought to have been drinking and taking drugs at the time of Miss Cunningham's disappearance.

Chapter Twenty-Nine

July 1999 – Maisie

It turned out that the three travellers had been carrying more than a bottle of spirits between them. The four of them sat around the crackling fire as the light faded, Maisie wrapped in an oversized hoodie, Kaz snuggled up next to Mitch. Keddie pulled out a familiar-smelling cigarette and lit it up.

'Where to next for you guys?' Maisie asked Kaz. 'When you're finished here?'

'Definitely no more hiking for a while,' Kaz laughed, pretending to rub at her feet. 'I'm done in. Maybe we'll head to Ontario, or Quebec. We'll decide when we get back to the trail head.'

Kaz passed her the joint without asking, as though she just expected that Maisie would smoke. She was grateful now that Ric had showed her how – it had been much easier to make a fool out of herself in front of him. She felt a jolt in her stomach – she wished he was here. Seeing Mitch and Kaz snuggled up in front of the fire – that could have been her and Ric if Sera hadn't pissed him off. It seemed obvious now that that's what had happened. They must have argued, maybe Ric had even gone ahead rather than back, he was probably camping at Carmanah, where she should have been.

Forget him, she told herself. It was a holiday fling. *You barely know him.*

And yet she knew, in the way young girls just know, that it would be a long time before she would move on from him. If she ever did.

'Are you two together then?' Maisie asked, emboldened by the weed she motioned to Mitchell and Kaz who were sitting close, legs and arms touching. Keddie was nowhere to be seen.

Kaz laughed. 'Kind of. I mean, no, not really, but we both enjoy each other.'

Mitch smiled. 'She means if we're both available and horny, we hook up every so often.'

Kaz smacked him on the arm. 'Not just that!' she objected. 'Like, if I need a hug, or a bit of affection, Mitch is good for that. Keddie is more aloof. But he's very good in bed.' She wiggled her eyebrows. Maisie had to work to stop her mouth dropping open. Mitchell snorted.

'You mean you sleep with both of them?' Realising how horribly judgemental that sounded, she began to backtrack. 'I mean, not that there's anything wrong with that of course... I just...'

Kaz was laughing harder now. 'It's fine,' she said, taking a sip of her drink. 'I get that that's not how women are supposed to act. We're supposed to be all, one partner for life, all virginal and shit. I'm just not really like that. I enjoy sex. Sometimes I just need a hug or a kiss, or someone to spoon with. And we all get on so well that it seems a shame to waste opportunities.'

Maisie couldn't wrap her head around what Kaz was saying. Here was a woman, only a couple of years older than herself, who knew exactly what she wanted from life, and wasn't afraid to take it, despite knowing that people didn't approve. Now that was a kind of freedom she couldn't even contemplate. The way she dressed, her hair, her unconventional life, Maisie envied it all.

'Do you get jealous?' Maisie asked Mitch. 'If she sleeps with Keddie?'

It must have been the combination of the weed and the vodka that had loosened her tongue to the point of asking such bold questions. She couldn't help it; she was intrigued by these people.

Mitch shook his head. 'Nah. We all get on great, but none of us are in love or anything. Or, if we are, we're too young to tie ourselves into it. Who knows, maybe one day me and Kaz will get married, or Kaz and Keddie, and the other one will realise that we've completely fucked up and lost out, but that's to worry about another day. I reckon Kaz will end up marrying some surfer dude before then anyway.'

'A surfer dude,' Kaz cackled. 'You mean a beautiful Wiccan who worships me in the moonlight.'

'You guys are Wiccans then?' Maisie asked. 'I wasn't sure if it was just a fashion thing.'

Kaz nodded. 'I'm Wiccan. Mitch is studying the occult – not that he worships Satan or anything, but he's all into true crime and wants to specialise in cults when he goes back to do his Psychology and Criminology course. Keddie hasn't decided what he wants to study yet.'

Maisie was just wondering where Keddie was when he reappeared into view, his arms full of firewood… and Seraphine walking alongside him.

'I found another lone wolf,' he said, dropping the wood into a pile. Kaz looked at Sera and Maisie thought she could see apprehension in her new friend's eyes. 'This is Sarah.'

Seraphine didn't correct him, her eyes were locked on Maisie's, waiting to see what she would do.

'We've met,' Maisie said, determined to take control of the situation. 'We walked a little way together.'

'That's what I love about these hikes,' Keddie said. 'You make new friends every day. Sit down, Sarah.'

Mitchell, who Maisie hadn't looked at since Sera's arrival, jumped up so fast, he almost knocked Kaz into the fire. 'Here,' he said, making space between him and Kaz, whose face now looked thunderous. 'You can sit next to me.'

'Thanks.' Sera smiled her angelic, cloud-parting smile. 'You're very sweet. I don't have any drink to contribute, I'm afraid.'

Typical, Maisie thought. *She's going to spend all night sponging off these now.*

'But I do have this.' She held up a clear bag filled with white powder and Keddie's eyes widened.

'Bloody hell,' he said, sitting down the other side of Sera. 'Looks like it's going to be a hell of a night.'

Chapter Thirty

November 2019

The security woman's name is Terry Baker, and her van is matt silver with an image of a camera lens inside an eye emblazoned on the side. I imagine the neighbours watching as she pulls up outside – I don't have to worry about lying to Rob: within a week, all of them will have CCTV. Keeping up with the Johnsons.

When Terry gets out of the van, I have to work hard not to look surprised. She's tiny, maybe only 5'2", with long blonde hair, a small button nose and green eyes. She looks like a Miss World contestant without the sequinned gown. Not quite the picture I'd had of her in my mind.

She must see the look that's on my face a hundred times a day because she laughs. 'I know, I don't look like your average security consultant.'

'I'm sorry,' I say, feeling annoyed at myself for judging her. 'You must get fed up with people saying that.'

'I don't mind,' she replies with a shrug. 'I quite like it when people underestimate me.'

My kind of woman. People have been underestimating me my whole life.

'I looked at your plans,' she says, looking around at the front of the house. 'And I think you're spot on with the positioning for the cameras. We should be able to cover the entire perimeter if you want?'

'And the car on the street?' I ask, remembering that the car is the reason Rob has agreed to all this. Well, technically he still doesn't know it's all this, but it will be a lot easier to explain if we can at least see the car.

'You have to be careful recording anything that isn't on your property,' she warns. 'Data protection. You can do it, but you have to have a sign up, and if anyone asks to see the footage with them on it, you have to let them. I have some signs in the van?'

I consider this. Yes, let him know he's being watched. 'That's great,' I say. 'Let's do that then. Do you want a drink?'

'No thanks, I'll be up and down the ladder for a pee if I drink too much coffee in the morning. I'll crack on.'

Any doubts I had owing to her model good looks disappear when I see her wielding her set of ladders as well as any man I've ever seen – better than my own husband in fact. He gets vertigo if he has to fetch the kids' ball off the roof of the shed, so I'm glad now, watching Terry scuttle up the ladders like Spiderwoman, that I enlisted outside help.

I go inside to try to get some admin done – really I should be in my studio replacing the commission I had to throw away, but I haven't been able to go in there since I found it had been broken into and I'm getting behind. Luckily I closed my Christmas orders months ago. It feels different in there somehow, not as safe anymore. And with all that business with Faye being on the bus, my chest has been in knots ever since.

I've barely slept all week going over and over what could have happened if Rob hadn't made it to the bus stop on time, wondering what would be next. But so far, nothing since the bus incident. Miss Murray had practically fallen over herself apologising the next morning at drop-off, which, if anything, made me feel ten times worse. She couldn't figure out what happened, it was someone else who took the call and the only thing she could think of was that they got the child's name wrong. Except no one was left at the end of the day who should have been put on the bus instead of Faye.

'And Rob is sure he didn't call and just forget?' she asked, an apologetic look on her face. Of course she'd want to find an explanation that absolved the school of responsibility, but the truth is, they did almost let a child be... God, I can't even think the word, but the school need to up their security. I just can't tell them why.

'Perhaps you should think about having a password for when people ring to change their pick-up plans?' I suggested.

Miss Murray looked at me in horror. 'Oh God, Laura, do you think it was someone calling to get Faye on the bus on purpose?'

'I don't know what to think, if I'm honest,' I lied. 'And I realise that in a school this small things like that almost never happen. Until they do.'

I felt terrible leaving her with those words ringing in her ears, but if it makes her check twice before letting my daughter out of her care again, then that's all I care about.

I hide away in the kitchen while Terry works and use my burner phone to google 'human remains West Coast Trail'. There are a few new articles, but they are only repeating what was said at the weekend, tests are ongoing, no further information, Canadian police are refusing to speculate.

Restless, I wander back outside with a mug of steaming-hot coffee in my hands to watch Terry measuring and drilling.

When she comes down from her ladder, she's holding something in her hand. She offers it out to me. 'I took your other camera down,' she said. 'You shouldn't need that anymore, the ones I've put up will do the same job.'

For a second, I have no idea what she's talking about. Then I see the camera she's holding out to me like an offering. There was already a surveillance camera on our roof.

'I didn't put that up there,' I say, and she frowns in response.

'Maybe your husband did it? Men are so helpful like that. More helpful if they remember to tell us though.' She rolls her eyes.

I should just agree with her and the conversation will stop, but I reply without thinking. 'He wouldn't do that. He's no good at this kind of thing, he wouldn't know what he was doing.'

She looks it over. 'It's solar-powered. Not a bad piece of kit, but not as good as what I've just put up.' When she looks at me again, her face is full of concern. 'If you didn't put it up, and your husband didn't put it up, then you probably need to contact the police.'

'I will,' I lie. Then a sudden thought hits me. 'What if there are more of these?' When could this have happened? Could someone have done this at night, with all of us inside? I think back to last month when we went to Rob's parents' for the weekend. Had someone been here then? Watched us leave and taken their chance? The idea is horrifying.

Terry tilts her head sideways. 'Are you in some kind of trouble? Do you know who did this?'

Maybe because she's been so kind to me, or because she's female, or just because I'm fed up with all the lies, I tell the truth without really thinking about it. 'Yes, I think I do. Someone I used to know, a man.'

It's all I need to say for her to assume that I'm being harassed by a crazy ex. She gives me a grim smile that tells me she knows what I'm going through and nods. 'I got into the security business because of my "someone I used to know",' she says, her voice full of sympathy. 'Look, like I said on the phone, I don't have any other appointments today. How about I give the house a good sweep for you, check for any more devices? Then I'll give you some details to give to the police, and the number of the agency that helped me with my problem. We'll get your new cameras and your doorbell up and running and I'll show you how to use them. I've got some spare attack alarms in my van too – just to make you feel safer.'

'Thank you,' I say, both grateful and ashamed. She assumes I'm like her, an innocent victim of an over-bearing, controlling ex. It couldn't be further from the truth. But I do need her help, and I have no problem lying to get it. This is about protecting my family. 'I'll make us a drink.'

–

While I'm pouring the drinks, Terry's head appears at the back door. I unlock it – yes, I am getting paranoid enough to lock the door every time I go through it – and let her in. She's holding another of the cameras.

'One in the back,' she says. Her face is furious on my behalf, but I just feel numb. So this is how Mitchell knows my schedule. How long has he been watching me?

Well, it's your turn now, I think. *I'm onto you.*

'Jesus,' I whisper.

'It's scary what people are capable of,' Terry says, shaking her head. 'Some of the things I've seen make me worried for the state of the human race. Husbands spying on wives, neighbours trying to catch one another out in parking disputes. I had one guy who wanted cameras putting up because every morning he'd come out and find human faeces on his front lawn. Someone was literally pulling down their pants and shitting on his lawn every day. He had cats and thought it was his neighbour trying to make a point about the cats pooing on their garden.'

'Did he catch them?'

She grins and takes a sip of her coffee. 'Sure did. It was his wife.'

Despite what's going on I can't help but laugh. 'His wife?'

'Yep. She wanted to get rid of their three cats, so she was trying to make it seem like his neighbours were waging an excrement war against him. Every night after he'd gone to sleep, she would creep out, lift her nightdress, and let one rip on the lawn. Seventy-five years old she was. You can't unsee some things, I'm telling you.'

We're both laughing now, but when she puts down her cup of coffee and gives me a serious look I know what she's about to say.

'Seriously though, Laura, you need to be careful. I don't remember the last time I saw someone going to the effort and risk of putting cameras on someone else's house.

You need to go to the police about this guy. That's way beyond a petty grudge.'

'I will,' I promise. 'I'll take care of it.'

Terry finishes her coffee and gives me details of the make and models of the cameras she's found and what I need to tell the police. Then she runs through the cameras she's fitted, how they work and installs the app on my phone for me to access them from wherever I am. The front doorbell camera has a motion sensor that reaches to the side gate, so if anyone breaches our garden, I'll get an instant text message.

'Will you be okay until your husband gets home?' she asks as she packs up to leave.

I promise her I'll be fine. I don't know how long I have before Mitchell realises that his cameras have been taken down, but I don't think he'll risk coming here in daylight. Besides, I'm not finished yet. I have more to do.

Chapter Thirty-One

Kaz wrapped the final band around the end of Maisie's hair and sat back on her feet. 'Voila!'

Maisie reached a hand up to touch the braids. Her scalp felt chilly, her head heavier.

Kaz stood up. 'Wait there. I have a mirror, it's only tiny but—' She dashed off to her tent and pulled out her backpack, started pulling things out of it and tossing them to one side.

Maisie looked over to where Seraphine was sitting, her head close to Mitchell's, deep in conversation. She'd hardly looked at Maisie once, let alone spoken to her. A rolled-up banknote and the remnants of the lines of cocaine sat at their feet. Maisie had shaken her head when it had come her way – a little weed she could handle, but she'd never tried anything harder and now didn't seem like a good time to start.

'Here.' Kaz handed her the small compact and Maisie edged closer to the fire, using the light of the flames to inspect her new look.

'It's awesome,' she grinned. She looked nothing like the girl who had joined the trail three days ago. She felt like a butterfly, emerging from her cocoon.

Keddie wolf-whistled from across the fire, and Sera looked up.

'Looks good on you,' she commented. 'I'm not sure what Ric will think though.'

'Who's Ric?' Kaz asked, raising an eyebrow at Maisie. 'I thought you didn't have a boyfriend?'

'I don't,' Maisie said, her voice firm. She glared at Sera.

Sera looked at her, as though she was thinking about something. She leant down and picked up the guide-book that the cocaine had been measured out on and tipped a little more on. Cutting it into a smooth line with someone's credit card – Maisie wasn't sure whose – Sera held it out to Maisie.

'Why don't you have some of this? To celebrate the new you?'

'No, thanks,' Maisie said, gesturing for Sera to take it away. 'I already said I'm not interested.'

'But I thought you wanted an adventure?' Sera remarked, her bottom lip fake pouting. 'Try new experiences? Take risks?'

'If you want a new experience, this is up there with the best,' Keddie said, his accent sounding really prominent now.

Maisie looked around at Kaz and Mitch, who were nodding encouragingly. Maisie noticed that Mitch's hand was on Sera's leg, his thumb gently stroking the inside of her thigh.

They've all had some, and they look fine, Maisie told herself. *How bad can it be? And this is the kind of freedom you wanted, the freedom to do things that other people your age do, drink, experiment…*

There was still time for Ric to turn up. She imagined his hand on her thigh the way Mitch's was caressing

Sera now, remembered his lips on hers, his warm tongue exploring her mouth. It wouldn't hurt to loosen up a bit before he arrived, would it?

'Fine,' she said, holding her hand out.

Keddie whooped, Kaz grinned. Sera smirked triumphantly.

'Let me show you,' Kaz said kindly. Maisie got the impression she genuinely wanted to help her have a good first experience. 'Sweep your braids back behind your shoulder, lean forwards and just inhale, pushing the note forwards.'

Kaz handed Maisie the note and she did as instructed. The powder hit the inside of her nose, making her sit back on her heels, coughing and spluttering.

'Woohoo!' Keddie whooped. 'Way to go!'

She looked at Sera, whose face was completely expressionless. Without saying a word, she turned to Mitch and whispered something in his ear. If he had a tail, it surely would have wagged off, the delighted look on his face. He nodded and glanced at his watch.

Maisie sat back, her head spinning. The fire seemed to be huge now, and it was making her hot... really hot. Her entire body felt awake, her skin was tingling. She let out a laugh, although she didn't know what was funny. Something must have been, though, because Keddie laughed with her, and then Kaz, and they were all laughing.

Kaz took another line of the cocaine and passed it towards Sera, who batted it away.

Don't you want to be free? Maisie thought, her voice so loud in her head that she wasn't sure if she'd shouted it. *Don't you want to be free, Sera?*

Chapter Thirty-Two

November 2019

I've managed the full day without calling the school to check that Faye and George are still there, but I still arrive a full thirty minutes early to get a parking space directly outside the exit. The last thing I want is for the school to start thinking I'm a madwoman, but if there's one thing I've realised over the last couple of days, it's that you are never as safe as you think you are. It only takes one bad person to blow a hole in your life. One person lurking, watching, waiting for you to slip up. I'm determined not to slip up again. If Mitchell wants me and my family, he's going to have to come out in the open and fight me for them.

Sitting in the car, I open up the app on my phone, where I can scroll through my cameras in turn, watching the entire perimeter of my house. All is quiet. I spend some time watching the camera that looks onto the street, see Gina walk past, probably on her way to the shop, and a couple of teenage girls whose school obviously let out earlier than the primary school. No shadowy, balaclava-clad figure.

When the kids come out, they are full of stories about their day. You can feel the excitement building in the play-ground, tomorrow is the first of December and as soon as December hits, the school goes into full-on Christmas mode. I don't know if even the teachers expect anything to get done. I hear one child ask their mum if the elves are coming tonight and I cringe. I'd forgotten all about bloody Elf on the Shelf.

Elf on the Shelf is the kind of thing that parents latch onto the first year. A toy elf arrives and every night, after the children are asleep, he comes to life and perpetrates increasingly naughty tricks and pranks. The first year our 'elf' wrapped the tree in Christmas wrapping paper, had a snowball fight with Faye's barbies and made snow angels out of flour. By the second year, however, the shine has well and truly worn off. Not for the kids – they wake up every morning delighted to see what the elf has thought of that night. No, it's the parents who wake up at three in the morning remembering they've forgotten to move the sodding elf. Who have to get up and creep downstairs, staring around the room looking for something funny and original to do with the demon toy before deciding to bung it in a cupboard and pretend it is playing 'hide-and-seek'. By year three – and if you hadn't guessed, this is year three in the Johnson household – you're left wondering if maybe you could get away with saying your elf has had a catastrophic accident on the way to visit and hold the bloody thing a funeral.

'I can't wait to see our elves again,' Faye announces, in an awestruck tone that tells me there's no way I'm going to get away with killing it off. And yes, she did say elves, plural. For some reason, Rob thought it would be a good idea to turn up with a menagerie of elves, despite the fact that he hasn't moved them once in the last two years.

'Well, if they're as naughty as last year, I might just send them back to Santa,' I play along, and Faye gasps, thunderstruck.

'You won't, will you, Mummy? I love Elfie and so does George.'

'Of course I won't.'

'Can we do the decorations tomorrow too?'

I stop short of sighing. It's not the kids' fault that my life is imploding and Christmas is the last thing I want to be thinking about.

'Ask Daddy,' I say, and they both cheer, knowing that Daddy's answer will be yes. Then Daddy will stand and watch while Mummy spends an hour moving the baubles around the tree to try to get them right.

–

'I had a prospective client today who said their wife went to school with you,' Rob says, handing me a glass of wine once the kids are in bed.

Automatically, my entire body goes tense. As far as Rob is aware, I grew up in the next county across, there's no reason why a prospective client wouldn't know me from my past. Only I know how impossible that is. When I went to school, my name wasn't Laura, and it was far away from here.

'Who was it?' I ask, trying to sound casual.

'His name is Mitch, Mitch Goodwin. I think he said her name is Maisie.'

Somehow I had been expecting him to say one of those names, but hearing it come from his mouth makes my blood run cold. Now Mitch is calling Rob's work? Pretending to know me?

'I thought the name sounded familiar, maybe you've mentioned it?'

I can guarantee that I've never mentioned the name Maisie Goodwin to my husband. If it sounds familiar, it's because he came across it in his early twenties in all of the newspapers, but I'm not about to tell him that.

What is Mitchell playing at? Is he trying to get me to confess? To slowly release enough information for my husband to piece together who I really am?

'I don't remember her,' I say eventually. 'I suppose she wouldn't have been Goodwin in school, if she's married now. But still, Maisie isn't a common name. Maybe she was in a different year.'

'Maybe.' Rob shrugs and doesn't seem bothered enough to push it. That's another thing that I love about Rob. He's so uncomplicated. He has no Facebook, Snapchat, Instagram or Twitter, because he says he can't stand the drama, and he has no interest in what other people had for breakfast, or how big their Christmas tree is. Unfortunately, my suspicious mind has always meant that I can't let things go that easily.

'Oh God, Rob, can you get the elves down please? The kids will be devastated if they don't come back tonight. Everyone at school is talking about it.'

'Not those pain-in-the-arse things again,' Rob says. 'Has it really been a whole year? I'll pop up to the loft when they're definitely asleep. Faye asks enough questions as it is.'

But by the time we've cleared the kitchen from our meal and put the kids to bed, I spend the entire evening trying to avoid thinking about Mitchell Dyke and completely forget about the damn elves.

'Mummy! Mummy! We need to see if the elves are back!'

Faye's words are the first thing I hear when I wake and my heart fills with dread. How did we forget the elves! I'd literally reminded Rob about them last night after dinner.

Faye and George are dancing around our bedroom and any minute now they are going to discover that their elf friends have not made an appearance.

'Well don't be mad at him if he's late,' I warn, pulling on my dressing gown. 'He has a long way to come, remember?'

'Look, I see one!' Faye is pointing at the window and I turn to see what she's looking at.

Sure enough, there's an elf dangling outside our front room window. Oh thank God! Rob must have remembered to do it after I'd fallen asleep. And that's a new one, pretending he can't get in. He's actually quite good at this.

'What's he hanging from?' Faye asks, getting closer up to the window. 'It's around his neck! Mummy, he can't breathe! Is he dead?'

I go over to where she's standing and take a look. There is a colourful beaded string around the elf's neck, and he's dangling from it like a noose.

'He's fine, sweetheart,' I say, cursing Rob for making a hash of it. 'I'll go and get him.'

'I wonder where the rest of them got to?' Faye muses as I traipse outside in my slippers and coat and pull down the elf from where he is swinging by his neck. The string has been attached to the window frame with a drawing pin. That's unusual for Rob, he hates me tacking anything to the woodwork. And what has he used to string it up?

It's a child's friendship bracelet, the type you can make at home with some brown string and beads. In-between the pink, white and purple beads are little charms: a teddy bear, an elephant. It looks so familiar that suddenly I know exactly what I'm going to find when I turn around the white beads. Letters printed on each one. Letters that spell S E R A P H I N E. This bracelet is identical to the one that belonged to Seraphine Cunningham.

Chapter Thirty-Three

Thread to discuss the disappearance of Seraphine Cunningham

Seraphine Cunningham disappeared from the West Coast Trail on 30 July 1999. She was reported missing by fellow hiker Maisie Goodwin, who raised the alarm after allegedly seeing Cunningham attacked by a mystery man at Cribs Creek. Police searched the area for weeks but found no sign of Seraphine apart from a ripped, bloodstained T-shirt she was believed to have been wearing. A bag containing her belongings was left at the campsite. When police searched it, it was found to contain several stolen credit cards and illegal substances. Seraphine is believed to have left home at the age of seventeen and had been travelling ever since. Her parents have never made any comment on the subject of her disappearance other than to say that they were 'estranged from their daughter and hadn't seen her for over two years'.

UPDATE: Human remains have been found near the West Coast Trail – could this be Seraphine at last?

Pinkyandthebrain

The whole thing is weird. Why weren't her friends and family looking for her?

Everyafter

She ran away from home a couple of years before she was killed. People are saying that she was selling drugs and upset the wrong people. Her family was rich and didn't want to be associated with her.

Happycamper

I know it was the 90s, but this case was botched from the start. What about the guy she was seen arguing with at the bus stop? How come police never tracked him down? There were a ton of witnesses who say she was travelling with a bloke. If he's innocent, he'd have come forward. Dyke was a scapegoat.

Therealslimshady

There's no real evidence this guy ever existed. It's a smokescreen. Her airline tickets were booked as a single traveller, she was booked on the trail alone. This guy never existed.

Happycamper

How do you explain the multiple witnesses?

Therealslimshady

Probably different blokes every time.
Happens all the time with these old
cases. Witnesses change their mind
over time. Witness testimony is
notoriously unreliable.

Happycamper

If you want unreliable
testimony just look at Maisie
Goodwin.

WhoframedMitchellDyke

If it is Seraphine, I hope Goodwin is jailed for perjury.
Hopefully the body will prove she was lying all along.

JustlikeJessieJames

How will it prove that? If Seraphine is dead, then
someone killed her. Dyke looks like the best
candidate to me.

WhoframedMitchellDyke

Seraphine died of an overdose and
Goodwin freaked out and hid her body.
She made up the story about seeing her
being killed and by the time Dyke was
arrested she'd gone too far to tell the truth
so she carried on lying her ass off.

JustlikeJessieJames

Nice theory, but you are missing one thing… evidence.

OzzyB

I think this is the most plausible theory I've heard.

Pixel8me

I always thought it was disgusting how the papers went after Maisie Goodwin just because she didn't want to give an interview the day after her friend went missing. Then when she did talk to the papers, they made her sound like a hysterical female. Any wonder why she didn't trust the media?

Happycamper

The police didn't trust her story either. More holes than a cheese grater. It was clear she was high as a kite in the interviews.

Pixel8me

So she took some drugs. Show me a teenager who didn't. We all know u did, Happycamper.

Happycamper

I never killed anyone though.

Chapter Thirty-Four

July 1999 – Maisie

She wasn't sure how long it was after that first hit of coke that things began to go wrong.

Maisie had been talking to Kaz – not just small talk, really talking, about the important things in life, although she couldn't seem to remember what they had been discussing now. But she felt listened to, important. Everything just seemed so... hopeful. She had things to say, and people who wanted to hear them. Maybe she should consider a career in public speaking, she could talk about the effects of depression on working-class families, or give a voice to teenage carers. For the first time ever, she felt as though she had a purpose, a calling.

She didn't notice when Mitchell and Sera disappeared, although later she would think that it had been some time since she had seen them. When she thought she saw Mitchell return on his own and go into his tent, Maisie got to her feet, stumbled slightly, steadied herself, then grabbed the torch that had been left on the ground to look around for Sera. She had been wanting to talk to her all day, to ask her what the hell had happened to make Sera seem so mad at her. Was she mad that Ric and Maisie had slept together? If so... why? Was it protectiveness over her brother, or jealousy, perhaps? Maybe she was annoyed Ric had monopolised Maisie's time, stolen her away. Perhaps that was why Sera had sent him away. Whatever it was, Maisie was going to sort it out. It was stupid for them to keep behaving like they barely knew one another when they had spent every minute together for the last three days. They just needed to talk it through and they could be friends again. They would have to be, if Ric turned up, because Maisie was certain now that things weren't finished between the two of them.

'Sera?' Maisie called, venturing into the forested area that cordoned off the beach. It was pretty dark in there, the moonlight casting through every now and then, and some glow from all of the fires on the beach giving the smallest of light. Maisie aimed the torch at the trees, it was a fairly decent one, its beam lighting up a good three feet in front of her.

The forest got dense quickly, and Maisie kept her beam trained on the ground in front of her. Wooden boards emerged and she knew she was on the part of the trail that she had explored earlier that day, that led towards the creek bed. The terrain was rough and graduated upwards – there was no way she could do it in the dark, especially with the drink and drugs she had in her system. She knew she should turn around and go back, but she also knew that Sera was out here somewhere and she wanted to speak to her, wanted to know what was going on.

She should have turned back. If she had turned back, maybe everything would have been different.

Chapter Thirty-Five

December 2019

Back inside, Rob is holding a devastated Faye, who is in floods of tears. George is crying too, but he has no idea what he's crying about.

'What's going on?' Rob asks me, and I hold out the elf.

'He's fine, Faye, I'm telling you. Go and tuck him into your bed because he must be freezing after being outside all night, then come and get ready for school.'

She seems mollified to find that the elf isn't 'dead', and takes him off me to give him a big hug. 'Come on, Elf, let's tuck you in nice and warm til your friends arrive. Come on, George!'

Rob gives me a relieved look. 'What the hell happened there? I thought we forgot to get the elves down from the loft? Next thing I know Faye's dragging me out of the shower to tell me that the bloody thing is dead.'

'I found a backup elf I'd bought and left in my studio,' I lie. 'But I must have been rushing too much to put it up before Faye woke this morning and the string wrapped around its neck. It looked like it was hanging, Rob, nightmare!'

I try to sound like it's a hilarious accident that we'll be reciting to friends for years, but all I can picture is the elf, swinging backwards and forwards ominously by its little neck. Mitchell had been outside our house in the night and my phone hadn't alerted me.

When I'm alone, I check it – there's a notification all right, I just hadn't heard it go off. At 3.28, a dark figure in a hood can be seen entering my garden and going in the direction of the front window, where they stay out of shot for six minutes before leaving. There's no telling if it's Mitchell or not, they have a hood that falls forwards over their forehead, and the bits you can see of their face are bright white, as if there is a glare coming from it.

I rewind the footage and watch it four more times as it gradually dawns on me that even hundreds of pounds of security cameras haven't made me any safer. If Mitchell Dyke had wanted to set a fire through my letterbox last night, I would have been fast asleep in my bed, none the wiser, and never woken up again.

Chapter Thirty-Six

July 1999 – Maisie

She hadn't turned back. And she had walked into her worst nightmare.

Eight hours later...

Maisie had been in the interview room of the police station for hours. She was exhausted. She blinked to dispel the spots of light dancing in front of her eyes and stifled a yawn – yawning wouldn't look good, like she was bored. She should be used to being tired, the baby still woke up at least once a night and her mum could never usually drag herself out of bed to take care of her, so Maisie ended up doing it, even if she had work early the next day. But this was a different kind of exhaustion, an emotional draining, as well as a physical one. Everything still felt like it couldn't really have happened to her, it couldn't be real. She kept touching her head where Kaz had braided her hair just a few hours ago. It felt like it had been weeks.

The police had contacted her mum, they said, but there was no way she could get over to Canada to be with her. She couldn't afford the airfare, and even if she could, there was no one to look after her sisters. Did she want to speak to her, the police had asked. No thanks, Maisie had replied. There wasn't any point.

'Tell us again where you were when you saw the man who was attacking Sera,' the detective opposite her requested. He was huge, with a neck so thick that Maisie wondered how he found shirts to fit. His dark hair was cut close to his head like he had spent his adult life in the military, and he had the most ridiculous moustache she had ever seen. It was a testament to how miserable she felt that even a comic-book moustache couldn't raise a smile.

The other officer − Canadian Mounted Police they were apparently called − was a tiny woman, who looked even smaller sitting next to The Hulk. Her blonde hair was pulled up into a slick ponytail and she wore round, rose gold glasses.

There was a pile of maps and photographs on the table between them and the thick-necked officer pushed one towards her now.

Maisie sighed. 'I've told you a million times already. I walked up here...' She pointed to the map. 'It was pitch black and I don't know how far I walked. I was yelling for Sera. The trees parted and I saw her in the moonlight. Find the place where the trees part and that's where I was.'

'The problem is, Maisie, the trees are very thick most of the way along that path. So, either you were there in those woods for longer than you're telling us, or Seraphine's attack happened earlier when it was still light. In which case, you waited hours to report the attack.'

Maisie sat back in her chair. 'You think I had something to do with it, don't you?' she said, her voice high-pitched and manic. 'You think I killed her? Well, I didn't. I'm telling you; I didn't do anything to her. Maybe I'm confused, it was so late and dark and...'

'And you were under the influence,' he reminded her and she cringed at the insinuation. *You're either a liar or a junkie, which is it?* 'We're just struggling to understand how you got mixed up in all of this, Maisie. By all accounts, you're a decent person, no criminal record, did well in school, never even missed a day of work. So how did you get mixed up with a girl who has a bag full of drugs and stolen credit cards?'

'I told you, I don't even know her!'

'And yet you say you paid for her bus to get here?' The woman raised her eyebrows.

'Well, yes but—'

'That's very generous for someone you've never met.'

Maisie could have screamed in despair. How did you explain something you didn't understand yourself? She still had no idea why she'd paid for Sera's bus fare, except that she'd just had that look, something that made you want to help her, to be near her. For a few short days, Sera had been like the sun, and Maisie had basked in her warmth. Now she was dead, and Maisie had been in the darkest place of her entire life, in a waking nightmare.

The detective was still looking at her for an answer.

'I suppose so,' she said weakly.

'Had you arranged to meet Miss Cunningham in Canada?'

'No, I already told you I never met her before.'

'So you saw her at the bus stop, paid for her bus fare to get to the trail and then what?'

'She said she thought that the money was in her bag somewhere, and that we should walk together and when she found it, she'd pay me back.'

'And you didn't find that strange?'

'Why would I? Sera seemed fun; she was nice. We were about the same age. I didn't mind walking with her. That's why you go travelling, isn't it? To meet new people.'

The detectives looked at one another.

'What about the man witnesses have said they saw both of you with at the start of the trail? Or the man Sera was seen arguing with at the bus stop?'

Maisie clenched her jaw. 'I didn't see her with anyone at the bus stop. She said she was alone, and she sat by me on the bus.' That was true, at least. 'Maybe she got chatting to a guy at orientation, I chatted to a few people as well. I already told you, that's what people do on these kinds of hikes. There's that sense of being in it together. You're all excited and a bit nervous... you just end up talking to anyone.'

'But it was just the two of you on the hike?'

Maisie thought now of the warmth of Ric's hand as he pulled her to her feet on the beach that first day. The sound of his laugh and the woody smell of his aftershave as they walked side by side, their bare shoulders brushing against one another. The taste of his lips on hers, then the feeling of him inside her, filling her up, his hands on her face, in her hair.

'Yes,' she whispered. 'It was just the two of us.'

'Do you need a drink?' the female detective asked. 'Shall we take a break?'

'Yes please,' Maisie said, the sudden kindness in such a hostile situation making tears spring to her eyes.

Once the thoughts of Ric had started, she couldn't stop them, like a slideshow running through her mind, his eyes suddenly dark as he looked into hers, his voice low as he told her to run, he would take care of everything. *Run, Maisie, I'll take care of it. You need to get out of here! Run! Run!*

Chapter Thirty-Seven

December 2019

To make matters worse, I hadn't been quick enough to hide the bracelet from Faye, who has decided that it was obviously a present from the elf – whose name must be Seraphine – and has insisted on wearing it to school.

I think back to the last time I saw its double, twenty years ago, and the memory makes me retch. A night I try not to think about and had been successfully not thinking about until recently. The night I became a murderer. Now it's going to be wrapped around my daughter's wrist for me to see constantly until she forgets about it, and I can 'lose' it somewhere.

Not for the first time since I heard that Mitchell had been released from prison, I consider how quickly I could convince Rob to move away. My job is one I can do from anywhere – although I really do love my studio and our beautiful home. The kids are so settled in school… it's just such a mess.

I can't sit at home all day, watching the street, wondering if Mitchell is out there somewhere watching me, or obsessing over what he's planning. I can't drive to the school and keep watch there either, not unless I want to find myself reported for strange behaviour outside a primary school.

It's less than a month until Christmas and I've done no shopping – that feels like a good way to keep my mind off things.

–

Town is much quieter on a weekday, and for a few hours I let myself enjoy wandering around the shops, picking up onesies for the children, the latest books from their favourite series, a Pandora bracelet and a couple of charms for myself. It might not seem very romantic, but I've always bought my own Christmas presents. I like to make sure I get something I want, and the enjoyment of shopping for them overrules any joy I might get from the element of surprise. I've never really liked surprises – I prefer to be the one in control.

When I've bought all that I can carry on the bus – my car still hasn't come back from the garage yet – I put off going home by stopping at one of the cafés on the high street and ordering a ridiculously indulgent hot chocolate with cream and marshmallows. I'm just watching the whipped cream sink into the chocolate when a voice says 'Laura?'

I look up to see the woman from last Saturday – the one who saved my daughter's life – standing over me, her arms full of bags.

'Hello,' I say, slightly taken aback. 'Cally, isn't it?'

'That's it. I hope you don't mind me coming over, I just wanted to see how Faye is.'

'Of course not! Do you want to join me for a drink? Or are you with someone?' I look around, but she shakes her head.

'I'm just doing some Christmas shopping,' she says. 'I'll grab a drink and join you if you don't mind? Can I leave these here?' She motions to her bags.

I nod and watch as she goes to order her drink. She's wearing the same long beige coat as when I last saw her, but this time she has on a red silk shirt underneath and a black pencil skirt. She looks like she's just come from the office.

'I'm glad you spotted me,' I tell her as she sits back down opposite me with a latte. 'I wanted to thank you again for what you did. I don't think you realised at the time just how important what you'd done was. You literally saved my daughter's life.'

She looks down at her drink; I've embarrassed her. 'I'd love to say that it wouldn't have come to that, but I couldn't stop thinking about it all night afterwards, about how easily it can happen. You always think things like that happen in other towns, not where you live.'

'That's what everyone thinks. Until it happens to them,' I say. 'The thought of what could have happened makes me feel sick. Did the police contact you?'

'Yes, there was a message after my appointment asking me to call the police sergeant. It sounded like they were taking it seriously, but they said they hadn't managed to catch the guy.'

'No, they didn't.' I think of Mitchell outside my house, hanging a toy elf from my window frame, putting cameras on my roof. 'He's still out there.'

'Terrifying. How is Faye now?'

'Oh, she's forgotten all about it,' I smile. 'Too taken up by Christmas and all that. What about you, do you have children?'

'No.' She looks down again and I curse myself for being insensitive. It's one of those questions that seems simple enough until you ask someone who can't have children, then it's like punching them in the face. 'I haven't found the right guy. I thought I had, but you know how these things go.'

'Plenty of time yet,' I say, but it sounds insincere to my own ears. She must be around the same age as me. I'm forty in February, and women of our age feel the pressure keenly. 'Have you been at work?'

I half expect her to tell me she's just been fired – feels like about my luck with small talk – but she nods.

'I took half a day to get my shopping finished. I work for the council, in those new buildings just down the road? It's too far from town to pop in on my lunch break, but I was owed a few hours.'

'What do you do for the council?' I ask, sipping my hot chocolate. It's still too hot and burns the tip of my tongue. Shit.

'Payroll,' she replies, rolling her eyes. 'I know, boring, right? What do you do?'

'I have my own gift design business,' I say. 'It's my busiest time of the year so I should be working non-stop, but since what happened with Faye at the weekend, I haven't really been able to concentrate much. I'm a bit worried, actually.'

It feels good to admit to someone that I'm struggling, even if I can't be honest about why.

Cally listens and makes sympathetic comments and I find myself enjoying her company. It feels like we've known one another forever; I haven't felt that kind of connection with another woman for a long time. There are some mums at the school that I like, but I've been so busy and turned down so many invites that I don't really get asked anymore. It was a bit of a relief when they stopped inviting me – one thing you'll know if you've ever had a big secret hanging over you is that absolutely everything becomes about guarding that secret. The closer I get to people, the more paranoid I become that I'll let something slip. Rob is the only person I've let in in twenty years.

When I glance at my watch, it's just gone two o'clock. 'Wow, I've got to get back for the kids. I'm on the bloody bus, then I've got to get a taxi to the school.' I've already told her about my crash, just not the reason for it.

'Can I give you a lift?' Cally asks.

'No, honestly, it's fine, thank you.'

She doesn't push the issue, even though I'd only said no to be polite. Damn politeness. Instead we swap numbers so that we can maybe do coffee again some time and I realise, with a small thrill, that I've just had a perfectly normal chat with another human being. Maybe I can pass as normal after all.

Chapter Thirty-Eight

October 2000

I THOUGHT I WAS NEXT

Sunday Echo

Maisie Goodwin, the friend of missing British backpacker Seraphine Cunningham, has told how she feared for her life after seeing her friend attacked by a male assailant on the West Coast Trail in Vancouver. 'I was certain that he'd seen me, and that he was coming for me next,' she told Martin Gerant of *The Daily Globe* in her first news interview since the attack. 'I was hysterical, a mess. The media cast doubt on holes in my story, but I was in shock.'

Her testimony led to the conviction of fellow hiker, Mitchell Dyke. Of Dyke, Goodwin says, 'He had been pestering Seraphine all night. I guess he didn't want to take no for an answer.'

Earlier this week, Dyke was found guilty of the kidnap and murder of Seraphine and sentenced to thirty years in prison, despite no body ever being found.

No-body convictions have been extremely rare in Canadian courts, however earlier this year, Timothy Culham was convicted of first-degree murder after the disappearance of 72-year-old Hugh Sinclair where no body could be found. Sceptics wonder if these two high-profile cases could set a precedent for convictions where there is no absolute proof of death.

Speaking out after the trial, one of the jurors said that the testimony of Goodwin was 'utterly compelling' and coupled with Dyke's confession that he had intercourse with the attractive victim immediately before her disappearance made it easy for the jury to convict.

Goodwin welcomes the result. Speaking of the scepticism with which her story was treated by the media and some of the RCMP (Royal Canadian Mounted Police), she said: 'I have spent the last year living with media intrusions into my life, to devastating effect. I thought I would be killed that night, and people wanted to doubt me because they wanted a news story. Thanks to the verdict, I can now try to move on with my life.'

Chapter Thirty-Nine

December 2019

When I get home with the kids, I feel completely deflated. For a couple of hours, I've been able to forget that I have a man stalking my family, and that I probably won't get to spend Christmas with my family because I'll be in prison. You can only keep thoughts like that at bay for so long though, before you have to come crashing back to reality, and in the kitchen at home, I sob quietly into my sleeve.

I want to be strong; I've always been strong. Ever since that awful night on the West Coast Trail twenty years ago, I've tried my hardest not to ever let myself think about what I did. It was him or me, I tell myself. I had to do what I did. And I did convince myself, for so very long. I allowed myself to make a fresh start, and when I met Rob nearly twelve years ago, I chose to allow myself to be happy, and to allow myself a family. Which I know I didn't deserve, but I've tried my hardest to deserve it. I've been the absolute best wife, mother and person I could be. We donate to our local food bank, we volunteer at the shelter every Christmas Eve, we do random acts of kindness and I teach my children that it's better to be kind than anything else. But still, I killed someone, and an innocent man went to prison because of me. Two people denied a family, denied the chance to be good and kind, or to raise children who might do great things in the world. It doesn't matter that I've become a good person now, I could donate enough soup to fill the Atlantic Ocean and those facts are still true. I am a murderer and a liar. And one day soon it will catch up with me.

So I have three choices. I can sit and wait for those things to happen, for Mitchell to turn up and either kill me, hurt my children or report me to the police and go to prison. I can come clean to Rob and hope he can forgive me and we can run away, make a fresh start, perhaps we can go where Mitchell won't find us, but I will always be looking over my shoulder. If he can find me once – and how did he find me? – he can find me again. And this option comes with the added risk that Rob tells me to go to hell and I have to leave without him, either steal my children, in which case he will call the police on me himself – of that I'm sure – or leave Faye and George forever. I won't abandon my children, not by choice anyway. And not by simply waiting to be arrested or killed, either. If I have to leave my children behind, it will be after I go down fighting, kicking and screaming in a hail of bullets.

So that just leaves option three. The way I knew this was going ever since my daughter was led out of a shop by a man I once had jailed for murder.

I have to find Mitchell Dyke, and I have to fight back.

–

Once the decision has been made, things feel clearer. First, I need to be able to protect my family.

After what happened in Canada, I became a different person. Not just my name, or my appearance – those were easy to change – I became harder-faced, more determined than ever not to let anyone hurt me. I'd been taken in by someone I'd thought I'd loved, left vulnerable by them and unable to protect myself. And I couldn't bear to let that happen again. So I bought a gun.

I trained with it almost daily, until I met Rob. After just a couple of months of knowing him, I packed away the entirety of my life and stored it in a lock-up outside of Reading, away from my new life and the person Rob made me want to be.

Where it all still is now.

'Mummy, George won't give me Bubblegum back!' Faye squeals, in a stark reminder that I'm not a hardened vigilante, I'm a mother of two. That side of me was so far in the past that it almost didn't feel like it had happened to me at all.

'George!' I shout, knowing that this half-hearted attempt to recover the kidnapped bear is not going to go down well with Faye. 'Give Bubblegum back to your sister!'

'No,' he shouts. Simple and unemotional, just no.

'Mum!' Faye screams and I sigh. 'Give it back, George.'

'Not that! Archie's broken his collar!'

God knows how he's managed it, but I'm sure I've mentioned already how much of an asshole our dog is. Somehow, he's completely shredded his collar, despite it being around the only place on his body that his teeth can't actually reach. Luckily, we have an old collar on the shelf in the cupboard. If he wears it too long, it irritates his neck – and now he's figured out how to destroy them, this one likely won't last long, but it'll do until I can get to the shop for a new one.

'Come here, you stupid mutt,' I say, but Archie thinks I'm trying to play and starts bounding around me like a kangaroo. 'Stop it! Archie, stop it!'

I manage to clip the collar around his neck just as the doorbell rings. I glance at the camera screen for our Ring doorbell to see that it's a delivery man. If it's Hermes, this might be the first time since we moved here that he's actually attempted to make a delivery rather than just wellying it over the back gate.

Archie immediately starts barking and jumping at the front door.

'Just give it a rest a minute, Faye, I'll sort it in a second,' I say, grabbing Archie's collar so he doesn't lunge at the delivery man as soon as the door opens. Death by licking is not another one I need on my conscience.

'Hi!' I say, breathlessly throwing open the door, a bit startled to see the young dark-haired lad still there after a full thirty seconds' waiting. 'I don't remember ordering anything.'

'Maybe it's a surprise gift,' he shrugs, not really bothered if I've ordered anything or not. He looks as though he'd rather be doing anything but delivering parcels. It's a large cardboard box with nothing printed on the outside except the address label. He leans down to take a photo of it on my doorstep.

'Is that for me?' Faye says, sticking her head around the door.

'It's my name on it, so stop snooping,' I say, glad of the distraction from her stolen teddy. As soon as she stops wanting it, George will get bored and drop it anyway. As long as he doesn't do what he did last time he wanted to wind her up and put it in the toilet. Especially now that he's started doing his number twos in the toilet without bothering to tell me – or flush.

I take the box into the kitchen, trying desperately to remember if I ordered anything online for the kids' Christmas presents. I dare not open it in front of Faye just in case, so I wait until she drifts back upstairs to get the scissors out of the drawer and slit the tape open.

You would think, with my current paranoia levels being at a hundred, that receiving a parcel I didn't remember ordering would have prepared me for something shocking. Maybe it's the fact that the kids have been arguing, and I'd been trying to restrain the dog that means my guard dropped for a minute. I realise afterwards that it could have just as easily been a pipe bomb, that I'd got off lucky really that the box hadn't exploded the minute I sliced into it. It doesn't feel very lucky though, as my chest constricts, and I feel like I can't breathe when I see what is lying in the bottom of the box.

Chapter Forty

July 1999 – Maisie

'Can you keep me here?' Maisie demanded. 'I'm a witness, not a suspect. Aren't I? Or am I a suspect now?'

'No, Ms Goodwin, you're still a witness.' The *for now* was implied. 'And you're free to go at any time. Of course, we appreciate your help and there's still a lot more we need to ask you, but—'

'I'm tired,' Maisie announced. 'And I need to get out of here.'

The female detective raised her eyebrows but nodded. 'Like I say, we can't force you to stay, but—'

'Then I'm leaving.'

Despite how desperate Maisie had been to get out of the police station, the minute she stepped outside, she wanted to run back in. The steps at the front of the building were crammed full of reporters, each one holding up a camera and a microphone towards her face. A cacophony of clicks and shouts of her name rose to meet her.

'Maisie! Can you tell us what happened to Seraphine?'

'Maisie! Can you tell us why Seraphine's parents aren't here?'

'Maisie! How long did you know Seraphine?'

Maisie turned around and shoved her way back into the police station. She put her hands on the desk where the detective was standing watching her, looking slightly amused by her reappearance.

'You have to help me,' she demanded. 'It's carnage out there. I'm an important witness! You have to get me past them.'

The thick-necked detective nodded slowly. She knew he'd told her his name, but she couldn't for the life of her remember it.

'Come with me,' he said, inclining his head to another door. 'Do you have somewhere to stay?'

Maisie shook her head. 'I was supposed to be on the trail for another three days, then I have a flight back to the UK.'

'You'll need to cancel that,' he said. 'We're going to need you around for longer than three days. I'll get Claire to book you a hotel for tonight, then we'll try to get your flight changed.'

The implication in his voice was clear. *You belong to us now.* And Maisie knew she wouldn't be allowed to pull another strop.

—

Detective Derek Barnes, that was the police officer's name, was true to his word. He took Maisie through the back of the station, gave her a jacket to put over her head in case any of the journalists had stationed themselves at the back entrance and had a car pull up as close to the door as possible.

Maisie chucked the jacket over her head, stooped low and ran towards the car door, which opened when she got close. She heard shouts of 'She's there!' and 'At the back!' But she managed to slam the door and Claire put her foot down before any of them could reach her.

The hotel felt like a slice of paradise. It wasn't the most luxurious in Canada, but after three days on the trail and almost eight hours in a police station, even the fact that it had a bath with hot water was heavenly.

Maisie turned on the hot tap and poured the hotel bath creme into the scalding water. She stripped off the plain grey tracksuit the police had given her when they had taken her clothes for testing and threw it in a heap on the floor. The water burned as she sank underneath, steam rising off her skin where it surfaced. She submerged her shoulders and her neck, feeling the tension ease. But when she closed her eyes, all she could see was Seraphine's eyes, wide with fear, her mouth open in a scream. Ric's face close to hers... *I'll take care of it... run... run... run!*

She opened her eyes with a gasp, the breath sucked from her lungs. How would she ever be able to close them again, without seeing Sera's face?

Maisie scrubbed at every inch of her skin until she was red and raw. She wasn't aware of when she began to sob, but once she started, she couldn't stop, and she lay crying in the bath until the water was cold, trying to resist the urge to sink below the surface and never come up.

–

Despite avoiding the media the day before, the next morning's papers were full of her face. Headlines such as 'How did she survive?' and 'What does the witness know?' screamed out at her from the front pages of the tabloids, each one accompanied by a picture of her standing on the steps outside the police station, her face stony.

Perhaps it had been a mistake not to speak to the media. Maybe she should have tried to get them onside, give them the story that they so desperately wanted, but it had been hard enough relating her lies to the police, let alone repeating them to the rest of the world. The police didn't believe her, she was sure of that, and if the media decided she was guilty... well, she knew what had happened to Lindy Chamberlain when Australia had chosen not to believe that a dingo had stolen her baby. Three years in prison before she was finally exonerated... and that didn't always happen.

Maisie deserved prison for what she'd done, she knew that. But she wasn't brave enough to face up to the truth. All she could do now was hope that Ric had kept to his promise to take care of everything and pray that Seraphine's body was never found.

Chapter Forty-One

The smell is the first thing that hits me when I open the lid. The vile stench of decaying meat is so rancid that I don't know how it hadn't seeped through the box and stunk out the entire delivery van. The odour propels me backwards slightly, making me gag.

What the hell is it?

The thing inside the box is round and pink, with lumps of white gristle running through it, and it's sitting on black tissue paper. I'm about to poke it when I see it move.

Oh dear God, it's moving.

I shoot backwards away from the box, banging my side against the edge of the kitchen worktop and sending the plate that was on there crashing to the floor. It shatters the eerie silence and I clasp my hand against my mouth to stop from screaming. The kids are watching TV upstairs and they will come running if they hear me scream. I can't let them see this.

How is it moving?

I lift a knife from the block and hold it in front of me for protection, like a sword. I have no idea how what appeared on first glance to be some rotten meat is *pulsating* inside that box, but I do know that it probably won't survive a knife attack if it comes at me. My mind spins through the possibilities. Could it be some kind of animal? Perhaps it has been skinned and left alive long enough to reach me. The thought of peering into the box to see a skinned rabbit or guinea pig staring back at me is almost too horrifying to comprehend. Surely no one could be that sick?

Whatever it is in there, I have to move quickly. I need to forget about my own fear and squeamishness because if Faye or George see that monstrosity, they will never sleep again. Or worse, knowing my daughter, she will insist we 'save' it and keep a hairless, skinless abomination as a pet. Eurgh.

I reach forwards gingerly and poke the box closed with the tip of the knife. When all four flaps are down, I slide the box gently from the table and move quickly towards the back door. Outside, I tip the whole thing upside down, fling the box to one side and stand with the knife braced to attack.

Instead of flying at me, the thing drops to the patio floor with a thump, followed by the black tissue paper, then hundreds of squirming white maggots that make me retch as they lay on the floor writhing over the lump of meat. A heart of some animal, either a sheep or a lamb by the size of it. The stench is still disgusting, and the maggots are repulsive, but I feel a wave of stupidity at the way I had allowed my imagination to run away with itself. It's just a juvenile prank to disturb me, nothing more. Mitchell is going to have to do better than this if he wants me to lose my cool.

I skewer the rotting animal heart onto my knife before Archie can come shooting out and eat it. For a dog that is so fussy about which brand of dog food we buy him, he certainly isn't fussy about eating anything else he comes across in the street or on the field. Fox poo, cow poo, mouldy old sandwiches – you name it, he's devoured it in the name of research. I don't think even the smell would put him off this, and the maggots would probably be an appetiser.

I push it down low in the outside bin, shoving it in-between two bin liners full of rubbish. Rob might not question a great deal in our lives, but the appearance of a maggot-infested animal heart might prompt an uncomfortable discussion or two. Wiping my hands on my trousers in disgust, I pull out the garden hose that's attached to the outside tap and spray down the patio, sending the maggots spinning satisfyingly off in a stream of water into the flower bed. I turn the soil over with Faye's miniature trowel and they too disappear.

Just the box left to deal with. The cardboard stinks so badly that I don't want to just stick it in the recycling. Burning it isn't really an option, so I hose it down until it's a soggy lump of cardboard mâché and roll it up into a sodden lump. Picking it up gingerly between two fingers, I cram that down into the bin as well.

'You won't break me that easily,' I shout to my empty back garden. 'I'm stronger than that. You should know by now.'

And satisfied that I've won this round, I go back into the house intending on cleaning up the broken plate. Instead I find Faye screaming that Archie is nowhere to be found.

Chapter Forty-Two

'We were hoping you might have remembered something more about the man you saw attacking Seraphine by now,' the police officer said. 'Now that the shock has worn off.' She held up a hand. 'I know you say it was dark, and we understand that. But you saw what was happening to her... so perhaps you saw what her attacker looked like?'

Maisie opened her mouth to say that she'd already told them she didn't see him, but she realised that was never going to be good enough. Until she gave some sort of description, she would be hounded by the police, and then by the media. If she described Ric and he was picked up by police... well, what he might say in retaliation didn't bear thinking about.

'He was tall,' she said, realising as she said it how weak that sounded. 'And thin.'

'Was he white?' Claire asked. 'Or black?'

'He was white.' Perhaps she should have said black... that would have taken Ric completely off their radar. It was too late now though. 'Really pale, I thought,' she added quickly, remembering Ric's tanned skin.

'What about his hair colour?' Claire said, her voice encouraging now that Maisie was finally giving them something. 'Was it brown?'

'No, not brown,' she replied, thinking of Ric's light brown hair. 'But not blonde either, actually.' She sighed, realising she was tying herself up in knots trying to avoid describing Ric. 'Maybe it was black.'

She saw the officers share a look. The room seemed half the size it had just a few days ago and the light grey wood-chipped walls seemed to close in with each passing hour. Maisie was tired... so, so tired, and her eyes hurt – there was something about the harsh, stark strip lighting in the room that was threatening to trigger the mother of all migraines. There was a slight pulse under her left eye that had been throbbing for the last thirty minutes. At that moment, Maisie felt as though she might say anything just to be allowed to get out of there and go back to the cheap but ultimately safe and comforting hotel.

'Are you sure about that?' Claire's eyes almost gleamed with anticipation. It was what they wanted her to say, there was no doubt about that. And Maisie would have years and years to regret what she did next, but at the time, she had absolutely no idea what she was about to set in motion.

'Yes,' she confirmed. 'I'm sure now. It was definitely black.'

They exchanged another look, then Derek slowly leaned forwards and opened the file they had in front of them. Maisie was half surprised to see that it contained anything at all, it had sat unopened for so long. She was even more shocked to see the photograph Derek pulled out of it and slid towards her.

'Do you recognise this man?' he said, his voice almost cajoling.

'Yes,' Maisie said truthfully.

'Could this be the man you saw attacking Seraphine?'

'No,' Maisie replied instinctively. 'No, it couldn't be him. He was really nice to us… He didn't look like he'd… No, I'm sure it couldn't have been him.'

'Forget what you think you know about him,' Claire said, frustration creeping into her voice again. 'Just concentrate on what you saw that night. You've already told us that Mitchell Dyke and Seraphine spent a lot of time together that evening, and that you saw them leave the camp together, that's why you went to look for her. Several others saw a man who fits Dyke's description walk off with a young girl into the trees.'

'Maybe someone came through the forest,' Maisie suggested. 'Maybe they weren't signed up for the trail.'

'But you'd been camping near Mitchell's group that night… hadn't you? You'd been drinking with them. So what are the chances that someone else matching the description of the man you were with that night snuck onto the trail and killed your friend. Unless…' She stopped and gave Derek a meaningful look.

'Unless what?' Maisie said, looking between the two of them. 'What? Unless what?'

'Unless you're lying to us, Maisie,' Claire said quietly.

Maisie felt the migraine that had been threatening to come breaking through at that moment, washing over her in waves.

'Unless you hurt Seraphine and you're trying to cover it up.'

'No,' Maisie muttered. She put her head in her hands. It was all going wrong. So, so wrong. Why had she raised the alarm in the first place? Why hadn't she just kept her mouth shut and done as Ric had said? 'No, no, no.'

'So tell us, Maisie,' Claire kept on at her and Maisie wished she would just shut up for a minute, give her a chance to think, to work out what she needed to say to make them go away and leave her alone, to make them let her get on a plane and go back to her boring, sheltered existence where all that she was expected to do in life was to change the baby's nappy and go to work at the café, serve bacon sandwiches and bitter coffee and never see another police officer this close ever again. To never have another police officer call her 'Maisie' in that way that was supposed to say 'we want to help you, we're on your side,' but instead just rhymed with 'guilty', so that every time they said 'Maisie' all she heard was 'guilty, guilty, guilty' and she knew that unless she put a stop to this now, unless she took charge and did something, that was all she was ever going to hear, from the police, from the judge, from the papers, from the rest of the world. Guilty, guilty, guilty. 'Have you been lying to us all along about seeing a man hurting Seraphine? Or could the person you saw have been the man in this photograph?'

'Yes,' she whispered, tears clouding her eyes and pain shooting through her temples. 'Yes.'

'Yes what, Maisie?' Derek asked, and his voice was hungry now, like a lover when he asks if you want it, if you really want it.

'Yes, it was him,' she said, the tears rolling down her cheeks and light bursting across her field of vision. 'He did it. He killed Seraphine.'

Chapter Forty-Three

December 2019

'He's gone!' Faye's screaming, tears running down her face. 'Archie's gone!'

'Hey, calm down,' I tell her. My daughter is well versed in both theatrics and hysterics. Archie is probably hiding from another of her games of 'invasion of the snuffle monster', where both Malibu Barbie and Sleepover Barbie work together to conquer the giant black snuffle monster that has taken over bedroomland. Archie doesn't mind the game until right at the end, where the barbies have to ride the snuffle monster into the cave of doom (her wardrobe). Now, when he sees the barbies come out, he makes a hasty retreat, leaving the mighty Georgeasaurus to be the bad guy.

'Have you checked the bathroom?' I ask. It is Archie's dream to one day be able to reach to drink out of the toilet bowl.

'He's not in there! The front door was open and he's gone!'

I freeze. We don't have a lot of rules in our house, but most of the ones we do relate to Archie, and not leaving the front door open is the first big one.

'Why did you open the front door?' I ask her, almost tripping over a pile of Duplo to get through to the front hall.

'I didn't,' Faye insists. 'It was just open. And I shouted, "Archie, what's this?" but he didn't come.'

My heart sinks. 'Archie, what's this?' never ever fails. The damn dog loves treats so much that I swear he can hear the treat tin opening from the field down the street.

'Get the treats,' I instruct, and I ram the slippers that I keep by the front door onto my feet. Running out onto the street, I scan both ways but can't see any sign of Archie. Panic rises inside me now as I picture him darting out into traffic.

Faye arrives at my side in seconds with the treat tin. She shakes it vigorously and we both shout, 'Archie! Archie, what's this?' over and over, but there is still no sign of him. I think about how long he might have been gone – since the delivery driver came with that horrible parcel, I must have left it open by mistake. That had been at least half an hour ago. Oh Lord.

'Run next door and ask Linda to come and get George.'

The last thing I need is to be searching for the dog and have George go missing.

I run inside and grab my boots and coat, and Archie's slip lead in case I need to lasso the little bugger.

'Laura, is everything okay? Poor Faye has just come over saying that George is missing?'

Linda from next door is here. Despite the fact that she comes over at least once a week for a cup of tea, or sometimes for food, I have absolutely no idea how old she is. She's older than me, but she could honestly be anywhere in-between forty-five and sixty as far as I can make out. Rob reckons she's on the older side and just looks pretty fantastic for her age, and from some of the stories she tells I'm inclined to agree. Whatever age she is, she must spend her day working out and having her hair and nails done because I've only ever seen her wearing leggings and hoodies, and I've never seen so much as a millimetre of roots in her bleach blonde hair. Now she looks as though she's been caught in the middle of a workout. Or, knowing Linda, sex. Her husband passed away five years ago, leaving her with a huge insurance payout and not much more to do with her time other than the aforementioned workouts and banging every unsuspecting tradesman that falls into her trap.

'God, no, sorry, Linda. Archie's missing. I was wondering if you could watch Faye and George while I go and search for him, please?'

'I'm coming with you,' Faye demands, and I don't have the patience to negotiate with her.

'No problem,' Linda waves me aside and walks in. 'You go and find the nuisance mutt; I'll take care of Georgie.'

'Thank you,' I say, and practically drag Faye out of the house with me.

'Are you going to call Daddy?' Faye asks as we bolt down the road, me hollering Archie's name every few steps.

'There's no need to call Daddy,' I snap. Where does this reliance on bloody men come from? Not from me. I've always proven myself more than capable of dealing with problems, and yet Faye's default solution is always to call her father. 'Archie's probably at the field and we'll have him back in a few minutes.'

It suddenly occurs to me that if the damn dog has run into the road, then bringing Faye probably wasn't the best of moves. I'd been in such a rush to get out and find him that I hadn't stopped to think. God, I hope the stupid mutt is okay.

Adrenaline surges through me as we practically run through the entrance of the field, only to find it empty. Archie is nowhere to be seen. I'd been so convinced that I'd see his black fur bounding through the grass that I sag forwards, leaning on my knees to keep myself upright.

'Where is he, Mummy?' Faye wails.

'He can't be far, sweetheart,' I say, but I know that's not true. He could be God knows where by now, and anything could have happened to him. He's microchipped, thank goodness, so the best we can hope for is that someone finds him and returns him to the vets.

'You need to call Daddy,' Faye demands.

I sigh and make the call.

'Laura, what is it?' Rob asks as he hears the break in my voice. 'Are the kids okay?'

'It's Archie,' I tell him, the seriousness of the situation only hitting me as I have to spell it out to Rob. 'He's missing. He got out and I don't have a clue where he's gone.'

'Shit,' Rob curses. 'How long has he been gone?'

'I don't know, over half an hour,' I admit. 'I think he must have got out when a parcel was delivered.' The parcel that I was so distracted by. For the first time since I saw the door open and the dog gone, it hits me that the timing of this might not be a coincidence after all. Mitchell sent the parcel so he could steal our dog.

'Oh God. I'll come home right now,' Rob says, and suddenly I wish I hadn't called him. If what I've just thought of is true, then I don't know what's going to happen next. I need my family away from this situation while I have time to think. Is it possible that Mitchell Dyke was at my front door after the delivery man left? Was this all part of his plan?

'Laura?' Rob's voice startles me – he's been talking to me without me even realising.

'Sorry, what?'

'I said will you start knocking on doors while I sort things here and come back? Perhaps he's got into someone's garden. He's probably eating the contents of our neighbours' bins as we speak.'

A spark of hope ignites in me. Of course, he'll have followed his nose. I'm overreacting. The door was left open – it isn't the first time. He's probably been in Linda's back garden all along.

'Good idea,' I say.

Maybe Faye is right, maybe I do need a man to fix my problems after all.

Chapter Forty-Four

It all happened so fast after that. The Canadian police wrote up Maisie's statement and had her sign it before she could change her mind – not that she could possibly change her mind now, of course. She'd said the magic words, what they wanted to hear and now everything was in freefall...

The arrest was announced the next day. They had swooped on Mitchell just in time – apparently his bags were packed to fly home and his flight was later that day. The newspapers used that as an obvious admission of guilt – why would he be running if he had nothing to hide? They made no mention of the fact that Mitchell and the group he was travelling with had already delayed their flights home once to help the police with their enquiries and had no idea why they shouldn't just take their flight home as planned. They certainly didn't realise that it would be on the front pages of every paper, with ridiculous headlines like 'Nicked in the Nick of Time'. The papers were also alluding to serious evidence of Mitchell's guilt in the forensic analysis, but Maisie had no idea what that might be because she knew he wasn't guilty. Was he?

Guilt crashed over her in waves when she heard the news of his arrest. She had known it was coming, of course. Derek and Claire had almost cracked open the champagne when she had agreed that it was probably Mitchell she'd seen on the dirt track that night with Seraphine. That it made sense, as well, because he'd shown her the most attention all night and at one point they had been getting extremely cosy in the entrance to Seraphine's tent – and hadn't they perhaps disappeared together for a while? In fact, the more Maisie thought about that night, the more she began to convince herself that Mitchell had been acting quite strangely, and there had definitely been something pushy about him. He had wanted Seraphine, she hadn't had to lie about that, and perhaps it was as the officers had suggested, that they had gone off together, Mitchell and Sera, and perhaps Mitchell had been a bit forceful, and Sera had said no. What if he'd assaulted her, then strangled her so she couldn't tell anyone? It happened, Maisie's mum was always telling her horror stories about women raped on nights out, walking home on their own, or getting into taxis alone. Maisie had always thought it was her mum's way of keeping her in – make her afraid and she wouldn't try to leave them, she wouldn't stay out all night, she'd always be there to feed the baby when she woke in the night. And now it had happened, Maisie thought, except not to her, but to Seraphine... Except it hadn't really happened, had it? Or had it? Maisie knew what had happened to Seraphine, didn't she? Perhaps Ric had been telling the truth, if Mitchell had attacked Sera and left her for dead, maybe she hadn't... maybe it hadn't been her after all. *Go now, I'll take care of it, run!*

And the police had told her they'd been suspicious of Mitchell from the start, and they'd said that another one of his friends had seen them kissing, Seraphine and

Mitchell… And the police, they had Mitchell's photograph in the file because he'd had her bracelet in his pocket, the one Sera wore. He said it had come off and he'd promised to fix it for her in the morning, but the police thought he was keeping it as a trophy, like the serial killers you saw on the news. They had other forensic evidence, it said so in the papers. So perhaps it was him after all, and perhaps what she'd seen… what she'd done, perhaps that had just been a drug-addled dream. Or a nightmare.

And that's how easy it was to delude herself that she had nothing whatsoever to do with Seraphine's murder.

Chapter Forty-Five

August 2000

'HE'S INNOCENT' FELLOW HIKER CLAIMS

Morning Herald

A fellow hiker of Mitchell Dyke, the man on trial for the kidnap and murder of British born backpacker Seraphine Cunningham, says there's no way he could be guilty. Dyke, who was twenty years old at the time of the hiker's disappearance, stands accused of murdering Cunningham on the West Coast Trail on 30 July 1999.

Kaz Rigby, who was travelling with Dyke at the time, claims that he was the kindest, nicest person you would ever meet, and that being turned down by Cunningham would never have pushed him to murder the nineteen-year-old. She ridiculed claims that the group were into satanism and Cunningham's death was part of a satanic ritual. 'So we wore black. Mitchell wants to study Criminology, he wants to help solve

176

crimes, not commit them. Wearing black isn't a crime.'

Of the police's star witness, Maisie Goodwin, Rigby said, 'I don't know if she's lying or if she's mistaken, but either way, she's got it wrong. Mitchell is not the one who should be on trial.'

Goodwin and Cunningham had met the group on the West Coast Trail the day before Cunningham's disappearance. It is claimed that Mitchell Dyke felt an 'instant connection' to the missing woman, a connection that, according to others, might not have been reciprocated.

'He barely knew her. Mitch isn't the type to be aggressive to women, or to hurt a woman because he got turned down,' Rigby insisted. 'I know he didn't do this. He's innocent.'

The trial is set to continue after the long weekend, with evidence yet to be given by star witness Maisie Goodwin, the woman who claims she saw Seraphine murdered by Dyke.

Chapter Forty-Six

December 2019

Rob has been back an hour. We've knocked on every house in the street, dozens of neighbours have come out to help us look and there's still no sign of Archie. Linda has posted on every local Facebook group, Faye hasn't stopped crying and even Rob looks like he's losing hope of ever getting him back. While she was stuck at ours looking after George, Linda has printed off a picture of the curly menace and has been sending them out with our neighbours. There's an actual search party going on and as I watch people knock on doors and encourage the occupants to check their gardens it hits me like a fire truck... Archie is gone. Perhaps forever.

'It can't be a coincidence,' Rob says for the fourth time. 'First someone tries to snatch Faye in town and now someone steals our dog. I don't understand it.'

I wish, for the first time ever, that I had the guts just to tell him what is going on. About Canada, about Mitchell, about everything I've done. I begin to cry for real and Rob puts his arms around me.

'I'm sorry, sweetheart,' he says. 'I'm being stupid. It's got to just be awful timing. What with what happened to Faye and now this, it just all feels so shit. I'm sorry, I didn't mean to upset you.'

I push my face into his chest and allow myself a few moments to recover, then we split up again and keep looking, under hedges, behind parked cars. I thrust Archie's picture at every passer-by I see, Rob is doing the same across the street. I see the couple who live across the road come towards us, shaking their heads.

'Sorry, Laura, we've been down Queensway and onto Rydal, but there's no sign of him at all. We'll go the opposite way onto Victoria.'

'Thank you, guys, thank you so much.'

Someone else approaches and I hold up the photo before realising it's Cally.

'Oh, wow,' I frown. 'What are you doing here?'

'I saw the Facebook post and came to help search for the missing dog,' she says. 'I didn't realise it was you – the post was by someone called Linda? Anyway, I'm terrible for not being able to resist a pooch in need.'

'That was my neighbour's post. Our dog's name's Archie,' I say. 'Little sod ran off when I took a delivery.'

'Did you see which direction he went?'

I shake my head. 'I must have left the door ajar and he escaped after I went back inside.' A thought occurs to me. 'Bloody hell, I didn't even think to check the doorbell camera.'

I pull out my phone and check the footage from the time that the delivery driver arrived. I see me carrying the disgusting parcel inside and shudder at the memory. As the door closes, I watch the hand of the delivery driver shoot out.

'What's he just done?' Cally asks, leaning over my shoulder to look. 'What's he holding?'

'It looks like paper, or cardboard,' I say, my heart starting to thud. 'He's shoving it in the door jamb, so the door doesn't close the entire way.'

So it wasn't an accident. No striking coincidence. I'm nowhere to be seen on the video when the delivery driver nudges the door open with his foot and Archie's head appears. He moves forwards and snuffles something up off the floor, then moves forwards another few inches.

'He's laid down treats,' Cally breathes. 'What an asshole.'

There's no point in walking the streets any longer. Our poor Archie has been stolen by the person who delivered me a rotting animal heart. There is no way the two things aren't related, and all I can think is that the man whose life I ruined has my beautiful Archie.

–

Rob calls the police as I try to round up all the people who have been searching for Archie to let them know there's no point. As I walk, I try to think about what I'm going to tell the police was in the delivery – they are going to want to know what I ordered so that they can trace the delivery company and find the driver. Except I know there was no order, no company, and the driver was a fake.

'I know it's stupid to ask if you're okay,' Cally says as she walks alongside me, 'but you seem like something else is bothering you. Is it just Archie? Because I can't help but think that the last time I saw you, someone had tried to walk off with your daughter, and today someone has taken your dog...'

'I know, you must think I'm the shittest person ever, I can't keep track of anything I care about,' I say, tears forming in my eyes. 'I don't deserve to have kids, or animals.'

'Hey, don't be silly,' she says, rubbing my arm. 'It's pretty obvious to me that someone has it in for you. An ex-boyfriend? Disgruntled employee?'

I wish, I think. If only it were that easy.

'Okay,' I say, stopping and turning to her. I have to tell her something, I want to tell someone something about what's going on, but I can't tell her the whole story – of course I can't. 'It's a guy, he's been stalking me. I can't tell Rob, because he'll want to know why I didn't mention it before, but I thought he would get the message and go away by now. I didn't think he'd take it this far.'

'You didn't tell Rob after what happened to Faye?'

'I couldn't,' I say, my voice almost pleading for her to understand. 'It was too late by then. And I didn't want him to think that it was my fault that Faye was in danger. He might think that I led this guy on, that it's my fault he's stalking me.'

'Look,' Cally turns to me and puts a hand on my shoulder, the gesture the kind of intimacy I've come to expect from this woman I barely know. 'I'm not judging you. I understand why you didn't want to mention it to Rob. But who is this guy?'

'Just someone I used to know,' I mutter, leaving the implication that Mitchell is an ex-boyfriend hanging in the air. 'What am I going to tell the police?'

'Do you know where this guy is? Where he might have taken Archie?'

'No,' I say. I'm annoyed at myself that I haven't managed to find out anything about where Mitchell might be. As much as I promised myself I wouldn't sit around and wait for him to hurt the people I love, that's exactly what

I've done. 'I've got no idea where he lives, or works, or anything.'

'Okay,' Cally thinks. 'What about the delivery driver. What was in the box?'

'A sheep's heart,' I say, and she cringes.

'Oh bloody hell. I'm guessing Rob doesn't know that?'

'No.'

'Tell him the box was empty,' she suggests. 'That you were wondering whether to report it as a scam to the police when you realised Archie was missing. They will think the empty box was delivered in order to steal the dog.'

'You're a *genius.*' We round the corner at the top of the street my house is on. 'Will you come in for a drink? Or am I being weird?'

'Just a quick one,' Cally says. 'In case you're a bit weird.'

I smile, but it's a weak one. I don't want to go into the house and face the hysterical children and quizzical Rob, but I don't have any choice.

The police don't seem to have arrived yet and when we walk in, Cally asks where the kitchen is so she can make us all a cup of coffee. I'd rather a gin, but I send her through and brace myself to see the children.

'Mummy, did you find Archie?' George bawls the minute he sees me, launching himself at my legs. 'I want Archie!'

'Not yet, baby, but we will,' I promise.

I look at Rob, who raises his eyebrows. He must know, as I do, that the chances of getting Archie back are slim, but he's putting on an ultra-brave face for the kids.

'We've been making posters,' he says, holding up a piece of paper on which George has been scribbling what is either a picture of Archie or a dinosaur. Faye's looks slightly more dog-like, just not our dog.

I force a smile. 'Wonderful,' I say. 'Those will have Archie back in no time.'

'Meanwhile,' Rob says, 'Linda has been plastering Archie's picture all over social media and it's been shared hundreds of times already. She's put it in every group in the area. I'm just gutted he didn't have that old collar on, the one with the hidden GPS tracker.'

That's when it hits me. A vision from just a few hours ago of Archie looking guiltily up at me with his collar half hanging off. Me clipping his old collar onto him – the one we had to stop using because it irritated his neck. The one with the GPS tracker inside.

'I know,' I murmur, an idea forming in my mind. 'How annoying.'

And just like that, I know how I'm going to find Mitchell. I just don't know what's going to happen when I do.

Chapter Forty-Seven

August 1999 – Maisie

She waited and waited for Ric to contact her, but he never did. She worried for days that he was mad at her for raising the alarm… that hadn't been part of the plan. She was supposed to go back down to the camp and get into her sleeping bag, try to sleep and in the morning tell everyone there had been an emergency and Sera had had to leave urgently in the night.

'What about all her stuff? Won't it look suspicious if she's left everything behind?'

'Hide her bag in the trees,' he'd instructed. 'Then tell them she didn't have time to take down her tent and that she asked you to do it for her. Who knows, they might even have moved on before you get up if you're lucky. No one cares about anyone on these trails, they just want to get on with their hike.'

Except it hadn't exactly gone that way. Maisie had stumbled back to camp, and by the time she got there in the pitch black she had been terrified and sobbing, a complete mess. Already her head was spinning, she could barely walk straight. She had tripped, practically landing on one of the other tents, and Kaz had come out, asking what was wrong with her, was she so hammered she couldn't walk straight?

'She's dead!' Maisie had sobbed, unable to stop herself. 'Seraphine... she's dead.'

'What?' Kaz had grabbed her arm to calm her down. 'What do you mean... what happened? How is she dead?'

'I don't know.' Maisie was shaking, her entire nervous system screaming at her. Her vision had blurred, was she going to pass out? Be sick?

'Where is she, Maisie?' Kaz was asking. 'We need to get help. Where is she?'

Maisie had just kept shaking her head. Her head was in-between her knees, and she could hear a low keening sound. She couldn't place where the noise was coming from until she had realised it was coming from her. At some point, she saw Keddie appear in front of her, pulling on his clothes.

'She says Sera is dead,' Kaz had been saying, her voice high-pitched and panicky.

'He was attacking her,' Maisie had said, more to herself than anyone else, but Kaz had heard those words and Maisie had realised she'd screwed up. 'He was... wasn't he?'

Even now Maisie didn't know what made her say it. Except that's what she had thought was happening, hadn't she? Ric was attacking his sister, Maisie had tried to help... Sera falling, then Ric saying, 'What did you do, Maisie? What did you do? She's dead, you killed her... she's dead...'

'Who was attacking her?' Kaz had asked.

Maisie had shaken her head. 'I don't... I don't know. We need to get help; we need to get out of here...'

'Come on,' Keddie urged. Mitchell was by his side now, looking terrified. 'Let's go. Which way?'

Too late she thought about Ric, trying to take care of Sera's body. If he got caught, it would all come out. What had she done? How could this be happening?

'That way,' she had said, pointing in the opposite direction from where she had just come. The men both took off and Kaz had run into one of the tents and brought out a hooded jumper.

'Here,' she'd said, passing it to Maisie. 'Put this on. You're shivering. You're probably in shock. We need to try to contact the police – I can get a bit of phone reception by the beach. Can you make it with me?'

Maisie had nodded, everything feeling numb. She hadn't been able to formulate a plan or think about what she was doing, and was grateful to Kaz for calling the police. The shock and fear had sobered her up, but she just wanted someone to take over, make it all go away.

Looking back, she knew that Ric was probably furious with her for not sticking to the plan and doing as she was told. Was that why he hadn't been in touch? Or was it just too risky? After all, none of the group they had met up with on the trail that night had seen Ric with them, it was in his best interests to stay away.

From what he had told her on the hike, Maisie hadn't expected Ric and Seraphine's parents to show up to look for their daughter, but she had expected their aunt and uncle to come to Canada. Perhaps they were older than Ric had made them sound, or they didn't have the funds to travel. The police were financing Maisie's own hotel stay, but that was probably because she was needed as a witness. It made her feel awful to think of Sera's aunt and uncle sitting at home worrying about her. Had Ric gone back to break the news to them?

It wasn't until the seventh day, the day after Mitchell's arrest, that Maisie began to realise she had been lied to, and not in a small way. The newspapers linked Seraphine to a wealthy family in the UK, whose only comment was to say that their daughter was 'estranged' from the family, and in their eyes had died a long time ago. 'We've done our grieving for our daughter,' a spokesperson said on behalf of the Cunninghams. 'We lost our only child many years ago.'

Our only child. No mention of Ric, or an aunt and uncle in Australia. Just a rich family and a bad-apple runaway daughter. So who was Ric? And why had they pretended to be brother and sister? They hadn't gained anything from it, except for their bus fare to the West Coast Trail. Was that it, was their lie just a cynical ploy to get money from some unsuspecting schmuck? Well, they'd found their perfect mark with her. They must have seen her coming a mile away. Plain, downtrodden, desperate. And maybe once it had been so easy to reel her in and have her pay their bus fare... well, why not go a little further? Why not seduce the poor little virgin, pull on her heartstrings a bit? What was their end game? Did they plan to take all of her money and leave her with nothing? Perhaps they would 'lose' their airline tickets and Maisie would be so desperate to help, she would pay their airfare.

You probably would have as well, she told herself in disgust. *You are pathetic.*

So what had gone so wrong? How had Seraphine ended up dead? God, Maisie wished she could remember it all more clearly. What she had seen... or what she had thought she had seen, why they had fought... how Sera had ended up falling. The only image she had was of her lifeless body on the trail, and Ric saying he would fix it all.

It was too late now, anyway. Maisie had her wish; it was out of her control. Someone else had taken over and everything had spiralled beyond her wildest nightmares. Mitchell Dyke was in custody and would go on trial for Sera's murder, and there was nothing Maisie could do about it.

Chapter Forty-Eight

December 2019

The app for the GPS tracker is on my laptop, and Cally looks up in surprise as I go storming into the kitchen, anticipation hammering through me. Shit, I'd almost forgotten she was here.

'Everything okay?' she asks, eyebrows raised.

Can I tell her? She already knows about my 'stalker', but if I tell her that I'm considering going to confront him, she will most likely try to talk me out of it, force me to tell Rob. On the other hand, after all of these years handling everything by myself, keeping my secret, it would be nice to actually trust someone. And I'm hardly going to tell her the real truth.

'I think I might be able to find Archie,' I say, putting a finger to my lips, then pointing to the other room where Rob and the kids are, to indicate not to react too loudly.

'How?' she asks, her voice low.

'He's wearing his old GPS collar,' I reply. 'But it's been ages since he wore it, it might not still be transmitting. I need to log on to my account to find out.'

'Well, Jesus, hurry up and do it.'

I can see we're both holding our breath as I press enter on the sign-in page and the large map begins to load on the screen. After about a minute, a flashing red dot appears.

'Where is it?' Cally asks. 'Where's that?'

'Boreham Warehouses,' I read, looking at the co-ordinates. 'Quickly, can you pass me one of those pens?'

She reaches across and passes me a pen from Faye's art corner, and I scribble the co-ordinates on my arm, hiding them under my jumper when the doorbell rings.

'That'll be the police,' I say. 'I'll have to take a look when they've gone.'

'Or you could just tell the police and let them go there?' she says, her voice sounding as though she knows there's little chance of that happening.

'I don't want to risk having to explain to Rob if the police uncover that I know this guy,' I say, perfectly truthfully. I'm not sure if the next part is a lie or not. 'You don't have to worry,' I tell her, trying to sound confident. 'He isn't dangerous. He's just trying to get my attention.'

–

The police are sympathetic but honest in telling us that they don't hold out much hope in dognapping cases. The best way to reunite a stolen dog is to raise awareness, the officer who looks young enough to have to rush home to do his homework tells us. Like Linda has been doing with her social media posts. We can also contact selling sites with his information and photos in case he's listed as for sale. I feel bad for wasting police time – I know Archie won't be listed for sale, and I'm just keen for this nice-but-useless boy to leave so I can go and find the man who is making my life hell. Rob can't stop asking questions, however, and the officer is too polite to tell him he has better things to do – or that it's past his bedtime.

Cally left us to it when the police arrived, making me promise I'll text her before I do anything stupid. I realise I haven't known her long, but she comes across as one of those ride-or-die type friends, the ones who will go along with you on the stupid stuff rather than try to deter you. I promised her I would, and I probably will.

Except I haven't told her about the gun in my lock-up, or how I'd already considered taking it out of storage before Archie went missing. Now I'm just waiting for my husband to go up to bed so that I can call a taxi to take me twenty minutes across Reading to where my old life is stored to retrieve it. The question is, will Laura Johnson, mother of two, personalised gift designer, know how to shoot a man?

This is it, I suppose. This is the moment where intention is formed. Premeditation, they call it. If I kill Mitchell Dyke with my old gun, I can't claim self-defence. I will have gone to that warehouse armed. What happens then is on me. Can I do it again? Kill someone, hide the body? Live with the guilt? This time there is more at stake than before, this time it is my family, my freedom, my life. I just can't lose them and I can't let Mitchell harm them. I know that I haven't been given a choice.

'You okay?'

Rob comes to me where I'm still sitting at the kitchen counter and strokes my hair, leans down and kisses my head. It fills me with guilt how kind he is being when this pain we are all feeling is my fault. I wonder what he would say if he knew that he was married to a murderer. Would his love for me overcome that? Would he still stroke my head, kiss my hair? I want to tell him, but the fact is that I don't know him well enough. I know everything about him – unless he's as good a liar as I am, of course – and yet I couldn't predict how he would react if I told him I'd killed someone nearly twenty years ago, if our love would be enough to survive. So instead I say, 'How are the kids?' and try not to cry.

'George is fast asleep on the sofa, he's all cried out,' Rob replies. He runs a hand over his eyes, they are red and blotchy from the strain of trying not to cry in front of the children. 'Faye is making more posters. I think she'd nod off if she hadn't taken full responsibility of the Find Archie movement.' He sighs. 'God, I hope he's okay. He must be terrified without us. We're all he's ever known.'

'He's a tough cookie,' I assure him, trying not to picture our baby boy tied to a radiator somewhere, anger for me being taken out on his tiny body. 'He'll be okay. And we'll get him back. I'll get him back, I promise. I'm so sorry.'

'Hey.' Rob wraps his arms around my shoulders and buries his face in my neck. 'It's not your fault. You weren't to know that asshole was going to take him. If I get my hands on him, I'll kill him.'

So easy to say. A turn of phrase, a throwaway comment. He doesn't mean it. I wish he did. For the first time in nearly twenty years, I miss Ric with a passion. I've never once wished Rob was like Ric, a man I came to realise was selfish, callous, calculating, only capable of lies and deception, looking after number one. And yet if Ric were here now, he would take care of this for me and make it all go away.

I go upstairs to bed with my husband and lie next to him waiting for his breathing to slow into that tell-tale sign of deep slumber before slipping out of bed and going downstairs to call a taxi.

Chapter Forty-Nine

August 1999 – Maisie

There was nothing more she could do. Mitchell Dyke's trial wouldn't take place for at least a year, and the police weren't prepared to fund her for any longer, so Maisie was to return home until she was needed to give evidence next year.

She had left under cover of darkness, Derek dropping her off at the airport in the middle of the night in an unmarked police car, so she wasn't given any trouble by the media. The press had taken to going home for the night by now: for the first week at least they had camped outside the hotel they had found out she was in, but once they had realised that she was unlikely to go wandering about in the middle of the night – and even if she did, she wasn't going to talk to them – they had operated on a daytime-only harassment.

'Look after yourself,' Derek said to her as he pulled her backpack out of the boot of his car. Maisie shuddered even now at the sight of it. She couldn't wait to get home and burn every last item in there, the bag included. She'd wanted to just leave it at the hotel, but she couldn't risk someone finding it, and uncovering some evidence she hadn't realised existed. She supposed this was how her life would be from now on, a dose of paranoia in everything she did. Derek handed her some cash. 'In case you want a snack or a drink or something,' he explained. He looked embarrassed and Maisie suspected that the money was his personal cash, and it wouldn't be going through the expenses.

Her face flushed. Derek had been good to her in the couple of weeks since they had first met. Initially, she'd hated him – and Claire too – but once she had ID'd Mitchell and taken herself off the suspect list, he had mellowed towards her, been kind even.

'Thank you,' she said, her fingertips brushing his as she took the money. They felt rough. She thought back to Ric's light touch, his smooth skin and was filled with a sudden pang of regret. Perhaps Derek interpreted the look on her face as a fondness or longing for him, because he snatched his hand back like it was on fire and cleared his throat. Maisie almost laughed at the absurdity of the situation. Her first trip away from home and she was being escorted back to the airport by a Canadian police officer. It still didn't feel like it was happening to her.

'You will remember what our lawyers told you?'

Maisie sighed. 'Don't say anything that might jeopardise the case. Don't speak to the defendant's counsel without speaking to you first. Keep you updated with my whereabouts so I can be called to give evidence,' she reeled off, her voice monotone.

'Perfect,' Derek confirmed. He looked at his feet, unsure how to end the interaction.

It was so surreal. They weren't friends, but he had been suspicious of her, outright accused her, then looked after her, calmed her down, reassured her. Jesus, she thought, Derek might depressingly be the most meaningful relationship with a guy she'd ever had.

'I'd better go then,' she said, hauling her bag onto her back. He looked relieved that she wasn't going to burst into tears or hug him. 'Thanks for everything. Especially this,' she gestured around. 'I don't know how we made it here without any press whatsoever.'

'You can thank Claire for that,' he grinned. 'She's leaked details of your leaving the country tomorrow at eleven.'

'She's a smart cookie,' Maisie said. 'Bye then.'

Derek held up a hand and she felt his eyes on her back as she walked through the automatic doors of Vancouver International airport. Did a part of him still suspect that she had been involved in Seraphine's death? Or was it pity he felt for her?

The airport was eerily still at this time in the night, and as she passed the large, darkened window of a closed shop, Maisie caught a glimpse of her reflection. It was funny, she thought, how this time just two weeks ago she had been in this exact airport looking every inch the chubby, soft-featured, plain-faced virgin. No wonder Ric and Sera had seen her coming a mile off. Not anymore though. In just two weeks, the woman who looked back at her was a slender, sharper featured version of her earlier self. She'd lost about a stone from the stress and sick feeling that had overtaken her most days, which had sharpened off her curves and plumpness, but it wasn't just her body shape which had changed. She couldn't quite put her finger on it, but there was a hardness about her face now, a knowing, worldly look in her eyes. Perhaps if Ric and Sera had seen this new version of Maisie Goodwin on that first day, they wouldn't have thought her such a pushover. In fact, she owed them a great deal, the pair of them. Because she knew now that she would never be treated like dirt by someone and let them get away with it again.

–

Maisie knew her luck had run out when she joined the queue for the boarding gate and saw the whispers and nudges, which evolved into full-blown staring by the time she was on the plane. She caught the woman next to her trying to take her photograph with a disposable camera at least three times before Maisie put her hood up and draped a plane blanket over her shoulders, hitching it up so it covered her face.

The nine-hour flight seemed much longer on the way back than it had on the way to Vancouver, probably because she was too scared to fall asleep in case she awoke to a camcorder shoved in her face while she drooled and snored.

When at last they touched down in Birmingham, Maisie wasted no time in making her way to the front of the plane, through security and to baggage claim. It was strange, she thought, that this was the first time in her entire ordeal that she wished she'd had someone with her to support her. That there was going to be her mum or a dad waiting for her, like a regular teenager would have. She suddenly didn't want to go any further, didn't want to discover what lay waiting for her beyond the arrivals gate. The Canadian police had been confident that no one knew she was going to be on this plane, and yet it didn't come as any surprise to her to hear her name shouted out as she walked through customs, the irony not lost on her that the press would most likely have a brilliant shot of her gaunt, tired face emerging from under a sign that read 'nothing to declare'.

To her surprise, though, West Midlands Police had been notified that she would be on the plane – thank you, Derek – and were awaiting her arrival.

'Ms Goodwin?' An armed officer approached her and Maisie flinched. *You're innocent*, she reminded herself. *These police are here to help you, not arrest you.*

'Yes?'

'You can come with us,' the officer said. Maisie had no idea what he looked like because every inch of him was covered with tactical gear, a helmet with a visor, a bulky stab vest. Presumably this was how the officers in the airport always dressed – either that or there was a serious threat to her life in this country that she had no idea about.

'Am I in danger?' she asked, unable to take her eyes from the gun clipped to his belt.

'No specific threat,' he said, and she sighed with relief until she heard his next sentence. 'But you are hot news at the moment. You might want to lie low for a while. We've got a vehicle waiting to take you home.'

Maisie thought about the press in Canada, screaming her name every time they saw her, yelling the most awful questions at her. Did you have anything to do with Seraphine's disappearance? Did you kill Seraphine, Maisie? Is it true you were covered in your friend's blood? Were you both taking drugs on the night she died? The woman she'd seen at the corner shop who had spat in her face, the warm saliva sliding down her cheek and dripping onto her T-shirt. The thought of encountering her old friends and colleagues, her mum, her sisters and all their questions terrified her.

'Do I have to go home?' she asked, an idea suddenly surfacing.

The officer shrugged. 'You're not under arrest,' he said. 'We're just here to get you away from the airport safely. Where you go is up to you.'

Maisie gave a thoughtful nod. 'In that case,' she said, thinking about the Cunninghams, and the daughter they had claimed was their only child, estranged from the family. 'I want to go to Nottingham. Can you get me there?'

Chapter Fifty

January 2000 – Maisie

She stood staring out at the water of the River Humber, a murky, mud-coloured mass that promised certain oblivion to those who entered. In her hand, she clutched a piece of paper that confessed her darkest sins and held the power to free an innocent man. Maisie realised that if she jumped with the letter still in her hand, or in her pocket, then it would be lost forever, unreadable if they ever even found her body. That was why she had brought the stone with her, not to weigh down her body – the rushing water would take care of that – but to hold the letter in place on the bridge until someone found it, probably the next day.

The wind was whipping her hair up around her face and she hoped that the flimsy paper would be secure enough under the rock. There wasn't much else she could do. She could have posted it to the police, of course, but what if she'd done that and something had stopped her from jumping off the bridge? She couldn't risk being arrested. As much as she'd hardened in the six months since returning from Canada, as much as she'd learned to fend for herself, look after number one, lie and deceive, disguise and fool – she knew she was no match for prison. The women in there, they were real killers, real gang members, unrepentant and evil. That wasn't her. She had taken a life… yes, but not in a planned, meticulous way. Not for her own gain. What had happened to Seraphine was an accident, and that's exactly what the letter said. A terrible accident that she couldn't live with any longer. And perhaps the media would go easier on her, once they realised that she had been so wracked with guilt over what she'd done, the lies she'd told, that she'd taken her own life.

She knew she wouldn't be the first to die by suicide on the Humber Bridge. In the nineteen years since its construction, there had been nearly seventy-five suicides. Seventy-five poor unfortunate souls who each believed the world would be a better place without them in it. Only in Maisie's case, of course, it was true. How else could you feel when you knew that an innocent man was quite possibly going to be jailed for a crime you knew in your heart he didn't commit? And that you were the only one who could tell the truth and save him? Her death could quite literally save an innocent life.

Except you don't know that Mitchell Dyke will be convicted, do you? the voice in her head whispered. *He might be let free. No-body convictions are so rare, the odds are stacked heavily in his favour. And then you'd be dead for nothing.*

'Well, I wouldn't care, would I?' she muttered out loud. 'Because I'd be dead.'

Still, the voice – her voice, of course, she wasn't ill enough to think that it was anyone other than herself thinking these things, trying to wheedle out of getting the job done – had a point. Surely she should wait until the trial was over before taking such drastic measures. If Mitchell wasn't convicted, then she had no reason to leave the note – no reason to clear the name of a man who had been found innocent in a court of law. Then she would have confessed for nothing. Her name would be plastered over all the papers again – her real name of course, not the one she went by these days. And all the people she'd met since moving away and starting again, they would realise they had been lied to as well.

And there was another reason, of course. A reason to keep living for as long as she possibly could – or, depending on how you looked at it, a reason to get her suicide over and done with. She cupped her hand around her bulging stomach, smoothing her T-shirt over the bump that was growing faster every day. Her baby. She knew in her heart of hearts that if she waited until Mitchell stood trial, if she waited to testify against him, her baby would already be born. It was one thing to end her life now, both of their lives, before her baby was born. She could almost convince herself she was doing the baby a favour, saving it from a life with a murderer and a liar. What kind of person would it turn out to be with her as a mother anyway? But once she had given birth, once she had held the baby in her arms and felt its heartbeat against her chest, laid with the baby's skin on hers the way she had seen her mother do with her sisters... well, there was no way she'd be able to hurt it then. So what options did that leave if Mitchell was convicted? One – to take her own life and abandon her baby, leaving it to the foster system, and eventually to bear the stigma of a mother who had confessed to murder, or two – forget the plan of confessing and try to move on with her life, put the past behind her and be the best mum she could be.

She imagined what her baby – *their baby* – might look like. Would it look like her? Or Ric? Would her punishment for what she'd done be to live every day with the ghost of the man who had helped her get away with murder? To be reminded on a daily basis of what she'd done in her child's eyes, or in their smile? Surely no life would be better than a life of purgatory?

Maisie didn't know how long she'd been there, standing on the side of the bridge, her fingers and toes tingling from the cold, but the sun had begun to rise a burning pink behind her. If she didn't make a decision soon, the cars would begin to arrive, people on their way to their daily commute in their normal lives. Thanks to Seraphine and Ric, her life would never be normal again.

Thanks to you, you mean, the voice said, its tone bitter. *Seraphine didn't ask to be murdered. And Ric was trying to help you. If it weren't for him, you'd be giving birth in prison.*

He had saved her, hadn't he? After all, he could have screamed blue murder – quite literally – and there would have been nothing she could do about it. He could have left Sera's body exactly where it was and let Maisie be arrested, walked out of there a free man. Instead he... well, she didn't know what he'd done exactly, but Seraphine's body had never been found, so he must have carried it far enough away from the trail that it wasn't discovered by searchers. Perhaps he even found a way to bury it, or submerge it in water. Or perhaps he left it somewhere the animals could take it away.

Maisie shuddered. She couldn't think about that. What she had to concentrate on was the fact that he had done what he'd done *for her*. To save her from the truth, from prison. And if that wasn't love, what was? And how exactly was she going to repay him? By throwing herself off a bridge, killing his child? Leaving a letter behind that implicated him in Seraphine's murder? What would happen when the police found him? He would be arrested, maybe even blamed for the murder, despite her confession. All of a sudden, the idea seemed ridiculous, horrifying.

No, she knew what she had to do. She had to protect Ric at all costs. And the only way to do that was to make sure Mitchell took his place in prison and find Ric herself. She would tell him about his child, and what she had done for him, the lies she had told, and he would tell her that he had loved her from the minute he saw her. The stuff about him and Sera being brother and sister – there would be an explanation for that, one they would probably laugh at one day. And when the nightmares came – which they often did – he would know the truth. She would never have to lie to him and pretend they were something else, their secret would cement them together. And he would hold her as she cried, and tell her it was okay, it was an accident, they had no choice but to do what they did. And they would never, ever leave one another. Together forever, their fates intertwined by that one night six months ago.

All she had to do now was to find him.

Chapter Fifty-One

December 2019

There's an almost blissful moment, that very first second when I wake up, that I forget what happened yesterday. I wait for Archie to notice that I'm awake and bound up onto the bed like he does every morning. Then there's the crushing realisation that Archie isn't here, that awful moment when I remember that he's gone, and it's my fault.

The middle-of-the-night taxi journey to the storage facility feels like a fever dream, and I slip out of bed without waking Rob, or looking at the wardrobe where the small red shoebox is mixed in with the other detritus of family life. If I don't see it there, maybe I can pretend for a short while longer that I am still Laura Johnson, innocent wife and mother. Last night's pilgrimage to another time of my life, to the person I used to be, might never have happened.

The taxi driver had asked no questions as we'd driven in silence through the city centre and out into the suburbs where the lock-up is located. I'd chosen the lock-up originally because of its remote location, but still, every small sound seemed amplified in the darkness and the silence. The shutting of the taxi door was a gunshot in the night, the roll of the shutter a low rumble of thunder. The face of the taxi driver an expressionless mask as I slipped into the back seat with the shoebox in a Home Bargains carrier bag. A fever dream, or a cold chill of a nightmare.

I take myself downstairs into the kitchen where I left my laptop on the oak dining table last night. There's a chill in the air and I pull my huge fluffy dressing gown around me and click on the kettle.

I love our kitchen diner. They were separate rooms when we moved in, stilted and formal until we knocked the wall through and discovered we had space for a dining-room table and a corner sofa at the end, making the perfect place for the kids to play and do their homework while I cook healthy and filling family meals. I did try, I think. I tried to live a good, normal life. But like the song says, there is always something there to remind me.

I log onto Archie's GPS tracker while the kettle is boiling. He's still there, in the warehouse I found him in yesterday. The dot has moved around the large building but not far. I realise that Mitchell, or whoever he sent to kidnap Archie, might have found the tracker and discarded it, I might show up and find nothing more than a collar on the warehouse floor. Or worse, Archie might already be dead. I have to be ready for that possibility, but it can't stop me trying. I allow myself a brief fantasy of me returning home tonight with Archie in my arms, telling Rob and the kids that I found him making his way home, that the wily little pup must have escaped his kidnappers like a Hallmark Christmas movie.

Once again, I curse myself for not having the guts to go there last night as soon as I'd picked up the gun, but that would have been a step too far for my bravery. Even now I wonder if I'll be able to go through with it. I tell myself that I'm only going to check it out – the gun is a precaution. I don't have to use it.

My phone vibrates and I check the screen. It's Cally.

Any news? Don't do anything stupid without me.

Not 'don't do anything stupid' full stop, just not without her. I knew she was my kind of woman. Should I take her with me?

No news, I type. *Archie still in the same place. I'm going there this afternoon.*

I don't mention the gun. Cally might be pretty cool, but I don't know her well enough to know how she'd feel about me packing.

I'm coming with you, she texts back immediately. *Too dangerous to go alone.*

You can't come, I reply. *But if I don't come back, then call the police and give them address.*

I'm coming.

I can't let her come. I honestly believe that I'm going to have to kill Mitchell Dyke and I can't have witnesses. Why couldn't he have just stayed away? I hadn't even known he'd been released; we could have both been living our lives right now.

Human remains found.

Well, perhaps not. There hasn't been any further news on the remains – police work in real life rarely moves as fast as in fiction – but it won't be long. Questions will be asked. Where will the answers lead? Back to me?

That's another bridge I'll have to cross when I come to it.

My phone rings and, thinking it's the police, I snatch it up.

'Laura, I've just heard about Archie, are you okay?'

It's Miss Murray, the school secretary. Even hearing her chirpy voice makes me feel better. Safer. It makes me think of a time a few weeks ago when all I needed to worry about was a forgotten permission slip or unpaid school lunches – both of which Tamra would sort for me on a regular basis.

'Not really,' I admit. 'We're devastated.'

'I can't even imagine.' We've brought Archie with us to school pick-up on countless occasions; everyone there loves him. 'I'm composing an email right now to spread the word around the school. And if there's anything else I can do you will let me know, won't you?'

'Of course,' I say, knowing that there is no way she would believe what I needed help with if I told her.

Chapter Fifty-Two

12 June 2000 – Maisie

She was sitting in a café feeding the baby when the woman approached her. As soon as she saw Kaz Rigby, Maisie recoiled.

'How did you find me?' she asked the girl whose face she hadn't seen in a year. Instead of black, she was wearing light blue jeans and a lemon hoodie. Her dreads had gone and in their place was a light brown bob. She looked much younger.

'The press are still hounding your mum. I told her I was a friend of yours from school and she told me where you were living. I've been wandering around here every weekend hoping to bump into you.' She looked at Maisie, hatred burning in her eyes. 'You know Mitchell is innocent,' she spat. 'How could you say those things about him?'

Maisie shook her head, placing a hand protectively around her daughter. 'You weren't there, Kaz,' she said, but even to her ears, her voice sounded weak. 'You didn't see what happened. I did.'

'I know you didn't see Mitchell killing anyone. I know him, he wouldn't hurt a fly.'

Maisie laughed, a cold, humourless laugh. 'You seem to have forgotten the first rule of life, Kaz. You don't really know anyone.' She leaned over and whispered, 'I learned that the hard way.'

'What is that supposed to mean?' Kaz said, frowning. 'What really happened out there on the trail? What did you really see?'

Maisie shook her head, stood up and placed her daughter into her pram, fixing the straps closed and tucking her bottle into the folds of the hood. 'You need to leave me alone, or I'll call the police. You're not supposed to harass witnesses. There's other evidence, it's not just my testimony.'

Kaz scowled. 'Mitchell is innocent. Don't you care about that? I've got lawyers working for us – he might not have any money, but there are good people who will help us for free. Because they believe in him. We'll get to the truth, then you'll be the one going to prison. Do you know how it feels to have someone you love torn away? Do you know how he calls me crying? Not for himself, but for the woman he's supposed to have murdered. He cries for her, even though he's the one who might end up locked up for the rest of his life. I want you to know that, Maisie. I want you to know that before you settle down to sleep every night, there is a man who might never get married, never have children, never experience another sunset on the beach because of your lies. Just you remember that when you put your baby to bed every night.'

Maisie opened her mouth to speak but was stunned into silence as Kaz turned and stormed away.

Chapter Fifty-Three

The Trial

August 2000

Derek had been on the stand for twenty minutes when the prosecution – a man called Henry Marshall – turned on the TV and played a video tape of a man walking towards a skip, throwing a black bag in and walking away. Marshall left it playing on a loop as he began to ask his questions.

'Can you please tell the jury what this footage shows, Detective Barnes?'

Derek cleared his throat. 'It shows Mitchell Dyke—'

Dyke's defence counsel, a Mr Harris, was on his feet in an instant. 'Objection! How does the officer know, without a shadow of a doubt, that that is Mitchell Dyke on the tape?'

'Sustained. Please be more transparent, officer.'

Derek nodded. A thin line of sweat began to form on the detective's forehead. He resisted the urge to wipe it away and betray his nerves.

'Sorry, ma'am. It shows a man we believe to be Mitchell Dyke, disposing of a black bin bag in a skip.'

'And in the interests of transparency, officer, can you tell the court what led you to believe that it is the defendant in this video?' Marshall asked.

'Well, firstly, because after Mr Dyke's arrest, one of the waiters from the hotel restaurant contacted police to inform us that he'd seen the defendant depositing a black bin bag in the skip at the back of the hotel. When we came to take the waiter's statement, we were informed by the manager of the hotel that, due to a spate of robberies, there was CCTV that now covered the entire perimeter, and they had isolated the footage of the night in question for our arrival.'

'So you had a witness who attested that this was Mr Dyke on the tape. Anything else?'

'Yes. We used the markers of the door and the skip to compare the height of the figure on the tape to that of Mr Dyke. They were a match. Also, when Mr Dyke was arrested, he was wearing a jacket that was identical to the one worn by the man in the security video.'

'Thank you. So when you say, "a man we believe to be Mitchell Dyke", you have several good reasons to believe that the man in the video is Mr Dyke?'

'Objection.'

'Quite, Mr Harris you have made your point. Make progress.'

'Your honour.' Marshall turned back to Derek. 'What did Mr Dyke say when he was asked if it was him on the video?'

'Mr Dyke refused to confirm or deny if that was him on the video.'

'Right. Can you tell me why this video is significant, Detective Barnes?'

'Because of the contents of the bag he's dumping in there.'

Harris shot up once more. 'Objection! The witness can't possibly know which black bin bag the man in this video deposited in the skip.'

'Overruled. Bring it up in cross-examination, counsel.'

Marshall jumped on his chance. 'How did you know which bag was deposited in the skip by the man in the video?'

'Because the black bin bag in question had Mitchell Dyke's fingerprints on it.'

'And what did that bag contain?'

'It contained Seraphine Cunningham's bracelet, and a T-shirt and pair of jeans believed to have been worn by the defendant, Mitchell Dyke, on the night in question.'

'Would that be this bracelet?' Marshall held up an evidence bag containing Seraphine's beaded bracelet, and his assistant waited to pass it around the jury.

'Yes, sir,' Derek confirmed.

The bracelet was the kind that teenagers used, a friendship bracelet, braided and filled with coloured beads. On alternate white beads were black letters that spelled out SERAPHINE.

'And these are the jeans and T-shirt found in the bag?'

Again, the assistant produced two evidence bags, larger this time, containing Mitchell's black clothing.

'Yes, and there was a belt.'

A fourth bag was produced, as though the moves had been choreographed, which they most likely had been.

'Is this the belt?' Marshall asked.

Derek leaned over and inspected the belt. It was black leather, with a heavy silver buckle in the shape of a snake's head. The snake's mouth was open showing sharp fangs, and a long-forked tongue.

'Yes, sir.'

'And can you tell me what your analysis determined about the belt specifically?'

'The belt was found to contain four long hairs caught in the fangs. Subsequent analysis found these hairs to be a match in colour and length to hair found in a hairbrush belonging to Seraphine Cunningham.'

'And these were found in the defendant's belt buckle?'

'Objection! There is no definitive proof that this belt belongs to the defendant.'

'Sustained. Rephrase,' the judge instructed.

'Sorry, your honour. Detective, were these hairs found in the belt buckle found in the bag that had the defendant's fingerprints on it?'

'Yes.'

'That was disposed of by a man identified by an independent witness to be the defendant?'

'Yes.'

'And was that belt shown to other witnesses who had been at the campsite the evening that Miss Cunningham disappeared?'

'Yes. Several people remembered Mr Dyke wearing it, on account of it being "pretty creepy-looking". That's a quote, by the way.'

'Thank you. Let's move on from the hair and bracelet. When you went to arrest the defendant, what was he doing?'

'He was attempting to leave the country.'

'Objection! The prosecution knows full well that the defendant was taking a pre-booked flight that had already been rescheduled in order to help with police enquiries.'

'Overruled. You'll get your chance with the witness, counsel. Having said that, can the prosecution refrain from coercing your witness into inflammatory statements.'

'Of course, ma'am. Did the defendant say anything at all during his arrest?'

'After he was read his rights, he said, "I didn't touch her."'

'And you took "her" to mean Seraphine Cunningham?'

'He'd just been told he was under arrest for Miss Cunningham's murder, so yes.'

'What else did you observe during your time with the defendant?'

'We had noticed, when Mr Dyke gave his witness statements earlier in the week, that he had sustained some scratches to his neck. When he was arrested, Mr Dyke had let a reasonable amount of stubble grow over where these scratches had been.'

'Did Mr Dyke give any explanation as to where these scratches came from?'

Derek looked down at his feet, his face flushed. He cleared his throat.

'Is there a problem, detective?'

Derek shook his head. 'No, sir, there's no problem. It's just that… when questioned, the defendant admitted he had engaged in sexual intercourse with Miss Cunningham. When he was asked about the scratches, he said Miss Cunningham gave them to him during consensual intercourse.'

'Thank you, detective. Let's talk for a moment about the scene. When you arrived at the place Miss Cunningham was last seen, what did you observe?'

'It was quite difficult to find, at first. Ms Goodwin wasn't a hundred percent sure how far she'd walked back to the campsite in the dark, so we couldn't pin down the exact crime scene. What we did find, whilst walking along the area Ms Goodwin believed to be the route she took, was a significant amount of blood soaked into the dirt just off the trail, and a T-shirt belonging to Miss Cunningham with more blood on it.'

'Was that blood tested?'

'Yes, sir. It was the same blood type as Miss Cunningham's.'

'Was there any blood trail, say, leading into the surrounding forest?'

'No, sir.'

'No blood leading back to the beach? Not even drops?'

'No, sir.'

'And did you find anything else during the search?' Marshall asked.

'Yes, sir. A bra and thong believed to belong to Miss Cunningham. They had been kicked into the brush a bit, and someone had tried to set light to them.'

'So if, as the defence would have us believe, there is "no body, no crime", and Seraphine Cunningham was not killed on that trail, she walked away with no T-shirt on and no underwear.'

'Yes, sir.'

Marshall paused to let the image settle in the minds of the jury.

'And what did you find on analysis of these items?'

'We found seminal fluid on all three items. That on the bra clasp was too small an amount to test, but the T-shirt and undergarments showed enough fluid to be tested. The tests came back as a high-probability match to Mitchell Dyke.'

'Was there evidence of any other party on any of these items?'

'No, sir. No evidence anyone else was there other than the defendant and the alleged victim.'

'No further questions.'

Chapter Fifty-Four

December 2019

I can't sit around and wait any longer. It's time to decide – do I give the location to the police or do I go there myself?

Human remains found.

I have to deal with this myself. Reason with Mitchell, try to make him see that he has his freedom now, he'd be stupid to risk it for petty revenge. And if that doesn't work? I'll do what I have to.

What's going on? Cally texts.

I haven't told her about the gun, nor am I going to. At the most, I'm going to get her to wait down the street for me, in case anything goes wrong.

Meet me here in two hours, I reply, sending her a picture of the street adjacent to the warehouse where Archie's dot is still flashing.

I pull on some black jeans and a long-sleeved black T-shirt, and cover it with my dog walking coat and hat.

'Can I take your car? I'm going to go for a drive around, see if I can spot the van or anything,' I tell Rob.

He pulls me in for a hug.

'You should stop torturing yourself,' he says. 'The police are doing everything they can.'

'Rob, it's a stolen dog, not an abducted child. They aren't exactly going to pull Inspector Morse out of retirement to find our cocker spaniel.'

He looks like this is the first time he's actually realised that the police probably aren't working day and night to get Archie back to us. I feel bad now, for bursting his bubble. Rob has lived the kind of sheltered life where if you have a problem, you call the police and they fix it for you. There is still justice in Rob's world. It's only me who knows how subjective the idea of truth and justice is.

'You're probably right,' he says. 'Do you want me and the kids to come with you? We can shove some fliers through doors or something.'

'No, no, it's fine. I just want some time to myself,' I assure him, knowing that it's the answer he wanted anyway. Three minutes of shoving fliers through doors and the kids will be whinging and moaning that they are cold/bored/tired – delete as applicable.

Rob looks predictably relieved. He kisses me goodbye, and I wonder what kind of person he will get when I come back – if I come back. Will this be the last time I see him? After today, I could be on the run, or in prison. Will Mitchell just kill me?

The thought makes me reconsider – as much as I can't bear sitting around and waiting to see what he's going to do next, I don't want to walk into an ambush. But the tracker in Archie's collar isn't obvious – there's no way he can know that I'm aware of where he is. I have the upper hand this time. And I have the gun.

–

Saying goodbye to the kids took an unusually long time. I'm a big hugger with my children anyway, I always vowed that they would get every inch of the love and attention I didn't get as a child, so I don't think they found it particularly weird, and Rob is assuming that I'm overly emotional over Archie. None of them realise just how big this moment is.

I linger at the front window, drinking in every inch of their faces, Faye and George watching *Moana* for the millionth time, Rob scrolling through his phone. All so innocent, all so normal. It makes me want to cry. It makes me want to burst back in and lock the doors, never let any of us leave the house again, just the four of us together. But Monday will come and the kids will have to go to school, Rob will have to go to work, and God knows where poor little Archie will be. There is only one way through this, and that's through it.

I touch the pocket where the gun sits, heavy and foreign-feeling. I check my phone, forty minutes until I'm due to meet Cally. The warehouse is at least a half-hour drive, so I have to go now.

Taking a deep breath, I walk down the path to Rob's car, leaving my precious family behind for what might be the last time.

—

I see Cally sitting in a car the minute I pull up. She's early, but then she probably hasn't been saying her final goodbyes. She thinks we're here to find out if my dog is inside – which is dangerous enough in itself and I have every respect for her for turning up. She's the kind of friend I would have wanted when I was younger, ballsy and determined. She reminds me of me, although I'm pretty certain she didn't have to go through what I went through to become that person.

She's engrossed in her phone and when I tap on the passenger-side window, she looks up in shock. I open the door and slide into the passenger seat.

'You didn't have to come,' I say.

'I don't think you should have come,' she says. 'But if you were stubborn enough to go through with it, I couldn't let you do it alone.'

We're parked up a street away from the warehouse, like true professionals. The gun in my pocket is practically burning a hole in my leg – I'm surprised she can't see it a mile off, it feels so huge.

'Well, thank you. What are you reading?'

'Oh, it's about that missing backpacker on the West Coast Trail. They found some remains, did you hear?'

If possible, my heart begins to thump even harder than it was before.

'I did hear something, yes. Has there been an update?'

'Yeah.' Cally holds up her phone for me to see the headline and there it is. The bridge I said I'd cross when I came to it.

HUMAN REMAINS ON WEST COAST TRAIL NOT SERAPHINE CUNNINGHAM

My eyes scan the page – the confirmation that the remains found on the trail are from an adult male, and not the missing traveller, Seraphine Cunningham. They have no clue yet who the remains belong to, just that they aren't from a nineteen-year-old girl. Which I already knew, of course.

Whatever it means for me, I won't need to cross the bridge today. That's how I learned to live for a long time:

deal with things as they occur, don't ruin today worrying about tomorrow. It's not always possible – you can't be prepared for disaster if you refuse to recognise that disaster might be on its way – but today I have enough to prepare for.

'Oh right, that must be a disappointment for her family. I bet they're desperate for answers.'

'I wonder who they do belong to then?' Cally muses, and I see his face, as clear as if he's standing in front of me now.

'I'm sure it will all come out sooner or later,' I say. But I'll cross that bridge when I come to it.

Chapter Fifty-Five

The Trial

August 2000

'Detective Barnes. My learned colleague earlier suggested that you have worked a great deal of homicides in your career. How many would that be, exactly?' Harris began the case for the defence.

Derek cleared his throat, a tic by now that clearly meant he was uncomfortable with the question. 'Eleven, sir.'

'Eleven. Well, that is a good amount. And how many of these were you a detective for?'

Derek's answer wasn't quite so loud now. 'Four. Sir.'

'Four. So that's four cases where you would be directly involved, as opposed to on the periphery?'

'Objection. The previous cases are not being tried here,' Marshall intervened.

'Relevance, counsel?'

'I'm attempting to clarify the glowing credentials presented by the prosecution, your honour.'

'I'll accept that. Objection overruled. Answer the question, detective.'

'Was there a question?' Derek said, looking annoyed. 'I heard a statement.'

'I'll rephrase, your honour,' Harris said quickly. 'Is it true you have only been directly involved in four homicide cases in your time on the force?'

'I'd say that was accurate, although it isn't only the detectives that can make a difference to the case.'

'I'm sure. And one more question in this line – how many of those cases have you been the lead detective?'

'One.'

'Just one?' The defence looked at the jury, and then back at Derek. 'This one?'

Derek hesitated. 'Yes, this one.'

'I see, thank you for clearing that up. And in your experience' – Harris said the word 'experience' as though it was in inverted commas – 'you have seen particularly bloody crime scenes, I'm sure.'

'A couple.'

'And would you say, in your professional experience, that in your previous cases that have involved blood, has there been more blood or less blood than this one?'

'I'd say more.'

'You'd say more,' Harris sounded pensive. 'And you testified that there was a bloody T-shirt and some blood on the ground found in this case?'

'Yes, sir.'

'And in your opinion, the alleged victim could not have survived such a loss.'

'That's right.'

'Would it surprise you to know that a human can survive up to around four pints of lost blood?'

Derek faltered. It looked for a second like he might have been caught out. Then he replied, 'It wouldn't surprise me to hear that, no.'

'But you didn't find anywhere near that amount, did you?'

'It's not our belief that Miss Cunningham bled to death.'

'Could you answer the question please?'

'No, we did not find four pints of blood. Sir.'

'Thank you. What physical evidence do you have, exactly, that my client was involved in a crime?'

'We have what we believe to be the victim's hair on his belt. We have scratches on his neck, and we have her broken bracelet in his possession. We have his semen on her underwear. And we have witness testimony.'

'My client has already admitted that he had consensual sex with Miss Cunningham, which would explain the hair and the semen. The bracelet came off during sex, and Mr Dyke put it in his pocket with the promise to fix it for her later. So can you tell me, is there any physical evidence that my client committed murder? Is there any physical evidence – aside from an unconfirmed amount of blood on the ground and on a T-shirt – that a crime actually took place at all?'

Derek looked between the prosecution and the jury, not knowing how to respond.

'Answer the question please, detective,' the judge prompted gently.

'No,' Derek said, his voice coming out loud and clear. 'Just a witness who saw the defendant kill the missing girl.'

Chapter Fifty-Six

December 2019

I convince Cally to wait in the car with the logical argument that if something goes wrong, there's no point in both of us being inside. She's to wait half an hour for me to text, and if I haven't been in touch, she's going to call the police. It's the only plan I could get her to agree to. Plus I had to promise that I wouldn't go inside the warehouse, I'm just going to look around, see if I can see Archie. But what she doesn't know won't hurt her.

The unit is huge, in fact it looks like it might have been several units once, more of a business park than a warehouse. There are no cars parked outside, no telltale fake delivery van or big sign saying BAD GUYS THIS WAY. It looks empty.

I check the app for Archie's GPS and there's the dot – right next to my location. It might look abandoned, but this is the place.

Taking a deep breath, I scan the perimeter, looking for a way in. There are huge gaps in the fence, but they all seem to have been secured with temporary fencing, like they use in a building site. There must be a way in if Mitchell has brought Archie here, though.

I find one at the back of the site. A wooden fence panel has gone rotten and the metal fencing put up to secure it has been kicked in and is hanging to one side. I don't suppose there's anything worth stealing in there so no one has been to fix it, the fencing is more of a precaution so kids don't get themselves killed while exploring the site. Well, kids and middle-aged housewives.

There is no way of getting in to the first three buildings I check out, but when I get to the fourth – what used to be an old carpet warehouse – the fire exit is hanging open.

Inside, the air is full of dust that cloys at the back of my throat and makes me want to cough and sneeze. There are still rows and rows of discarded carpets, forming aisles that make the place look like a labyrinth. I can't hear anyone, or see any sign of Archie, and I've used ten minutes of my half an hour just finding a way in.

I make my way through the rows of carpets, some are standing up straight like soldiers guarding the abandoned building, others are laid down and look like the slightest sneeze might set them off in an avalanche of beige and paisley. There's no one in here, that much seems obvious. There's a door at the back that leads to a staffroom. It looks like the *Mary Celeste*, mysteriously abandoned. There is a mug on the side that has a thick layer of dust on the rim and a tea bag still inside. The cupboards are full of plates and cutlery and there are men's magazines stacked up on the table.

I'm about to move on when I hear a small yap.

Archie.

Chapter Fifty-Seven

The Trial

August 2000

Transcript of evidence given by Dr Rowley Jacobs, expert on the occult and cult-related crime.

MR MARSHALL for the prosecution.

MARSHALL: Dr Jacobs, could you tell the jury what you do for a living please?

DR JACOBS: I'm a consultant. I offer advice and insight into non-traditional groups.

MARSHALL: Non-traditional groups? Such as?

DR JACOBS: Such as gangs, cults...

MARSHALL: And when you say cults, does that include what is known as the occult?

DR JACOBS: They are two distinct groups. Not all cults practise the occult, that is, Satan worship.

MARSHALL: But you study both.

DR JACOBS: Yes, sir, I do.

MARSHALL: You've reviewed the items put forward that were owned by Mitchell Dyke, is that correct?

DR JACOBS: Yes, sir.

MARSHALL: That is the book created by Dyke known as his Book of Shadows, *The Satanic Bible* by a Mr LaVey, a belt buckle in the shape of a serpent, a pentagram necklace and the picture of the man found inside the book.

DR JACOBS: Aleister Crowley.

MARSHALL: Excuse me?

DR JACOBS: The picture, it's of Aleister Crowley. He's probably the most famous occultist in mainstream media.

MARSHALL: And what does Mr Crowley say about human sacrifice?

DR JACOBS: He said, 'Those magicians who object to the use of blood, have endeavoured to replace it with incense. But the bloody sacrifice, although more dangerous, is more efficacious. And for nearly all purposes, human sacrifice is best.'

MARSHALL: So the defendant is carrying with him a picture of a man who advocates for human sacrifice?

DR JACOBS: That is Aleister Crowley in that picture, and he said those words, so if the picture belongs to the defendant, then yes.

MARSHALL: And what about this Book of Shadows found in the defendant's possessions? What can you tell me about that?

DR JACOBS: The Book of Shadows is personal to each individual owner. It charts their own journey through the practice of witchcraft.

MARSHALL: And is this Book of Shadows synonymous with satanism and the occult?

DR JACOBS: Not at all. These books are often used by pagans, or Wiccans, which has nothing to do with satanism. It's white magic.

MARSHALL: Okay, so did anything you saw in Mr Dyke's Book of Shadows set it apart from that of a white witch, or Wiccan?

DR JACOBS: Yes.

MARSHALL: And what was that?

DR JACOBS: For a start, the Sigil of Lucifer drawn on the inside of the cover.

MARSHALL: I'm sorry, the what?

DR JACOBS: The Sigil of Lucifer. It's the triangles with the V shape underneath, and the curled-up ends.

MARSHALL: This one? (Prosecution holds up a book for the witness.)

DR JACOBS: Yes, that's the one. It's supposed to be used to call forth Lucifer.

MARSHALL: And I'm guessing your average Wiccan doesn't want to summon the Devil.

DR JACOBS: No, they do not.

MARSHALL: Okay, so we have a Devil-summoning sign. Anything else?

DR JACOBS: At several instances, there are the symbols for Chaos Magic – that's Crowley's symbology. That's the circles with the arrows coming out of them. Then there is this squiggly one, (the witness points to another symbol in the book) that's the symbol for sulphur, that's to represent fire and brimstone.

MARSHALL: And these aren't just your opinions, are they, Dr Jacobs? These are well-known symbols for satanism? If I asked ten other experts, they would all say the same thing?

DR JACOBS: Absolutely. These symbols are widely recognised and not really up for debate. Of course, if you were to see the symbol for sulphur in an alchemic text, you might not specifically associate that with the Devil. Similarly, the picture of the goat inside the back cover might not raise eyebrows in a drawing of a farm, but in this context is clearly used to depict Baphomet.

MARSHALL: Excuse me, Baphomet?

DR JACOBS: You don't pronounce the 't'. It's French, it's said like Bath-o-may.

MARSHALL: Okay, thank you. So who is Baphomet?

DR JACOBS: Baphomet is a deity originally worshipped by the Knights Templar. A depiction of Baphomet as a goat-headed creature by Eliphas Levi was used by Anton LaVey and Aleister Crowley in their work and it became mistakenly synonymous with satanism. Perhaps this is because the Greek god Pan was often used to represent the Devil, and he also resembled a goat.

MARSHALL: And this Baphomet creature is depicted in Mitchell Dyke's book?

DR JACOBS: Yes.

MARSHALL: Following in the footsteps of famous satanists?

HARRIS: Objection, your honour – the prosecution cannot possibly know whose footsteps my client was following when he drew those cartoons.

JUDGE: Sustained. Strike that question from the record.

MARSHALL: Apologies, your honour. Dr Jacobs, are you aware of the date the alleged crime took place?

DR JACOBS: Yes, July thirtieth.

MARSHALL: And is there any significance in that date, to your knowledge?

DR JACOBS: Well, in the occult calendar, the twenty-ninth was a blood moon. The week beginning Monday the twenty-sixth was the event known in the occult calendar as the Grand Climax.

MARSHALL: And could you explain to myself and the jury what the Grand Climax is please?

DR JACOBS: It is a ritual of blood and sex in which occultists pledge themselves to Satan and offer up sacrifices.

MARSHALL: A ritual of blood and sex. Can you be more specific?

DR JACOBS: Each coven celebrates the Grand Climax in different ways. What I can tell you is that it is a time of sacrifice, ritualistic sex and debauchery. A time when chaos ensues. A time of murder.

MARSHALL: And this murderous, bloodthirsty ritual happened to be occurring the same week that the defendant, who has a book full of occult symbology, meets and has sex – by his own admission – with Seraphine Cunningham in the forest?

DR JACOBS: From what you've told me, yes, those dates correspond with the Grand Climax perfectly.

MARSHALL: Thank you, Dr Jacobs, no further questions.

Chapter Fifty-Eight

December 2019

The noise is coming from behind a door at the back of the unit. Instinctively, I run to it and push it open, realising too late how stupid I'd been to throw open a door without knowing what was behind it, without even taking my gun out of my pocket. What was the point in bringing it if I was going to leave myself so vulnerable?

The relief I feel to see mops and brooms, and shelves filled with decades-old cleaning products, and Archie, the only living thing inside, is palpable. He's crouched in the corner, a lead attached to a shelving rack, but he doesn't look harmed. When he sees me, he rushes forwards as far as the lead will allow, the units creaking their displeasure at his frenzied attack. He is yapping and his tail is wagging like crazy. There is a sharp smell of urine, but no dog poo, so someone must have been letting him out. He isn't bleeding as far as I can see, and he looks okay.

Thank God.

I kneel down in front of him and he jumps at me, licking my face. I'm so pleased to see him that I don't even mind when he pees excitedly all over my knee.

'It's okay, baby, I've got you now,' I tell him, unclipping the lead to unwind it but keeping hold of his collar.

He begins to buck and bark, and I'm trying to calm him down when I see the arm come down over my head and wrap around my neck and I feel the pressure on my throat.

—

When I open my eyes again, everything is dark. As my eyes adjust to the light, I realise that I'm still in the cupboard, but someone has closed the door. Archie is tethered again to the shelving unit and my arms are twisted awkwardly behind my back; my wrists bound together. My ankles have been tied too.

Mitchell.

Archie is whimpering by the side of me, his head on my leg. I wish now that I'd spent more time training him, perhaps I could have convinced him to bite through these ropes.

How could I have let this happen? I stormed in here, so convinced that I was GI Jane or Xena Warrior Princess and then the first trap laid out for me and I'm hogtied and trapped in a cupboard. What a pathetic idiot, thinking that because I acted impulsively and overwhelmed someone once upon a time, I could walk cold-blooded into an unknown situation, find the man who had spent twenty years in jail because of me and shoot him in cold blood. Whatever made me even consider it?

My only hope now is Cally. My half an hour is bound to be up, and with any luck, she's called the police, or driven back to my house to get Rob – not that I think he'd fare any better against Mitchell. Prison will have changed him, hardened him, whereas I can't imagine Rob ever having it in him to fight someone.

Archie lets out a bark and I rub my knee against him, telling him to shush. What is Mitchell planning to do with me now? Just let me starve to death in here? Leave me locked up in this cell the way that I left him in his, I suppose. Or maybe he'll come back and shoot me with my own gun.

My gun. I can't help but hope that Mitchell didn't think to frisk me before he tied me up. Not that a gun will be much help as I starve to death. I move my leg up and down, there isn't anything heavy there. He's taken my gun.

'Oh Archie,' I say to the dog, who has curled up and gone to sleep now that his mum is with him. He doesn't seem to realise that the danger hasn't passed.

I pull at the cords that bind my wrists, but it just seems to tighten them. They bite into my skin and I grit my teeth in pain. Maybe if I just shuffle to the door, I can find a way to loosen these ropes. There could be knives in the staffroom – could I shuffle there before Mitchell returns? But before I can get halfway across the floor of the cupboard, I hear a voice calling my name and I have the sickening realisation that Cally hasn't called the police or gone to get Rob. She's come in after me. My last hope, and she's probably going to end up dead. We're all dead.

'In here!' I shout, desperately praying she can get me loose and we can make a run for it before Mitchell returns. Where has he gone anyway? He must be planning on coming back for me, otherwise why take the chance of leaving me alive? 'In here! Help!'

She yells my name again; I think she's heard me, but she can't make out where my voice is coming from.

'In here!' I yell. 'Hurry!'

There's a pause and then a banging on the door. 'Are you in there?'

'Yes! Yes, in here!' I shout. What's taking her so long? She's right outside.

'It's locked,' she calls. 'Stand back.'

I can't bloody stand at all, so there's no hope of that, but I'm far enough away from the door that she won't hurt me if she manages to break in.

'Have you ever kicked in a door before?' I call to her.

'What do you bloody think?' she shouts back, and there's a loud thump, but the door doesn't move. Clearly not then. 'Wait, I'll go and look for a key.'

It seems like forever until I hear her voice again.

'I've got it! It was on the table in the staffroom.'

The door opens and Cally bursts through.

'Where is he?' she says, her voice desperate. 'Where's Mitchell?'

She realises what she's said the minute his name is out of her mouth. I look at her in shock, hearing her say his name like that, so familiar like she'd known him a lifetime. Or perhaps a lifetime ago. And all of a sudden, it's like I can see her face differently now. A face I've seen before, back when I was a different person. And so was she, clearly. Nothing about her is instantly recognisable from the girl she used to be, from her hair to her svelte figure, to her designer clothes.

'Kaz?'

She smiles and it's the smile of someone who has been to hell and back. Someone who has done what they have had to, to survive. It's a smile I recognise as my own.

'I'm surprised you remember,' she says, giving a little finger wave. 'Hello, Seraphine.'

236

Chapter Fifty-Nine

The Trial

Late September 2000

It was the day. The day that at least two countries – Canada and the UK – had been holding their breath for. The star witness testimony.

Maisie took the stand, certain that everyone could see how much she was shaking, from her toes to her hair.

The questions began easily, as the prosecution, Mr Marshall, had warned her. How did you meet Sera? What made you decide to walk together? Was anyone else with you before you met the defendant and his friends?

The questions only began to get harder when he started to ask about that night.

'Mr Dyke and his friends have testified that the two of you were camping separately?'

'That's right,' Maisie tried desperately to refrain from picking her nails. She'd done that in practice and Marshall had warned her how it made her look like she was lying. That was the last thing she wanted. The media had been hellish enough to her as it was. They hated her. It was because she wouldn't talk to them, she hadn't trusted them and she'd been right not to. And if they thought she was lying now, they would make her life hell again.

Maisie had spent the last fifteen months trying to rebuild her life without the media following her every moment of the day, reporting on her every movement as if she was some kind of celebrity. Why did anyone care when she'd given birth? And, of course, the timing was difficult – she managed to 'leak' that the baby was early and deflect some suspicion, but that hadn't stopped the more salacious papers speculating that there had been some sort of love triangle between her, Mitchell and Sera, and the baby was the result. The truth might have been closer than they could have known, except it hadn't been Mitchell that the two girls had shared.

Maisie hadn't been able to find Ric in the year since their baby had been conceived, but she had been able to discover that he and Sera were definitely not brother and sister. She had found out everything she could about Seraphine Cunningham, and she had never had a brother. She was a liar, a thief and a con woman, and she deserved to be dead. Maisie had no guilt about that anymore. Sera had sealed her own fate when she had decided to lie and steal from the wrong person.

'And why was that, if you'd become such good friends?'

Maisie snapped back to the present. Shit, she hadn't been paying attention.

'Sorry, can you repeat the question please?' She looked over to the judge, her eyes imploring. 'This is quite difficult for me to relive. I'm sorry.'

'Don't worry, Miss Goodwin,' the judge assured her, and Maisie remembered she was here as a witness, not the defendant she should be. 'You take your time, and if you need a break, we'll stop.'

The police had treated her like a celebrity since she'd arrived back in Canada, but not in the same way as the press. The press was an intrusion, distrustful and accusing, always looking for the next salacious story. The police had treated her like she mattered, and she supposed she did. This was the biggest trial of the decade – a rare 'no-body' murder trial – and if she messed it up, there would be no chance of a conviction. For the first time in her life, Maisie was important.

No, that wasn't true. She was important now, to her little baby girl. That was what really mattered. When this show trial was over, when she was back to a no one in the eyes of the police and the press, her baby girl would still need her more than anyone else. Ironic really, that she'd gone to Canada to escape her responsibilities at home and ended up bringing back the biggest responsibility of all.

'Thank you,' she said.

'Miss Goodwin, the question was why you and Miss Cunningham were camping separately if you'd become such good friends?'

'I think she'd become tired of me,' Maisie said, truthfully. 'She said she was used to travelling alone, maybe she just didn't like me chirping in her ear the whole time.'

'So there was no big fight? The defendant and his friends have testified that the atmosphere was quite icy between the two of you.'

'Well, I don't know why they would say that,' Maisie said. 'It's a bit of an exaggeration. I was cautious around her that night, sure. I liked her and I didn't want to rub her up the wrong way anymore.'

She stopped, realising she was talking too much. Keep it short, Marshall had said. Don't babble. Nothing too complicated, you risk tying yourself up in knots. It was almost as if he knew she were lying and was coaching her. Although she supposed that was an occupational hazard – assume every witness was going to screw your case up somehow.

'Okay,' the defence counsel said easily. *He doesn't want to look like he's badgering me*, she realised. *But that doesn't mean he will go easy on me.* 'Let's talk about that night. You hadn't met Mr Dyke and his group before, is that correct?'

'Not really,' Maisie corrected. 'We met really briefly at orientation.'

'Apologies. What was your first impression of the defendant and his friends?'

'Well,' Maisie looked down, 'I thought they were a bit different. I don't mean in a horrible way,' she said quickly, looking at the jury. 'They just dressed differently. I'm not really used to it where I come from.'

'They were dressed all in black, weren't they? It made them stand out, made them look scary. Different.'

'Well, yes,' Maisie said. 'But I didn't care that they looked different. I wasn't being stuck-up or anything. I said hello, then when we met up, I was drinking with them and that.'

'More than drinking, wasn't it?'

Maisie froze. She couldn't lie, she'd already admitted in her police statements that there had been drugs. She wished she'd never said that bit. 'Yes,' she admitted. 'A bit more.'

'What else was there? Weed? Cocaine?'

'Both, yes.'

'And when did Miss Cunningham join you?'

'Before the drugs. She bought them with her, actually. Keddie brought her over and she had them.'

'Not Mr Dyke?'

'No,' Maisie shook her head. 'But he fancied her straight away, you could tell.'

'Did that upset you?'

Maisie frowned. 'What? No. I didn't fancy him at all. He wasn't my type.'

'And what about her?'

Maisie didn't understand what he was saying. 'I suppose, yes, she looked like she fancied him a bit.'

'I mean,' the defence counsel said gently, 'were you attracted to Miss Cunningham? Sexually, I mean.'

'Wait, what?' Maisie hadn't been expecting that. In all the scenarios they had discussed, this hadn't been one of them. 'No. Definitely not. She was a friend.'

'A friend you barely knew. A friend you had quarrelled with. Had she flirted with someone else, is that why you had fallen out? Was she threatening to ditch you for Mr Dyke? How did you feel when they went off together, after all the time you'd spent with her?'

'Objection!' Marshall shot to his feet, and Maisie thought he looked as panicked as she felt.

This was all wrong. It wasn't like that at all. She should tell him about Ric, about how wrong he was, but she'd spent so much time protecting him, denying he existed so he wasn't accused of anything, if she told everyone about this now, it would make her look like a liar.

You are a liar, the voice in her head said.

'Sustained. Counsel, please let the witness at least answer a question. This is not *A Few Good Men*.'

The jury tittered at that, and the defence counsel coloured. It broke the tension slightly and Maisie took a few deeps breaths. It was fine, this was his job, to poke holes and twist things. She could do this. She just had to say what she saw.

'I was not attracted to Seraphine,' she said, loudly and calmly. 'Despite the amount of Cher in my music collection.'

The jury tittered slightly again, and the prosecution looked calmer.

Out of his flow, the accusations seemed ridiculous, that she had gone on a hike and embarked on an illicit lesbian affair and murdered her lover in a jealous rage. If he tried to repeat that show, he would be the one who came out of it red-faced.

'It's dark, on the trail at night, is it not?' Harris picked back up.

'Very,' Maisie conceded.

'And you admit you had been drinking and taking drugs.'

'Yes.'

'Then tell me' – the defence counsel looked her in the eyes as if he could see into her very soul – 'how can you be sure of what you saw. How can you be certain that you didn't see the defendant and Miss Cunningham engaged in the throes of passion? How can you be certain that it wasn't consensual, albeit a bit rough, sex you saw?'

It had been coming back to her, bit by bit, sometimes in dreams, sometimes as she fed their baby in the middle of the night, somewhere between sleeping and waking. Seraphine's hair falling down around her face, his hand on her chin, grabbing at her neck as he rammed into her from behind, her mouth falling open in an O of pain… no, of pleasure. Her eyes wide as he swelled inside her, moaning as he came inside her. It wasn't possible, they were brother and sister, he was hers, not Sera's, hers…

'Um… because…' Maisie faltered.

She saw Sera's face as Maisie flew out of the greenery at her, grabbing at her hair, pulling her onto the floor. How dare she! How dare she scoff at Maisie, treat her like dirt, act like she was an inconvenience, when Sera was the liar, the bitch!

Maisie folded her hands into her lap and looked at the jury instead of Mitchell Dyke's defence counsel as she said the words that would seal his fate, and free her at the same time. 'Because men having consensual sex with women don't usually smack them around the head with a rock.'

Chapter Sixty

December 2019

HUMAN REMAINS ON WEST COAST TRAIL NOT SERAPHINE CUNNINGHAM, POLICE ANNOUNCE

The Echo

The human remains found weeks ago on the West Coast Trail in Vancouver have been confirmed to be those of an adult male, in a revelation that shocked those who were certain that the remains were those of nineteen-year-old traveller Seraphine Cunningham who went missing in 1999 whilst hiking the trail.

'The bones found are definitely those of an adult male, of between twenty and thirty years of age,' forensic anthropologist Mary Morris said in her statement to the Canadian media this morning. 'Further tests will be needed to confirm how long the bones have been there, and how far they might have travelled from the original placement of the body. There are definite signs of animal intervention and it is thought that the remains may have been dragged off the trail into the forest by cougars or wolves.'

It is believed that recent high rains may have dislodged the remains from their resting place and washed them further towards the trail, where they were discovered by hikers who had ventured a short way off the boarded path.

Canadian police have yet to release a statement regarding who they believe the remains might belong to. Seraphine's parents declined to comment.

Chapter Sixty-One

The Trial

Late September 2000

The courtroom was silent as the jury filed back in one by one. Maisie watched their faces, each one as blank as the next, each refusing to look Mitchell in the eye.

There was no one here for Seraphine. Of course, the press would say that the entire nation was turned out for her, she was the reason they were all here, this girl that no one had ever truly known. But she had no family in the gallery, no mother and father. And, of course, no Ric.

Maisie had been stupid to hope that he might turn up. Except there was no danger for him, now, was there? After all, the evidence had been given, no one had believed in the existence of a male companion, and even if they did, a year later, no one would recognise Ric anyway. Everyone was focused on the man in the dock, Mitchell Dyke.

Mitchell looked different after a year in prison, but then who wouldn't? He had let the black grow out of his hair. Underneath the dye, it was a light brown colour that suited him much better. He was wearing a smart suit instead of the all-black outfit Maisie had last seen him in and there were no pentagrams or snakes in sight. But it was his eyes that showed the real difference. His eyes had a haunted, deadened quality that Maisie knew she would never understand. Because, thanks to Mitchell, she would never see the inside of a prison cell for what she did.

It was an accident, she told herself over and over, as the foreman of the jury stood up and confirmed that they had reached a verdict. *It was an accident. None of this is my fault. I didn't mean for it to go this far.*

She said a silent prayer to a God she didn't believe in to save Mitchell, to the jury to find him innocent and let them all be free of this nightmare.

'And on the count of murder, do you find the defendant guilty or not guilty?'

'Guilty.'

And there it was, it was done.

Maisie stood up from her seat in the gallery and left the court by the rear exit, without looking back.

Chapter Sixty-Two

December 2019

My skin tingles at hearing someone call me by the name I gave up so long ago. Seraphine Cunningham, daughter of Alyssa and Marcus Cunningham, disappointment, fuck-up, criminal. That was me then, not anymore.

Archie begins to bark, the sudden noise pulling us both back to the present moment.

'We have to get you out of there,' Kaz says, looking over her shoulder. 'We can do the catch-ups later.'

This throws me off guard again. 'What? Get me out? But I thought… I assumed…'

She snorts. 'You assumed I was behind this? From what you said before, I thought you knew that Mitchell was out and looking for you?'

'Well, I mean, that's what I did think until about ten seconds ago. What are you even doing here if you're not helping him?'

'When I last saw him just after his release, he said he thought you were alive, and that he was coming to "wipe the slate clean",' she says, leaning over and pulling at the knots on my wrists. 'I thought he meant that he was going to kill you. I understand why he's so mad at you, obviously, but the last twenty years, he's got through his ordeal in the knowledge he was innocent. If he kills you, he's no better than the police and the newspapers said he was. And he'd go back to prison.'

'What made him realise I was alive?'

'I have no idea,' she says. 'One day he didn't know and the next he did.'

'I actually never said he did anything,' I point out, pulling my left hand free as she gets to work on my right. 'I ran away. I had no idea anyone even thought I was dead until much later. I was already in Wyoming before I found out that Mitchell had been arrested for my murder.'

'So why didn't you come back? Make a phone call? If you were still alive, then he never would have been convicted. All you had to do was tell people you weren't dead.'

'It wasn't exactly that simple,' I say, as she frees my right hand. I flex my fingers and they start to cramp up as the blood flows back into them. 'I was in deep for some drugs money with some pretty horrific people. If they thought I was dead, I was safe. Plus…' I trail off, not wanting to say anymore. Okay so she's freeing me, but that is to stop Mitchell from doing something stupid and going back to prison. She has no reason to be loyal to me and telling her what happened that night would only give her more fuel for the bonfire she already has on me.

'Plus what?'

'Nothing. Can you help me get these off my legs? My fingers have seized up.'

'Yeah, here. Oh shit.' Her back straightens and she presses a finger to her lips.

'What?' I mouth silently.

'I hear someone,' she mouths back, pointing to the direction she came in from. 'What shall I do?'

Archie whimpers.

'Untie me,' I hiss.

She shakes her head frantically and grabs at the ropes she's just taken off my hands.

'Wind these around,' she mouths, gesturing at my hands, and before I have time to object, she ducks out of the cupboard.

Without hesitating, I wind the ropes around my wrists as instructed, doing a pretty good job of making it look like my hands are still tied. I lie back down and close my eyes just as the door to the warehouse bangs closed behind someone. As gingerly as I can, I begin to rub my ankle up and down to loosen the ropes that bind them.

Footsteps echo across the floor from the direction of the door. I don't dare open my eyes. If Mitchell thinks I'm still unconscious, he might go away again for long enough for Kaz to get my legs untied. If I thought Archie was any kind of guard dog, I'd have let him free to defend us, but unless death by bad breath and licking is a thing, he's going to be no help. I'm just glad he's lying quietly now, unable to fathom what's going on.

The footsteps are getting closer. I hold my breath, not daring to breathe too heavily. Oh God, he's going to kill me. My only hope is that Kaz has found a weapon, something she can hit him with. Will she be brave enough? It's not easy, finding the strength to hit another human being, hard. I should know. Perhaps she's already run away, perhaps she will call the police. Perhaps she will come back with Mitchell and shoot me with my own gun.

Chapter Sixty-Three

July 1999 – Seraphine

She was cold. Her clothes were wet and muddy, and she felt utterly miserable. Maybe it was all this pretending to be some sunny, adventure-loving, bohemian surf chick, it was fucking exhausting. Whose idea had it been to come on this bloody trail anyway? It must have been Ric's; she would never suggest anything so stupid. Actually… it had been Maisie's idea really. They had been standing at that bus stop with a fuck-ton of stolen coke in her bag, arguing over a deal that had gone *very* wrong when Maisie had inserted herself right in the middle of their conversation. She'd heard them say something about losing money and had assumed that Sera had actually lost her purse. Then she'd offered to pay their bus fare and pointed to the bus for the West Coast Trail.

'It's perfect,' Ric had murmured to her. 'They will never think to look for us there. We'll just be like every other dumb tourist hiker on the trail.'

'And how are we paying for this little trip?' Sera had asked.

Ric had raised his eyebrows. 'The same way we pay for everything else. Do you still have those credit cards we stole?'

'Well yeah, but if they check their statements, we're fucked,' she'd said. 'We can hardly escape on a trail that has one beginning and one end.'

'Right now, prison is preferable to the people you have managed to piss off,' Ric had replied, his eyes dark. Sera had never seen him afraid like this. It made her realise just how badly she had screwed up this time, getting cold feet and running out on the deal with the drugs they owed to Very Bad People in her bag. But hadn't it been his idea to shave some off the top of that very stash? And hadn't the reason she'd got cold feet been because Ric had decided to rip them off in the first place? 'And I'm sure our new friend won't mind helping us out a little,' he'd finished.

'Not when you've seduced her, you mean,' Sera had raised her eyebrows. 'I swear sometimes you enjoy that part more than the marks do.'

'You know you're the only one for me,' he had winked at her and she'd remembered why she had fallen for him in the first place. How attracted to him she'd been when she'd seen him in a bar in Costa Rica, stealing wallets from rich old women. How she'd managed to steal every last one of them from him, and how they'd ended up having hot, dangerous sex in the villa he was staying at with one of his rich benefactors while she was having physio on her knee on the patio underneath the balcony.

They had been inseparable ever since, travelling from country to country on cloned credit cards and stolen travellers' cheques. They were Mickey and Mallory without the bloodshed, fuelled by sex and danger. The problem with sex and danger was that sooner or later the sex grew stale and the danger grew old. The stakes needed constantly to be raised, from pickpocketing, to stealing from shops, to breaking into villas and hotel rooms. They would eat at a different hotel buffet every day, only rarely being challenged by the staff, until even that wasn't enough of a thrill, so they began eating at fancy restaurants in stolen clothes before running out on the bill at the end. And the next day they would move onto a different town, then a different country. The only thing that wasn't fake about her was her passport, but Ric had introduced her to a guy who got her a new one anyway, just in case. No one had looked for Seraphine Cunningham in so long that she didn't see the point in a fake passport, but, of course, it had come in handy much later.

And now she was cold. And wet. And muddy. And she had no idea where Ric had got to, or how long he was going to make his point for.

She wasn't sure why she hadn't wanted Ric to have sex with Maisie. Usually she was well aware that women were much more pliable once they had given into him in that way: for a lot of women, sex made them lose their common sense, and half the time their dignity. Perhaps it was because sex had never been a big deal to her, she had always been able to separate physical needs from emotional, and so she'd never minded if Ric needed to sleep with a woman to get them some extra cash, or food, or a place to stay. And yet this time, it felt different. She had found herself getting more and more jealous as the pair of them garbled away behind her as she pretended to dart around enchanted like some permanently amazed Disney princess. At one point, she'd even started to hum one of the songs from *Cinderella*, but, of course, neither of them had noticed. They wouldn't have noticed if she'd stripped naked and started swinging from the endless, boring trees.

She hadn't been able to let it go. For some reason, Maisie had bothered her more than the others ever had. Perhaps it was the way Ric had looked at her when they were walking together, the same way he looked at Sera. Or maybe it was her stupid doe-eyed naivety that bothered Sera. Because she knew she could never be that innocent. Ric would never be able to see her as pure and unsullied, and maybe that's what she wanted. So she'd argued with him, refusing to believe that anyone would be this utterly besotted with him after three days if he hadn't been shagging her after Sera retreated into her tent alone. Then she'd asked him how he'd feel if it was her spending her nights in someone else's tent, and maybe she'd give it a try. And the next thing she knew, he was leaving. A punishment for the things she had said, showing her that he was still in charge. She knew he'd be back – he'd left her on her own before to show her how much she needed him, to teach her a lesson. And if he wanted to march off with their spare tent and camp by himself, then good luck to him. Idiot.

Even the tents had been a stroke of luck. They had only had one, and they were planning on ditching that as soon as they had managed to blag a place to stay in Canada. Then when Ric had announced they were brother and sister, they had realised they would probably need an extra one, and with only minutes to sort something out, he'd simply picked up someone's bag as he'd walked past them on the way to the bus. They had been waiting for a different bus to the other trail head and by the time they had noticed their bag was missing they probably assumed they had left it at baggage claim and gone back for it. Either way, Sera and Ric were on their way to the trail with a new set of camping gear.

'I wonder where Ric has got to?' Maisie asked for what felt like the gazillionth time. This girl was truly, truly desperate. It was her first time away from home and Sera almost felt guilty that she was being so spectacularly led down the garden path by them, but needs must, and their needs were greater than hers. She probably had plenty of people she could call on to get her home once she realised the rest of her cash was missing, Sera had no one.

'He'll catch us up,' Sera resisted the urge to sigh. It was getting harder and harder to keep up the Pollyanna act with this one.

'I was going to carry on through this campsite and stop at the next one,' Maisie said, hitching her bag further onto her shoulder.

Ric had warned Sera about this on the very first morning after they had been in the sea. It was important to Maisie that she felt like she was in control, he'd said, that she gets to make the decisions. He was like that sometimes, thinking he was bloody Freud, psychoanalysing people. She'd gone along with it and it had seemed that he was right, Maisie had practically orgasmed in her pants when Sera had asked if they could join her at her choice of campsite, but enough was enough.

'I'm staying here,' she announced.

Maisie looked startled, already she'd got used to being a decision-maker, it appeared. Well, she was going to have to get unused to it, because Sera was knackered, and needed a drink and, now that Ric was gone, some of the powder they had stashed in her pack.

'Oh,' Maisie said, looking around. There was nothing wrong with the campsite they were at, Sera thought. Cribs Creek, it was called, and plenty of other campers had decided it was satisfactory. 'Carmanah Creek is only four kilometres away,' she commented, her tone cajoling. 'And it's a lot quieter.'

Sera wanted to punch her. At that moment, she decided that Carmanah Creek could have a four-star hotel and a masseuse on site and she'd still be staying where she fucking well was.

'Well, I'm staying here. You can go though. Ric and I might catch you up tomorrow or something.'

It was obviously the right thing to say. Maisie wasn't about to risk Ric turning up at Cribs Creek and leaving his 'sister' behind to catch up with his new shag partner. Maisie seemed to be in an internal debate with herself – let go of her new-found decision-making freedom, or put her foot down and go on alone.

'You're right, I'm knackered too,' Maisie said, and despite a thrill at her small victory, Sera's overwhelming feeling was disappointment that Maisie was going to stay with her. A big part of her had wanted rid of their annoying new cling-on, money or no money. And she didn't feel like she'd care a whole lot if Ric didn't turn up either. Perhaps it was about time she went it alone for a while.

Chapter Sixty-Four

December 2019

The door opens and there he is. Mitchell Dyke, the man who has spent the last twenty years in prison for my murder. He has my gun in his hand.

'Oh shit,' he mutters when he sees me. What does *oh shit* mean?

I hold my breath as he comes towards me. He doesn't know that I'm not bound anymore, and I don't know if the safety is still on that gun. It's a gamble, but as he leans down towards me, I scream and throw myself at him.

The gamble pays off. Mitchell is caught off guard and is thrown backwards, the gun flies from his hand and doesn't shoot me in the face. Note to self, safety is on. I make a grab for the gun before Mitchell even knows what has happened. Archie leaps up again and starts barking like crazy.

'Get back!' I scream, clicking the safety off and pointing the gun at Mitchell. 'Stay the fuck back!'

Mitchell gets to his feet and backs away, his hands in the air. 'Hold on, hold on, Sera.'

'Don't call me that!' I shout, my heart is pounding and adrenaline rushes through my veins.

'I'm sorry,' he says, hands still up. 'I didn't come here to hurt you.'

Kaz chooses that moment to reappear in the doorway, a Stanley knife in her hand. She looks between me and Mitchell, confusion on her face. 'What's going on?'

'What does it look like? He came back for me, but I was ready for him.'

'What do you mean, came back for you? You think I tied you up?' He looks at Kaz. 'You tied her up.'

Kaz looks at me and shakes her head. 'Nuh-uh. It wasn't me. I swear.'

'She's lying. It wasn't me,' Mitchell says. 'I had no intention of hurting you. I just wanted to talk to you.'

I think of the look on his face when he saw me tied up, his words... *Oh shit.* Why did he say that? He'd looked as though he had no idea I'd be tied up there. Oh God, who the hell am I supposed to be able to trust?

'Why else would you be stalking my family if you've no intention of hurting us?' I ask him.

He looks confused. 'I don't know what you're talking about. I haven't been stalking you.'

I jab the gun in his direction. 'You tried to walk off with my daughter!' I shout. 'You had her put on the bus so you could get her off before we realised. Then you stole my dog! Is that not your idea of stalking?'

He shakes his head. 'I didn't do any of those things. Why would I do that? I've just got out of prison; I've got no desire to go back in. Despite what the whole world thinks of me, I've never been a violent person. You just managed to disarm me in ten seconds flat.'

I frown. He must be lying, but he sounds so convincing. 'Then why are you here? And how did you get my gun?'

'It was on the floor outside the door there,' he says. 'I came to find you because I want to clear my name. You're the only person who can do that. I didn't want to hurt you; I want you to help me. And to warn you.'

'Warn me? About what?'

'About her,' he points at Cally, or Kaz, as she was once known. I only knew her for a few hours, had barely spoken to her. Her hair had been in dreadlocks, if I remember correctly, and she had been dressed like Mitchell in all that black nonsense. Nothing like this well-put-together, businesslike woman in front of me. 'I made the mistake of telling her I thought I knew where you were. Then when I saw you together in the café, I knew she'd got to you first. I wanted to approach you, but I didn't want to scare you off. If you ran... I'd never get people to believe you were still alive without you to prove it.'

'I didn't come to hurt you,' Kaz says, shaking her head. 'I told you, I came to stop *Mitchell* from hurting you – the last thing I wanted was for him to go back to prison after all these years waiting for him to get out. I just wanted to keep an eye on you both, stop him if he tried anything stupid. He stopped answering my calls, so I started following you to see if I could get to him. Then I saw that man walking off with Faye and I thought he'd set that up to get you to confess. If he had your daughter, you'd have to tell the truth.'

'So both of you came here today with my best interests at heart?' I scoff. One or both of them is lying, I just don't know which one. They both have reason to want to hurt me: I took away the chance of love from one, and the liberty of the other. 'So which one of you brought Archie here?'

I swing the gun between the pair of them. Mitchell puts his hands up and Kaz takes a step back.

'It wasn't me, Sera, I swear,' Kaz says. 'I only came here to make sure Mitchell didn't jeopardise his chance at a future. I didn't want to hurt Archie. Or Faye. I wouldn't hurt a child, no matter what you've done.'

'Admirable,' I say. I don't want to have to shoot her. I like her. *Liked* her. As Kaz and as Cally. But she's been lying to me, pretending to save Faye and help me find Archie when all along she knew who I really was. 'I just want you both to know,' I continue, taking a slow step back, 'that I didn't ever want you to go to prison for killing me.'

'But you still didn't come forward,' Kaz says, her face screwing into a scowl. 'You've just been living your best life while Mitchell was denied his. You could have come forward and had him released at any time.'

'It was weeks before I even knew I'd been reported missing.' It's a relief to be able to say this out loud, to make my excuses to someone other than my conscience. 'I just wanted to get away. All I did that night was run away.' It's not strictly true, I did something much worse than that, but it doesn't make any difference to what Mitchell went through, it doesn't involve them. 'I ran into the forest until I came to a dirt track and hitched a lift with some old guy in a truck. I had no idea I was supposed to be dead until I saw a headline and an awful old photo of myself weeks later.'

'Why didn't you come forward after then?' Kaz asks.

'I didn't think I needed to. I was presumed dead, and I didn't particularly mind. The reason I ran in the first place was because I owed money to some horrible people. I just left. I didn't even know Mitchell had been arrested.'

'All this time?'

'No, obviously not all this time. I found out, but by then I didn't think I could come forward, I thought it was too late. I might be arrested for faking my own death and wasting police time and all that. Plus, if the gang we owed drugs to found out I was alive, they would want their money and I didn't have it. I needed to be dead.'

'So you let them convict an innocent man.'

'It's not like I'm the one who accused him in the first place,' I say, but she's right. I let Mitchell sit in prison for half of his life, knowing there was no way he could be guilty of murder. I've never claimed to be a good person. I was a terrible person when I was Seraphine. I try to make up for it now I'm Laura, but how do you make up for a wrong without putting it right? And wasn't I still prepared to kill to preserve my secret? I tried to tell myself it was to protect my family, but it's not. My family will survive without me. I've been trying to protect me, looking after number one. Just like I always did.

'You weren't the one who put me in prison, but you can clear my name now.'

I sigh. I just want this to all go away and be back with my family, curl up against Rob and sleep for days. I can't stand the thought of giving up that life. 'You're out now. Can't you just go and live your life? Does my life really have to implode? Who even told you where I was?'

'You want him to live the rest of his life as a convicted murderer, so you don't have to tell your husband you're a liar?' Kaz says, her voice incredulous at my selfishness. Because, yes, that's exactly what I'd like and I know how selfish it sounds.

'Not just a liar,' a voice comes from behind us, and I forget about the potential danger from Kaz and Mitchell and wheel around. 'A murderer too.'

Chapter Sixty-Five

1999 – Seraphine

Her victory was short-lived once she realised how small and cramped Cribs Creek campsite really was and remembered that she had no idea how this stupid tent was supposed to go up. Ric had put it up the other nights, and now she couldn't even get practical Maisie to help her because she'd made it clear she wanted some space. It was lucky, really, that Sera had always been so good at enlisting the help of strangers, otherwise she would have been sleeping outside that night.

As the man in the tent next to her spot finished putting her tent up, Sera glanced over to where Maise's was – of course – already finished and saw she had begun chatting to a couple of guys and a girl. They were all wearing black and looked like Satan worshippers or something. The girl had her hair in dreadlocks and was wearing what looked like a pentagram around her neck. One of the guys looked like he was wearing eyeliner, for God's sake. The other one was kind of cute though. Was Maisie really going to move on so quickly? Her and Ric must both be losing their touch.

Sera opened her tent and got in without bothering to thank the man who had put it up for her. She thought that maybe she heard him mutter 'you're welcome', but that was just typical of people, wasn't it? Only bothering to help someone out for the praise and gratitude afterwards. People were just innately selfish.

She left the zip open so she could see Maisie and her new friends. God, she couldn't wait to get to the morning and get the hell out of there. She might pretend to twist an ankle and get herself airlifted out. Ric had probably just kept on walking and would be out of this godforsaken place before morning. He wasn't one to stick to the rules: only hike in the daytime, beware wild animals. How dare he just leave her here? She was absolutely done with him this time. In fact, she was done with this whole joke of a lifestyle. What had ever made her think that stealing, conning and dealing drugs was glamorous in the first place? She definitely didn't feel very glamorous right now, up to her tits in mud and mozzies, that was for sure. She was going to go somewhere and find an actual job, live like a normal person for a while. Maybe she'd even go home and make up with her mum and dad.

It was an hour later when she saw one of the boys that Maisie was with walking past her tent. Boy was right too. Although he looked slightly older than her, he could hardly be classed as a man. All that teenage angst. He probably lived in his mum's basement listening to Nirvana and Marilyn Manson or whatever these Satan types listened to. Still, she was bored to tears, and so when he walked back past, she made sure she was outside of her tent ready to bump into him. Literally.

'Oh God, sorry,' she said, pretending not to have seen him. 'I haven't broken your foot, have I? Fat lump I am.'

He looked her up and down, as expected, and his eyes widened with every inch he took in. Sera was used to this reaction – it was so predictably boring. Still, being on her own in the tent for the next fourteen hours was bound to be even more boring.

'Don't worry about it. I'm Keddie,' he said, holding out his hand.

'I'm really sorry, Keddie,' Sera said, taking his hand, giving it a small shake and keeping hold. 'I hope your foot doesn't hurt too much. I've got something that can take the edge off, if it does?'

She bent over, knowing that his eyes would be firmly on her backside, and reached into her rucksack. Men.

'How about it?' She waved the bag of coke and when his eyes widened and he gave a nod, she slipped it into his hand. 'How about we share it?'

'Absolu— Oh shit.' He looked as though he'd only just realised he wasn't hiking alone. 'I'm here with my friends. I'd better not abandon them. You want to come and join us?'

'Sure,' Sera agreed, painfully aware of how desperate she sounded. She had spent all day wishing the cling-on Maisie would get lost, now look at her, a pathetic little sap, bribing her way into joining them. Keddie didn't seem to notice her desperation though, and if he did, he didn't seem to care. Maisie probably wouldn't be happy to share her new friends, but it served her right for thinking she could get one over on Sera so easily. She probably fancied that other one – what a cheek to replace Ric so fast! Well, Sera was back now, so she could just step aside and see how it was really done.

–

And that was how it was done. She'd been with the group an hour before Mitchell – that was the name of the better looking of the two boys – had slipped his hand under the blanket he'd offered her and begun to stroke her leg in slow, light strokes. She had to admit, with the buzz from the drink and the coke, it actually felt pretty nice. And it wasn't like she had anything else to do tonight.

'You wanna go do some sightseeing?' she murmured.

His eyes lit up like a kid in a candy store. He nodded and stood up, pulling her to her feet. By now, Maisie had come out of her sulk at seeing Sera and was talking animatedly to the witch girl, and Keddie had drifted off to talk to some other campers, realising early that he'd lost the battle for Sera's attention.

'I don't get it,' Mitchell said as they left the beach behind and joined the forest trail. 'Girls like you don't usually go for guys like me.'

'You have no idea what I'm like,' Sera muttered, venturing deeper into the trail. She stopped short. 'What was that? Did you hear something?'

Mitchell looked around and shook his head. 'Can't hear anything. Do you want to go back?'

She turned to look at him, his long hair slicked back, his Metallica T-shirt and his black jeans. She traced a finger along the buckle, an ornate snake's head, its tongue flicking out over the belt. 'You're different. All that stuff about Wicca and the Devil. Do you actually believe any of that?'

Mitchell shrugged. 'I don't know. It's Kaz who's into all that stuff really. Me and Keddie, we just… we just want to…'

'You just want to feel like you belong.'

Mitchell nodded. 'I guess. I bet that makes me sound like a right sissie.'

Sera reached up and touched his face. The moonlight broke through the clearing in the trees above, casting shadows all around them. There was that noise again – a movement in the bushes off the trail. She didn't react this time. She'd seen what was out there. 'I don't think you sound like a sissie. I've never fitted in anywhere in my life.'

She leaned up and softly touched her lips to his. He responded, pushing into her more urgently, reaching up to touch the back of her hair. He smelled of whisky and weed, and something more innocent, Lynx Africa or one of those other cheesy smells the boys from school used to smell of. He was a thousand miles from the kind of man Ric was. Mitchell was vulnerable and unsure, hiding behind his tales of bloodsucking and Devil worship.

Sera dropped to her knees and began slowly loosening the snake buckle. There was a crack in the trees beyond and Mitchell whipped around, snagging Sera's hair on the belt.

'Ow, fuck!' she exclaimed.

'God, sorry, are you okay? There's someone out there...'

'There's no one there, just relax,' Sera said, rubbing her head where the hair had been ripped out at the root. She eased down Mitchell's jeans and felt his erect penis straining at the fabric of his boxers. Sera stood up and placed her hands on his chest. 'Do you want me, Mitchell?'

The look in his eyes was part lust, part terror. She could see how much he wanted her, and how much he didn't want to fuck this up. He nodded, bringing his mouth down to kiss her neck. She held onto his shoulder with one hand and pushed down her jeans with the other.

Sera took his hand and slid it in-between her legs and he moaned with pleasure into her neck. He shoved his fingers inside her, clumsy and overeager, nothing like Ric, with all of his experience and his smooth ability to bring her to climax, and yet this was just as exciting because she was the one with the power here. She was the one in control.

She looked into the trees, over Mitchell's shoulder as he pumped away with his fingers and moaned 'Is that good?' into her hair over and over. And that was when she saw him again. So it had been him, watching her from the trees. Her eyes locked onto his in defiance. She knew he'd lied to her about fucking Maisie, she knew him too well. He couldn't resist making women fall for him, control was his drug. Well, not anymore. Two could play that game. And Sera thought she might as well enjoy it.

'Oh yes,' she moaned, loud enough for Ric to hear from his viewing spot. 'That feels so good. I want you inside me.'

Mitchell didn't have to be asked twice. He freed his erect cock from his boxers and lifted Sera slightly against the tree. She gasped for real as he entered her, her nails digging into his neck so hard they left livid red scratches behind, and closed her eyes as he thrusted, once, twice, three times before coming with a feral groan.

Sera opened her eyes and locked onto Ric's as he watched her clinging onto Mitchell, gasping theatrically. *I hope you enjoyed the show*, she told him with her eyes. *That one was for you.*

'God, you are amazing,' Mitchell said as he pulled up his underwear and jeans. 'Was that okay for you? Did you come?'

'Of course I did,' she lied. 'You were great.'

'Right, um, sorry it didn't last very long. You're just so… and I got carried away. I'll make sure it lasts longer next time.'

Next time? Sera refrained from raising an eyebrow. The poor idiot actually thought there would be a next time.

'Look, you'd better get back. I'll come back separately – I don't want people talking about us.'

Mitchell looked uncomfortable. 'I don't want to leave you out here. Let me walk you back and I'll wait in the trees for a bit.'

'No,' Sera said, her voice sharp. 'I've got my torch, I'll be fine. These woods aren't exactly full of serial killers, are they?'

Mitchell still didn't look sure. 'I guess not.'

'Look, you go back to camp, I won't be long. I'll see you in the morning, maybe we can spend some time together alone before you have to go?'

Mitchell smiled. 'I'd really like that.'

'Me too,' Sera smiled back and watched as he walked back along the trail to their camp. Then she sat down on a rock and waited for Ric to come.

Chapter Sixty-Six

1999 – Seraphine

Ric came, of course, through the trees over to where she was sitting. Sera knew she smelled of Mitchell's childish body spray and sex.

'Pervert,' she said, without turning to look at him. 'Did you enjoy that? Did you touch yourself watching him fucking me?'

'Oh, is that what he was doing?' Ric's voice was sardonic. 'I thought he was looking for his watch inside your cunt.'

Sera flinched at the vulgar term. He must be really pissed off; Ric never spoke like that.

'Liar.' She stood up to face him. His eyes bored into hers, dark and dangerous. 'You were turned on. Admit it.'

'I didn't have time to get turned on. Your schoolboy was over and done before I could get started.'

Sera let out a laugh, knowing she'd got to him. She reached up to touch his cheek and he caught her hand in his fist and squeezed. She yelped.

'That hurts,' she said, trying to twist her hand away. 'You're hurting me.'

'What, and you think that little performance just then didn't hurt me?' Ric tightened his grip and twisted. Sera winced. 'You think that didn't rip my insides out?'

She set her jaw, refusing to show him how much he was hurting her. Ric hardly ever got angry, but he was the possessive type. She'd had to watch him seduce countless women in the name of making them money, but he hated to see her so much as flirting with another man. She knew in that moment that she'd crossed the line. What had she been thinking?

She hadn't been thinking. The drink and then the drugs… Oh God, what was he going to do when he found out about the drugs? He was going to be even angrier when he knew she'd shared the last of their stash around.

'Let go please,' she said, her voice even. To her surprise, he let her wrist go.

Sera turned to leave, not knowing if he would follow her or not. If he came back to camp, they would have to resume their little game of brother and sister – he would go straight back to screwing Maisie, he would probably be more open about it this time, after what she'd just done. Well, let him. She'd already decided she was done with him after this anyway.

'Where do you think you're going?' he said, grabbing the sleeve of her T-shirt. It had begun to rain, cold drops splashing through the canopy of trees above. Sera shivered, all of a sudden feeling the cold.

'I'm going back,' she said, trying to shrug him off, but his grip on her T-shirt was too tight.

'Back to lover boy?' He let out a laugh. 'I don't think so. You're mine, Sera. And it's my turn.'

Sera frowned. 'What do you mean, your turn? Don't be such a dick, it's raining and I'm cold. Come back with me if you want, but stop messing around.'

But something in his eyes had changed, they were colder now, his expression was harder. Without warning, he raised his hand and smacked her around the face. Sera was knocked down into the dirt, yelling out in pain.

'Fuck, Ric! That really fucking hurt! What are you—'

But her words were cut short as he levelled a kick into her stomach. Winded, she doubled over, gasping for breath. Tears sprung to her eyes. He'd never so much as laid a finger on her before. What the hell was he going to do to her?

She was still struggling to breathe when he pulled her to her feet.

'Do you get it now? You. Are. Mine. To do whatever I want to. Did you think you were being clever, fucking that idiot with me watching you? You must have been pretty sure I wasn't going to kill him for putting his filthy hands on you. In you.'

'I didn't think you'd care,' Sera rasped, still holding her stomach.

'Well, you were wrong. And now it's my turn. Take off your T-shirt, let me see you in the moonlight.'

Sera scowled. 'I'm not taking my shirt off, Ric. It's cold and raining. Can we just—'

He raised his hand to hit her again and she cowed.

'Okay, okay, please don't hit me.'

'Take off your shirt.'

'Ric—'

He stepped towards her and grabbed the hem of her T-shirt, yanking it up roughly over her chest, dragging her arms upwards. He wrestled it over her head and threw it on the ground next to her. 'Stop fucking arguing with me.' He looked her up and down, gripping her arm and moving her further into the moonlight. 'I had been missing this so much.' He ran his hand over her stomach, and she flinched. 'I'd been looking forward to touching these again.' He wrenched the cup of her bra down, exposing her breast to the rain and cold air, doing the same to the other one.

Sera began to cry.

'What are you crying for?' he scoffed. 'You've never been bothered about getting your tits out outdoors before.' He reached out and squeezed her nipple hard. 'Tell me, Sera, whose are these?'

'Yours,' she said, a sob escaping her throat. 'Only yours. I'm sorry about him, I was just trying to get back at you for Maisie.'

'Oh yes, Maisie,' Ric said, a mean smile crossing his face. 'Now, there's a nice girl. A dependable girl. Not some dirty slut, fucking goths in the filthy dirt.'

'I didn't me—'

'Shut up. Get those off.' He pointed at her shorts.

'He'll be back if I don't go back to the campsite, he'll be worried about me.'

'What, now that he's had you? Unlikely. Boys like him only bother before they've got their dick wet, not after. I'm the only one stupid enough to let you cling on to me. Now take off your fucking shorts before I do it for you.'

Sera unbuttoned her shorts, not wanting Ric to hit her again. He was just punishing her, she knew that. If she went along with him, he would get bored and let her go back. She pushed her shorts to the ground. Ric reached out and grabbed at her lace thong, ripping the side open. He motioned for her to turn around.

'What are you doing?' she asked, her voice unrecognisably small.

He shoved her shoulder around and unhooked her bra, discarding it on top of her shorts. He took out a lighter and set fire to her thong, dropping it on top of her shorts and bra.

'Ric!' Sera shrieked. 'What the fuck are you doing? What am I going to wear back to camp? Can you just stop this now, you've gone too far.'

'Too far?' he said, his voice a low whisper. 'Too far?' He moved behind her and grabbed her hair, shoving her against the same tree she had just had sex with Mitchell against. 'You must have forgot what I said. You're mine, Sera. You belong to me, and I'll go as far as I want to go.'

The tree trunk was rough against her chest and face, her hair caught on the bark and snagged in the branches. Pain ripped through her as he shoved himself roughly into her, again and again. They had had rough sex before, but it had never been like this. It had never felt like hatred and spite. Tears streamed down her cheeks and she slumped against the tree trunk, waiting for it to be over.

Chapter Sixty-Seven

1999 – Maisie

Maisie stumbled through the forest, calling Sera's name over and over into the trees. Moonlight lit the path, but beyond the forest line was pitch black. She felt like she'd been walking forever when she heard voices and saw Sera's blonde hair through the trees.

They were off the main path in a clearing bathed in moonlight. Sera was leaning against a tree, she looked completely out of it, and behind her... was that Ric? It was Ric, and he was strangling Seraphine.

Without thinking, Maisie screamed and ran towards them. As she reached them, Ric was standing up straight and Seraphine was naked, leaning against the tree for support, her eyes open but not seeing anything.

'Get off her!' Maisie shrieked, grabbing at Ric, pulling Seraphine away. Maisie stumbled; her arms flailed out sideways. She grabbed at thin air, but it was no use, there was nothing to break her fall. Seraphine slammed into the tree and fell to the ground like a dead weight, Maisie landing on top of her. Maisie jumped up as quickly as she could, but Sera lay on the ground unmoving. Blood began to seep from somewhere underneath her, pooling under her body.

'Oh God,' Maisie whispered. 'What have you done? What the hell were you doing to her?'

'What have I done?' Ric knelt down by Seraphine's side. 'Don't you mean what have you done? I found her out here, naked and out of it. I think she'd been having sex with some guy. I was trying to stand her up and the next thing you come charging over and slam her against the tree. Oh Jesus. I think she might be dead.'

Maisie looked down at her friend's naked body in horror, at the blood. She couldn't be dead; it was just a fall. She'd just fallen, that was all, she'd get up and they would get her help and it would all be fine. Except…

Ric picked up her wrist. He looked at Maisie, his eyes wide. 'There's no pulse. You killed her, Maisie. She's dead.'

Maisie felt the entire universe drop from under her. There was no way she could be dead. This could not be happening. It was the drink, or the drugs – she'd never taken drugs before and now she knew why. They messed with your mind, made you hallucinate, made you think you were going mad. She put her hands to her face.

'What about all her stuff? Won't it look suspicious if she's left everything behind?'

'Hide her bag in the trees,' Ric replied. 'Then tell them she didn't have time to take down her tent and that she asked you to do it for her. Who knows, they might even have moved on before you get up if you're lucky. No one cares about anyone on these trails, they just want to get on with their hike. I'll be in contact when I've managed to sort this mess out. Go Maisie, run!'

Maisie looked at her friend on the floor again. This couldn't be happening.

But it was. Ric was pushing her shoulder, urging her to run, and so she ran. Back through the trees to camp, where she let out a blood-curdling scream.

Chapter Sixty-Eight

December 2019

When she steps out of the shadows, I'm relieved to see her, and shocked. Has she followed me here?

'Tamra,' I say, lowering my gun slightly. What must she think is going on? A mum at her school pointing a gun at her. Except… 'Wait, what did you say?' Confusion grips me. 'Did you call me…'

'A murderer,' she says, her voice cold. And there's a hint of an accent that I've never heard before, somewhere in Manchester? 'That's what you are, isn't it?'

'You,' Mitchell says, looking at Tamra. When I frown, he explains, 'She's the one who told me where you were. She came to the prison before I was released and told me she thought you were alive. Who are you? What are you doing here?'

'Yes, what are you doing here?' Kaz asks Tamra, her face a furious mask. 'Wait… does your mother know you're here?'

'How do you two know each other?' I look between them, confused. Does Kaz have kids at my school?

'You don't know who she is?' Kaz asks me.

'Ha! Of course she doesn't,' Tamra says with a barking laugh. She points at me. 'Why would she? My mother meant nothing to Seraphine Cunningham. You meant nothing to her, any of you. She walked away from you all without a second thought.'

'Only it was your mother who lied,' Kaz says, her voice full of hatred. And I know why. I realise now who is standing in front of me, and how far she's gone to wheedle her way into my life. Maisie Goodwin's daughter.

'She had to,' Tamra replies, turning to me. 'Because *she* faked her own death and left my mum to pick up the pieces.'

'How do you know her?' I ask Kaz. I've purposely never looked up Maisie, not just because I didn't want a search history to bite me in the arse, but because I wanted to forget any of it ever happened. I had no idea that she had had a child, maybe more than one.

'I kept tabs on Maisie for a long time,' Kaz replies. 'I tried to convince her to admit she was lying for a while, but it was no use. I still don't understand why she had to tell everyone Mitchell killed you. Without her testimony, you'd still just be another missing person. They wouldn't have got a no-body conviction if she hadn't said she saw him kill you.'

'She said it because she thought she'd killed me,' I say. 'She accused Mitchell to save herself.'

Tamra Murray, Maisie Goodwin's daughter, smiles at me. But it's not the warm, sunny smile that I've come to know from the sweet school secretary. It's a cold, calculating smile.

'Did you snatch Faye?' I shake my head. 'No, it was a man, he was seen—'

'Tsssk,' Tamra makes a noise of derision. 'He's no one. Just someone very easy to manipulate. Someone very willing to accept the sob story of the poor school secretary he's sleeping with. I told him Faye was my niece and that you wouldn't let me see her. How heartbroken I was. He'll do whatever I need him to. Deliver parcels, steal dogs. Take on a new graphic designer...'

Rob's client, the one who said his wife was Maisie Goodwin.

'I don't understand why you came here, why you orchestrated all of this. Your mum got off scot-free after what she said about Mitchell,' Kaz says.

Tamra looks furious. 'I *can't believe* you still think my mum is more to blame than she is,' she says, taking a fierce step towards me.

I jab the gun at her. 'Stay back!'

Tamra just laughs.

'You called me a murderer,' I say. 'Why?'

She leans on the door frame of the cupboard. She looks far too casual for someone who has a gun pointed at her. 'Human remains discovered on the West Coast Trail, Sera. Who do you think those might be?'

Human remains found.

'You know who they are.' It's a statement, not a question. She knows.

'My mum has a friend who is a retired police officer in Canada,' she says. 'She helped him out in a pretty famous murder case.'

Mitchell growls and steps towards her.

'Don't,' I say. 'She's not worth it. Don't let her rile you up.'

'They knew the remains were male pretty quickly,' she continues. 'But they didn't want to release the information straight away, you know what the police are like there. They don't want it to have anything to do with your case, that was closed a long time ago. Mum knew though.'

'So she knew it wasn't me. How did she know it was him?'

'Him who?' Kaz demands. 'What are you two talking about?'

Chapter Sixty-Nine

1999 – Seraphine

Sera lay on the floor, her eyes closed and her head thumping and pain ripping through her side. Her entire left side felt wet and sticky. Ric was kneeling over her. Had that been Maisie flying out of nowhere, or a hallucination? When Ric had been raping her, she had felt as though she was leaving her body completely, and the next thing she knew, she was being pulled away and was flying towards the floor. Then everything had gone black for a few minutes, and now it was just her and Ric again, as if Maisie had never been there. Maybe she hadn't. Maybe Ric had hit her again and she'd blacked out, imagined the whole thing. What had she done to her side?

'You can get up now.' Ric pressed something to her side and she realised it was the T-shirt she had been wearing. 'You've landed on something sharp and it looks deep, but it's not going to kill you. We need to get you out of here. Here, take my jumper.' She felt something land on top of her. 'We need to head back the way we came as fast as possible. Are you listening? Your little "play dead" act fooled her. Now we get out of here and we have a blackmail plan set up for life. She'll pay anything now she thinks I've disposed of your body for her. Not what I was expecting, but I'll take it.'

Sera didn't understand a word of what he was saying, but it didn't matter. All she knew was that she couldn't spend another minute with the man who had attacked her, raped her, burnt her clothes. Now she had seen this side of him, and he expected her just to carry on like nothing had happened? He was certainly acting like it hadn't. She didn't know what she was going to do, though, so instead she stayed where she was.

Ric leaned in closer to her. 'I know you're alive,' he whispered, his breath sour in a way she had never noticed before. Who was this man? Certainly not the man she had known before this hike. 'So fucking get up and help me.'

'It hurts,' she groaned, not able to work out what hurt more, the cut on her side or what Ric had done to her. She hurt all over.

'Here.' Ric rummaged through the pack he had stolen when they first got to the trail. 'There's some bandages here. Put that T-shirt down.'

Ric dressed her wounds as though nothing had changed between them. Sera couldn't help but flinch at his touch, but he didn't comment, perhaps assuming that it was the pain.

When the cut on her side was bandaged, he pulled her to her feet. 'Now we have to go.' He opened the pack again and threw her some shorts. 'Cover yourself up.'

She had no idea where they were going, or why. Why were they leaving everything behind?

'I don't have my stuff. My shoes. My feet will be ripped to shreds.'

'I wonder how much I can get out of her?' Ric mused, ignoring her pleas completely. 'I mean, she thinks she's a murderer, that's got to be worth a bit in blackmail.'

So that was it. They were just going to disappear and Maisie was supposed to think Sera was dead. No one else would even realise she was missing, except Mitchell maybe, but he'd only known her a few hours. Ric had it all worked out so quickly, it was terrifying really. Had he always been a psychopath? Of course he had, just not to her before. The amount of times they had disappeared from places in the past, this was nothing. If it hadn't been for the brutality she'd just suffered at the hands of the one person she thought she could trust, this would just be another adventure for the pair of them. Bonnie and Clyde, taking off in the middle of the night.

'Maisie doesn't have any money though,' Sera said, although she may as well have been talking to herself. Twigs and stones bit into her feet, but she only half registered the pain anyway. Her entire body hurt, what was one more cut, another graze?

She followed him for what felt like hours, pushing their way further away from the West Coast Trail and into the trees. Sera had already decided she had to get away from him. Nothing could be the same after this, after she knew what he was capable of. It was as though the scales had fallen from her eyes and there was no way to undo it. She would run – not now, she couldn't outrun him in this state, but as soon as they found civilisation she would—

Her thoughts cut off as she tripped, falling to her knees amongst the bracken and twigs and broken tree stumps. 'Ow!'

'Oh Jesus Christ,' Ric muttered. He walked over and prodded her with his foot. 'Come on! We need to get as far away as possible.'

He loomed over her, leaning forwards to pull her up and in that moment she saw him attacking her, over and over. How many times would that happen, now he had done it once?

Sera's hand slid over a large rock. Now. She could end this now. Without thinking twice – for surely that would have stopped her – she picked up the rock and smashed it into the side of his head.

Ric went flying backwards, holding his head. Blood was pouring from between his fingers. He looked shocked, confused. He looked the same way she imagined she had when he had first struck her.

Before he could react, Sera moved over him and swung the rock again. This time, when it connected, Ric yelled out in pain. It was a perfect sound. She hit him again, and again, until there was a pool of blood beneath his head and he was no longer shouting.

Sera dropped the rock. She looked down in horror at what she'd done and began to shiver. She realised she was probably going into shock and opened up Ric's pack, looking for anything to calm her down. She took a swig of whisky from the hip flask in there and pulled out a pair of his jogging bottoms. They were far too big but better than the half-burned denim shorts she'd had to pull on hastily when they left the trail. Pulling them on, she looked back down at Ric. Should she try to hide his body? They were far from the trail, and no one had any reason to look out here. Still, she would feel better if he was at least covered up.

She grabbed his arms, but he would barely budge. She guessed that was where the term 'dead weight' came from. How the hell was she going to move him? She bent down and pushed the side of him. His body rolled over slightly and she pushed again, harder this time. He fully rolled over, so she did it again, and again. She dragged him for a while, feeling the strength come back into her arms again, then rolled some more. The trees were so thick now, she couldn't see a thing, and several times she grazed her hands and arms on branches or trunks.

When she simply couldn't do it anymore, she pulled her lover's body into a ditch. She took what little money there was in his pack, an energy bar and the rest of the whisky. She was bruised and sore, exhausted and terrified, but running was her only option, she had killed a man with her bare hands, and now she alone was liable for the drug debts both of them had accrued. If tonight had taught her anything, it was that she wanted to live. So she ran.

Chapter Seventy

December 2019

'Ric. If that was even his real name,' Tamra says, looking at me for confirmation.

'It was to me,' I say with a shrug. 'But I suppose I don't really know. He was a con man, a liar, a swindler. Whatever your mum has told you about him is lies. She only knew him a few days, he wasn't a good person. He stole drugs, got us into a mess with some bad people.'

'He was good to my mum,' she says.

What on earth did you tell her, Maisie? Why is she so upset over a man who died before she was born? Unless...

'He was your father,' I guess. 'They slept together on that trail.'

Her face sets in anger. 'And I'll never get to meet him. Because of you.'

'He raped me that night, Tamra. That's why I fought him. That's why I ran and never looked back. Your father wasn't a good man. I'm sorry.'

The words come out cold and Tamra takes a breath as though she's been slapped. Mitchell lets out a gasp.

'Liar,' Tamra growls. 'You lying bitch.' She takes a step towards me, and I hold up the gun.

'Stay back,' I warn.

She laughs again and I'm certain she's gone mad. If she knows I've killed before, then why isn't she the slightest bit concerned about the gun? Unless…

I turn and pull the trigger at the wall. The gun clicks but doesn't fire.

'You took out the bullets,' I say.

There is a maniacal grin on her face, and she nods. 'Yep. I left it there to see if Mitchell would shoot you, given the chance. I mean, technically you're already dead.' She looks at Mitchell this time. 'If you want to kill her, you can. You've already served a sentence for her murder; they can't lock you up twice for it.'

'That's not even true,' Kaz tells her. 'He absolutely can be locked up for it. The films lied to you,' she shrugs. 'Soz.'

Kaz says this so confidently that I'm certain she's looked it up. It makes me wonder if she'd have let Mitchell come and kill me if she thought he couldn't be tried for it.

'I wouldn't anyway,' Mitchell says, and he's looking at me, not Tamra. 'You had your reasons for what you did. I don't blame you.'

Tamra lets out a puff of air like she can't believe what she's hearing. 'You must have a magical vagina, Seraphine,' she says. 'And a lying bitch mouth.'

'I'm not lying about Ric,' I promise her. 'I know what I did wasn't right, but he did rape me. And so I killed him, and I hoped the cougars would eat his body before the police could find it. And I've lived with that every day since. As well as the knowledge that I could have saved Mitchell just by picking up the phone and telling the authorities that I was alive. I know what I've done, and I deserve whatever comes my way.'

'Touching,' Tamra sneers. Maisie must really have done a number on this kid. Have they both been obsessed with Ric this whole time?

'Where is your mum?' I ask her. 'Let me talk to her. I can reason with her, get you both help.'

'*She killed herself,*' Tamra hisses, and I realise now why she's so angry. 'She spent years looking for my dad until she finally located someone who had sold him drugs in Vancouver. He sent her to a document forger who said he hadn't seen Ric in years. But he had seen *you*. Twenty years of thinking that you were dead, and that she sent an innocent man to prison to protect me, her daughter, from being born in prison and taken away, only to find out that she hadn't killed you that night. The whole time you were alive, and she'd done the unthinkable for nothing. It cost her a few grand, but he gave her the name he'd put on your new documents. Laura Johnson. It took her another two years until she actually found you, thanks to that business you set up. And then she couldn't deny it to herself anymore. She knew what he'd said was true. You were alive and Mitch had been innocent all those years.'

Oh God. My legs threaten to buckle underneath me. *Maisie is dead.* Another life gone because of me. Will this never end?

Chapter Seventy-One

December 2019

'I wanted to know you,' Tamra says, stepping forwards fully into the cupboard now and taking the gun from my hand. 'You were like some kind of myth to me growing up. Mum would get drunk every night and alternate between you being the best thing since sliced bread and the reason I didn't have a father. I never really understood her inebriated ramblings until she told me one night what she'd done to you. The guilt she'd lived with all these years for your death. Then someone actually found my dad's remains and she knew what you'd done. I was amazed she stayed sober long enough to track you down, but it was her new addiction. Like finding dad had been for all those years. Perhaps she intentionally overdosed that night or maybe it was an accident. Either way, she'd have had a normal life if you had never pulled your little disappearing act.'

I want to tell her that Maisie could never have had an ordinary life once hers had collided with Ric's. He would have taken over her life the way he took over mine. But I don't want to make excuses for my past anymore. This is too much. Let her kill me.

She loads the bullets from her pocket, and I stand and wait, like a prisoner at a firing range. Mitchell and Kaz do the same, and I wonder if they're as tired of this life as I am, or if they are just too stunned to react.

I close my eyes and wait for the shot. Will I hear it? I think I will: sound moves faster than a bullet, I will hear the crack and then, hopefully, nothing. All I can hope for is that she shoots me in the head, rather than somewhere I will stay alive for longer.

But first I hear a different sound. Archie is barking all of a sudden, as though he senses the danger I'm in. It pulls me back to my senses, Archie's bark reminds me of home, and home reminds me of Faye, and George, and Rob. They are the ones I live for. If I die now, it will all be for nothing. They will be without their mum. I can't give in that easily.

'No!' I yell, as Tamra loads the last bullet. She doesn't have time to pull it up and fire, it isn't even loaded properly yet. I land against her, shoving her backwards out of the cupboard. As she falls, she grabs my hair and yanks me out with her, both of us sprawl to the floor.

Tamra is on her feet faster than me, slamming the cupboard door shut and turning the key. I hear Mitchell and Kaz banging on the door and Archie barking. I pull myself to my feet to unlock it with the key she's left in the lock, but Tamra throws her full body weight at me, screaming. I hit the wall and feel all the wind leave my body. Gasping for breath, I grab at her face, her hair, anything I can get hold of. My fingers close around her jumper, but as I pull on it with all my strength, she twists sideways and flings me to the floor. She kicks me in the stomach and pain sears through me. Then the blows rain down, kick after kick in my side, in my face. Everywhere hurts and instinctively I curl up into a ball to protect my head, face and stomach. Still she doesn't stop, kicking me in the shoulder, the side, the back of the head. She's going to kill me.

And then she stops. I can hear her panting, but I can't get up, everywhere hurts too much. It's not like in the films where the hero takes a pasting, then jumps up and carries on fighting. I can feel warm sticky blood trickling from my nose, I suspect more than one of my ribs might be broken and the way I'm breathing, all raspy and low, it's possible I've got a punctured lung. I think I might be dying.

The sharp stench of gasoline brings me to my senses. So that was her plan all along. Lock me in and watch me burn. Only now it's all gone wrong and I'm out here and the people who came to rescue me are in there, with my beloved Archie.

As I lie on the cold concrete floor, unable to move, I think about every decision that led me to this place. All the lies I've told, all the people I have hurt. I think of Ric, whose betrayal was never sleeping with Maisie, but treating me like I belonged to him, like I was his to use. And Mitchell, who, even knowing he had been wrongfully convicted, cried over my death. There are good people and bad people in this world. Ric was a bad person, although it doesn't excuse what I did to him. Mitchell is a good person, and now, as I smell the smoke filling the warehouse, I know he will die in here because he came to find me, to save me from Kaz — or so he thought. He's given me his life a second time. And as I lay here dying, I know that the final thing I have to do in my life is to give him his back.

Tamra has long gone, fleeing as soon as she has set the fire. It feels like it takes forever, the whole place is filling with hot black smoke now, but inch by inch I shuffle on my side towards where I know the store cupboard is. Archie is still barking, and I can hear Mitchell and Kaz yelling for help. When my fingers touch the cold wood of the door, I fight through the excruciating pain to press myself up against it, pull myself to a crouching position, high enough to turn the key that's still in the lock and press down on the handle. The door opens inwards, and I stumble forwards and hit the floor.

Epilogue

'We wish you a Merry Fishmas and a Happy New Year!'

'Mum! George keeps ruining it, saying Fishmas!'

George giggles and I could swear that he's doing it on purpose to wind his sister up. He looks at me for support, his massive blue eyes beseeching.

'He's not doing it on purpose,' I assure her. My chest seizes up and I bend double in a fit of coughing.

'Are you okay?' Rob leans over my hospital bed, where I've been for the past eighteen days, ever since Mitchell Dyke pulled me from the smoking wreckage of the abandoned warehouse, and pushes the hair from my face. Tinsel is strewn around the end of the bed and Christmas cards line my bedside table, along with piles of magazines and bars of chocolate. Not a grape in sight – how well my friends know me.

The doctors say it's unlikely I've sustained long-term damage; I wasn't in the smoke for long enough and my lung wasn't punctured by Tamra's attack, just three of my ribs broken. I might even get out by Christmas Day if I'm lucky, but Rob will be cooking – not so lucky.

Lucky. I suppose that's the story of my life. As I lay on the floor of that warehouse, waiting to die, I felt Archie's wet tongue licking my face, and the strong arms of Mitchell Dyke, the man whose life I ruined, pulling me to safety. He could have left me there to die. *I* would have left me, but then he's always been a better person than me.

They found Tamra's body in the wreckage two days later. She died a hero. After the way I had ruined her life I felt like it's the least I could give to her. I told the police that I'd suddenly remembered the GPS tracker on Archie's collar and Tamra had come with me to try to rescue Archie. We hadn't noticed the fire until it was too late and Tamra was trapped.

Mitchell and Kaz left before the police arrived to avoid any possible association between him and Maisie's daughter. And when the police went through her things in the tiny one-bed flat she had rented, they found her mother's diary, obviously written before she'd realised I was still alive. Maisie had confessed to my murder, so, as far as the world will know, I am still dead and Mitchell is innocent.

The remains of Richard James Hadley were identified by dental records and his killer is still at large. Ric had several aliases, but it seems that he'd at least given me his real name. At the time of his death, he had been wanted for questioning in three horrific attacks on women – not including mine – fraud and drug charges. I had never known just how bad he was because I'd chosen not to look, caught up in the Bonnie and Clyde lifestyle we had together. It was always going to come to a head, I just never could have imagined how brutally, and how far-reaching the consequences would be.

I know that I should step forward and clear Maisie's name, like I should have cleared Mitchell's, but life isn't that easy. In a novel, I'd end up being a changed person, one who puts others first after a lifetime of keeping such a selfish secret, but in real life you have to make difficult choices in a heartbeat and live with them forever. I know this because as Mitchell pulled me from the wreckage, I heard a woman's scream. I heard Tamra's scream. I don't know why she was still in the building, whether she'd had a change of heart and was coming back to unlock Kaz and Mitchell, or if she'd left something incriminating inside, but I know I heard her.

Mitchell paused. 'What was that?' he asked.

Kaz looked at me and for a second I knew she'd heard it too. The fire was roaring now, no doubt helped along by the rows of carpets inside catching alight like flaming dominoes. The smoke was overwhelming, we needed to escape, *now*.

'Nothing,' she said, a little too quickly. The look on her face told me that she'd heard the scream and she wasn't going to risk losing Mitchell again. We both knew he'd go back in for her.

And once again, I had a choice to make. Half-conscious, bleeding and beaten, I chose to give his life over hers.

'I didn't hear anything,' I murmured, before closing my eyes and hearing Kaz's small sigh of relief.

Now we have another secret, but I'm good at keeping those.